——A——
FORGOTTEN
EVIL

—A—
FORGOTTEN
EVIL

SHELDON RUSSELL

cennan

PUBLISHED BY CENNAN BOOKS
an imprint of Cynren Press
101 Lindenwood Drive, Suite 225
Malvern, PA 19355 USA
http://www.cynren.com/

Printed in the United States of America on acid-free paper

ISBN-13: 978-1-947976-13-9 (pbk)
ISBN-13: 978-1-947976-14-6 (ebk)

Library of Congress Control Number: 2018965799

This novel's story and characters are fictitious. Certain
historical events, locations, and personages are mentioned,
but the characters involved are wholly imaginary.

COVER DESIGN BY Tim Barber

Prologue

J ust north of the Washita River, on a small knoll, a crude
gravestone stands alone on the windswept Antelope Hills.
Scratched onto its face with rude and coarse hand is a fleur-de-
lis, hurried, perhaps, against imminent danger, or forgotten evil,
or some awful and blinding sorrow. No name, no date, marks its
time, no sign to claim its silent watch. People stand with hands
in pockets and wonder, who might it be who has lain so long in
this place? From the canyons below, the ceaseless winds grieve
through the seasons but do not give up their secrets.

Chapter 1

Despite Caleb Justin's best efforts in building the coffin, dirt dropped through a pine knot hole and onto his father's blue suit. In its eddy were the corruption and detail of death, the realities and ugliness of man's lot as he is lain at last into the silence of the earth. But it was the dampness from the grave, cool and stringent in the spring morning balm, that weakened Caleb's knees and caused him to lean against the giant maple tree to catch his breath.

From the dock below, the *Belle of Louisville* backed into the river, its paddle wheel slapping against the green water, its throaty whistle rising into the morning quiet, its engine toiling against the drift of the river. Like giant insects, the steamers clawed up and down the river, their appetites insatiable, their craving for fuel endless, their stacks black and belching.

Each day, Caleb and his father cut the wood and stacked it on the dock, selected and sized and readied. Each day, they received their due, counted in currency by the captain himself, and each day, they returned to the forest once more. Now it would never be the same, the last of his father's wood loaded and stacked just hours before the accident, before his death beneath the tree. Nothing would ever again be the same.

The stink of moss and fish churned from the shallows as the *Belle* struggled into the mighty Ohio, caught in its power and current. Caleb turned again to his shovel.

Baud Moss reached for his makings and dabbed at the perspiration on his forehead with his shirtsleeve. No matter how hot or miserable, he wore his sleeves and neck buttoned, his straw hat squared. He, too, was a woodcutter, from upriver, and one of the few people Caleb and his father knew in the forests that banked the Ohio. The fact that he was colored mattered little to Caleb, or to his father, or to Baud for that matter, and they shared a raft tied in the backwash a few miles upstream.

"You all right, son?" Baud asked, touching off his cigarette, the smell of sulfur filling the air.

"I'm all right," Caleb said, setting his shovel into the dirt with his foot.

"It's a hard day a man buries his father," Baud said, "and one he ain't likely to forget."

"Sorry to take you away from your cutting, Baud. I'll make it up when I get things in order."

"Some things ought not do alone," he said, "and I figure burying your pa is one of them."

But taking up a man's time in these parts was a problem, this Caleb knew, because time was money, and a man with as many kids as Baud needed every penny just to survive.

"There's a partial cord of oak down on the south branch, Baud. You pick it up on the way home."

Baud, drawing on his cigarette, looked down on the river and watched the *Belle* splash away like a man floundering in the depths.

"Thanks the same," he said, squashing the cigarette under his foot, "but I come bareback, didn't I. Besides, that's your wood, Caleb. I got plenty boys to help me, and you ain't."

Filling his shovel, Caleb tossed the dirt onto the casket, its thud irrevocable against the pine, and a pain twisted like wet rope within his core.

"I still got his axe," Caleb said, "the one hand-forged out of that plowshare, you remember?"

"Oh, sure," Baud said. "Wasn't no one used a axe like your pa. Fall a tree with a dozen licks, couldn't he, chips the size of saddle blankets, and not even a sweat. He was a horse, your pa, and a man to reckon with." Tossing in another shovelful of dirt, Baud locked his fingers over the handle and studied his feet. "Reckon you're just like him, Caleb. Course, you're young, maybe even a little scared. When a man dies, the son steps up to the grave, don't he, and there ain't no one between him and death no more. It's a unsettling feeling for boys what think life goes unchanged." Turning back to his work in earnest, he added from under his hat, "That's what eternity is, I'm thinking."

By the time they finished, the sun rose above the trees, setting the Ohio ablaze. Sweat soaked Caleb's shirt and glistened in the pocket of his throat. With his hands, he sculpted the last of the dirt over the grave, warmed now, like flesh.

"Guess that's it, Baud," he said, dusting his hands. "Guess it's done."

"A man ought to have some words said over him, Caleb. It's fitting, you know."

"I ain't got no words, Baud, just a emptiness, like I've been turned upside down and shook out on the ground. Maybe you could say something."

Turning his back, Baud looked down on the river for a while before taking out his makings again. When his cigarette was rolled, licked, and tucked in the corner of his mouth, he said to the river, "God, take this woodcutter in, if you've a notion. He was a good man, as you know, even though not much for talking, or praying either, I figure. He's left a good boy who'll require some looking after, I 'spect. Amen."

"Amen," Caleb said, "and thanks, Baud."

Baud gathered up his mule, kicked a leg over, and pulled himself upright.

"You got no kin at all, boy?"

"No, sir, just pa and me was all that was left."

"You're welcome at my place, but guess we know it wouldn't work out."

"Thanks, Baud," he said, picking up his shovel. "If you ever need a hand—"

Baud brought his heels up into the mule's ribs and disappeared into the trees.

From behind the door in the cabin, Caleb retrieved his father's axe, its six-inch blade honed sharp by stone and oil. Even the handle his father had made, carved from hickory and shaped to his hand. Many a night, Caleb had watched as his father sat by the fire, working at the blade, checking its sharp with a brush of his thumb.

He searched out a cypress in the backwash. He squared off, the feel of the axe warm and strong, like the touch of his father's hand. Chips surrendered under the force of his swing, great slabs that gave way under the power and accuracy of his cuts. When the cypress creaked, groaning in defeat, he stepped back to judge its direction and to await its plummet into the brush. The beat of his heart throbbed in his foot, and he waited for it to pass.

Afterward, he sheared away the limbs with short but powerful swings of his axe, and then from the heart took his wood, splitting it into slabs for his cross. By choking the handle, he shaped and cleaned the pieces, shaving them smooth and perfect with the razor edge of his blade. Satisfied at last, he lashed them together with rawhide, holding his cross to the blue of the sky. Later, when the wood was cured, grayed, and enduring, he would carve his father's name.

How long he sat at the grave amid the whisper of leaves, the angry clamber of crows, the sweetness of the honeysuckle that grew in yellow curtains along the riverbank, he didn't know. And when the sun rode high, the smell of decaying fish wafted from the valley, the distant but certain scent of death.

The accident had been sudden, the shift of a great oak, heavy and green and filled with spring rain. In that moment, Caleb knew it was too late: his father caught, the immense weight, the unforgiving stump, the eyes full of surprise and sadness and despair.

With his fingers he'd dug at the earth to free his father of the crushing weight, to spare him what no man deserved, to cradle him against the injustice and cruelty and agony of this world. But even as he dug, the smell of death, the bloodied sand, the bowels spilled and hopeless in the heat, told him it was too late.

Only then did the pain of his own broken foot wash through him, pooling hot and wet in his mouth. Pulling off his boot, he'd examined his foot, crushed from the limb that had saved his life. The big toe jutted to the side, its angle unnatural, its color dark and bruised. Gritting his teeth against the pain, he'd straightened his toe, waiting for the nausea to pass before tying it to his middle toe with a lace from his boot.

Like a cougar, piteous and worn, he'd dragged the body home, pulling it at last onto the rough planks of the cabin porch. Bewildered and weary, he'd tried to focus, to think, to decide what must be done. There was his father's bed, against the wall, beneath the window, where the morning sun broke, and a blanket to cover his face. But what of the blood, the smell, the horror beneath the shirt? Perhaps he could leave him just there on the porch, subject to the evil and darkness of death. There was Baud Moss, of course, who would come if he asked, but so far away and now with night upon him.

In the end, he'd stayed with him there, curling alone against the wall of the cabin as the moon slid through the blackness of the night.

Chapter 2

Each morning, Caleb rose at dawn as was the way, ate corn mush and syrup, drank black coffee from his father's favored cup, dressed, and made his way to the stable, but living alone was harder than he'd expected, the silence, the absence of laughter, the longing for a human voice in the vastness of his world.

Alone, even the most routine jobs mounted into exasperating and complicated tasks. One morning, he'd spent twenty minutes just catching up the belly band on Ben's harness. By reaching under, he could loop the strap through the buckle, but by the time he'd gotten to the other side to feed it through, it had fallen out again. In a rage, he kicked the feed bucket across the stable, his damaged toe erupting in pain and dropping him to his knees.

Craning his neck, Ben peeked white-eyed from behind his blinkers at the madman loosed upon him.

With one cutter, there was no longer a load of wood each day to place on the dock, but a load every third day instead. To make up the difference, Caleb increased his hours, leaving and returning in the dark, but even then, he was unable to keep up. It was he alone who trimmed out the limbs, loaded the wood, fed the mules, and managed for supplies from the steamboats.

Sometimes, even in his weariness, he would wait at the dock after they'd loaded the wood, just to hear the voices, the men as they cursed and kidded and teased. On occasion, a lady would appear at the helm, her face shaded by a parasol, or sometimes one would walk down the gangplank, the trim of her ankle, the smell of her perfume in the dankness of the air.

To make matters worse, his big toe stiffened, the joint frozen and useless, his gait now awkward in the absence of its spring. At night his back ached from the work and heat, from the ungraceful bent of his pelvis, and from the stress of the incessant blows of his axe. Blisters ballooned on his hands, burst, and ballooned again, until at last they hardened into unfeeling calluses.

But it was nights that he dreaded most, the hours alone in the cabin with naught but the fire and the memories to haunt him. Even his mother's books, worn and frayed now, gave him no pleasure, and he would sit in the darkness, rocking in his father's chair until weariness drove him at last to bed. At times the smell of perfume lingered long into the quiet hours, and he slept not at all, a fever burning hot and unexplained within him.

There were so many things that he could not do; his food tasted of copper; his clothes were wrinkled and sour; his bed was a jumble of blankets, sandburs buried in their fringes. Try as he may, he could not break an egg, the grit of shell fragments gagging him over his plate. Having failed to strain the cow's milk, his white gravy smelled of manure, and his biscuits shattered like dirt clods when he crumbled them onto his plate. Sometimes in the night, he would sit upright, his gut a seething and rumbling cauldron, poisoned by vermin or some unknown disease that had survived the ferment of the kitchen.

But each day, he rose again in the darkness to harness Ben and Sophie to the wagon and make his way into the forest. Summer turned to fall as he worked at his wood, the first color of gold high in the reaches of the oak grove. As the days shortened, cooling under the sun's drift, Caleb's melancholy grew.

He returned to his father's grave on such a day, the cypress cross now gray and settled from the summer's heat. After carving his father's name, he cursed God and all that He was for taking his father. There was a sweetness in his blasphemy, and he dared God to take his own life that minute.

Afterward, he wept for the first time since his father's death, a wound unhealed, and when there were no more tears, he lay on the ground next to the grave and looked up into the sky. There was within him a longing, a yearning to know what lay beyond the green expanse of his forest, the only world he'd ever known. When a cool wind swept from the north, he stood, pushing back his hair, still wet from tears, and made his way to the wagon.

He grew strong over the months and under the demands of his axe, his muscles knotting beneath the thin cotton shirt. When, on a clear night, the first chill of winter froze his water bucket and sent him in search of his coat, he discovered how much he'd changed, his old jacket stretching tight about his shoulders, his arms dangling from the too-short sleeves. He found his father's coat in the wooden chest, smelling still of smoke and mule, and he slipped it on. There was a sadness in him at its fit.

That night, as he sat before the fire, he honed his father's axe, checking its sharp, its shine against the firelight, and knew that something had changed, something profound and immutable in the course of his life.

By dawn's light, Caleb drove Ben and Sophie under the lean-to that served as stable, tack room, and part-time henhouse for the chickens his father had purchased off a river peddler.

As usual, Ben ducked into the wrong stall, dropping his head into the corner to avoid the harness. Caleb whacked him across his ears with a stick he kept by the door for just such purposes.

"Get out of there, you ole son of a bitch," he said.

Outside, Sophie waited, being the lady she was, and knowing all too well Ben's intractable ways.

Once they were in their correct stalls, Caleb filled their troughs with corn using an old scoop shovel, its handle long ago broken from prying rocks. Soon enough, the mules settled in to breakfast, the grind of their jaws powerful in the tiny stable, the smell of corn, the heat of their bodies in the cool morning. The chickens clucked as they worked at the bits of corn that spilled from the troughs. Caleb loved to listen to the mules eat and sometimes wasted precious cutting time doing just that.

When Ben finished eating, he blew cornmeal from the corners of his trough with powerful snorts of his nostrils and stomped his front feet at the chickens, who in turn accommodated him with alarmed squawks and a cloud of feathers that floated about the stalls.

Caleb tossed the belly band under Ben so that he could fasten the rope and pull it through. He eased himself back around just as Ben turned his rump, dragging the belly band beneath him.

"Here! Whoa, you son of a bitch," he said.

It was a refrain his father had used often in regard to Ben, and it came natural to Caleb now in such moments. Snorting cornmeal, Ben craned his neck at the words.

Caleb squatted down and could see the belly band lying just beyond reach.

"Whoa, boy," he said again, patting Ben's rump to reassure him, to let him know he was going to stretch his arm under him. As he strained to gather up the belly band with the tips of his fingers, he spoke to Ben in that calming voice. "Whoa, now. Whoa, boy. There we go, ole Ben."

Above him, Ben's appendage, a tool of amazing variation, lay sheathed and sightless. When Baud's mare came in heat down in the oak grove one day, the astonishing proportions had been revealed, the magnitude of which could render a man mute for a lifetime, so for now Caleb worked with concentration at the belly band.

"Whoa, boy. There's the good ole boy," he said again, stretching for the belly band.

At what point he appreciated its weight, he couldn't be certain, so absorbed was he on the task at hand, but there it was, the size of a man's forearm and as warm as fresh milk on the back of his neck.

"Yeow!" he screamed, jerking his head up into Ben's belly. Ben vaulted back and onto Caleb's bum toe.

"You son of a bitch!" he yelled in disbelief, the pain in his toe now exquisite beneath Ben's hoof.

Ben watched on with wide eyes, his ardor retreating under Caleb's rude behavior.

Freed at last, Caleb lay against the stable wall, foot in hand, rocking with agony and with a decided notion to club Ben senseless with the broken scoop.

But logic, and Ben's contriteness at the prospect of a beating, won out, and so it was that Caleb worked out the week, his poor toe crushed and throbbing at the end of his boot. Still, by week's end, he'd met his quota, his wagon filled with walnut, his foot now numbed into submission.

That Saturday morning, he rose, his breath visible in the cold morning air, and rubbed the stiffness from his hands. He dressed in his cleanest clothes, dancing from one foot to the other. He combed his hair in the small mirror that hung on the back of the cabin door. It was, as usual, an impossible task, his hair straight and black and unruly to the finish.

Giving up, he tossed the comb onto the bed and examined his face in the mirror. Perhaps it was not such a bad face, weathered from the sun, and with the rough-hewn angle of his father's nose, but then it was a man's nose, devoid of daintiness and pretension. And on his chest were the first signs of hair, sure evidence of impending change. What a girl might think, he did not know, but to him, such meager evidence of manliness was unconvincing, and he turned from the mirror.

After his close encounter with the beating, even Ben cooperated with harnessing, and by the time the sun had set the river ablaze, Caleb was on his way to the dock with his load of wood. It would be the *Belle of Louisville* at nine o'clock, her great stacks smoking, her red wheel slapping from around the bend.

She was his favorite, and the busiest of all on the Ohio. Folks of all natures packed her decks, most from Cincinnati on their way to Louisville, others south to the Mississippi and parts unknown. There were businessmen, and gamblers, and soldiers, sometimes whole families with their trunks and kids, with everything they owned on their way to a new life. There were colored folks, too, most scared, some angry, but all searching with newfound freedom. Best of all, on occasion, there would be a lady smelling of perfume, or leaning from the rail, or flashing the white of her ankle against the green waters of the Ohio.

It took him longer to stack out now, having to move each piece of wood himself as many as three times as he unloaded from the wagon, but by the time the whistle rose into the morning quiet, he was finished and waiting atop his cord of walnut. This was his favorite moment, because now his job was done. It would be the deckhands who would load his wood, who would carry his bounty into the steamer's belly, and the captain himself who would count out his pay.

As the *Belle* swung to shore, the great paddle stopped, reversing against the current to slow the steamer's speed. The whistle blew again, its sound piercing Caleb's chest and setting his heart to pounding. Within moments, the *Belle* was tied off and the gangway secured.

Above him, the deck churned with soldiers, the blue of their uniforms, their bawdy laughter, the smell of their pipes as they smoked away the morning. These were men of adventure, of experience and knowledge and remote to the world in which Caleb lived. Where they were going and where they had been Caleb could not know, but he knew his own place, and in the scheme of things, it was small enough indeed.

The first hand off was a white man, young, like Caleb himself, but tall and thin and with dangling arms. A red bandanna was tied about his head. There was a swagger to his step and a look of mischief in his eye. Following him were a half dozen colored men, stripped to their waists against the boiler's heat.

Sticking out his hand, he said, "Howdy. Name's Joshua Hart. Captain says he wants hardwood or none at all."

Climbing down from the wagon, Caleb pushed back his hat like his father always did and shook Joshua's hand.

"Caleb Justin," he said. "She's walnut for the most part and hard as rock. There's a full cord, some to boot. Won't take but a stick from here to Louisville."

"That a fact?" Joshua said, motioning for the men to load her up.

"Cut every one myself, so I ought to know."

"You cut all the shade trees, too?"

"No, sir. One's right over there."

"There's a slack bushing on the paddle wheel, and I ain't standing out here in the sun all day while they check it."

As Joshua made his way toward the shade, Caleb followed behind. Feeling the need to pick up the silence, he said, "I don't have much time for shade since my pa died."

"That bushing's got to be packed, as I see it," Joshua said, leaning against the tree trunk.

Sitting down, Caleb pulled up his legs and propped his elbows on his knees. "Guess you know a lot about running the river?"

"Don't take a genius to see when a bushing's slack, does it?"

"Suppose not," Caleb said, "though I ain't never seen one myself."

Slipping off his bandanna, Joshua dabbed at his brow.

"Whew, boy, does this shade feel good. I ain't been out that boiler room since hell was born." Leaning over, he picked a grass stem and stuck it in the corner of his mouth. "Been eating hog slop, too, no better than them colored boys. Don't seem right, do it?"

"Where you from?" Caleb asked.

"Cincinnati," he said.

"Why, that's just upriver. I near walked to Cincinnati myself cutting wood."

Sticking the piece of grass between his teeth, Joshua shrugged.

"See them soldiers up there?"

"I see them," Caleb said.

"See that little son of a bitch with the walrus mustache and walking stick?"

"So?"

"Well, that's General Phil Sheridan on his way to Fort Leavenworth."

"You don't say?"

"That's right, General Sheridan himself, this here nation's biggest hero. He's been up to Somerset parading around for all to see what a mean son of a bitch looks like what comes back from the war."

Caleb shaded his eyes and looked him over.

"Don't look like no hero, does he, not that I've ever seen a hero."

"Well, heroes always look that way," Joshua said. "But he's a mean son of a bitch and no man's friend. Just ask any one of them soldiers up there, and they'll tell you the same. Some say he's going to clean up the West just like he cleaned up the South, by killing everything what moves and burning the rest. When Sheridan's done, there won't be a Indian left west of the Ohio. That's what they say."

Caleb checked on his wood. It hadn't taken long for that many hands to move what had taken him a week to cut.

"How is it you know so much about Sheridan?" he asked.

"Because that's where I'm going, too, all the way to Fort Leavenworth to join up with the Seventh Cavalry."

"No you ain't."

"That's right," he said, spitting out the piece of grass. "I run off, didn't I. Got a job on the *Belle* and been eating smoke and sweating like a pig all the way from Cincinnati, but it's a Indian fighter and a hero I'm going to be, you just wait and see, a mean son of a bitch just like ole Sheridan up there, providing I don't die of heat stroke or get poisoned on carp."

"It's a fair way to Fort Leavenworth, I'll bet?"

Joshua took hold of a limb overhead and let his body droop as he watched the last of the wood go up the gangplank.

"A fair way they say, though I ain't never been." He looked down between his arms. "You say your pa's dead?"

"Felled under a tree," Caleb said, looking away. "Same tree near took off my own foot."

"Thought you idled a little when you walked, like a winged duck."

"Some maybe."

"Damn shame about your pa."

"Wish he was here," Caleb said, "but wishing never cut no wood."

"Leaves a man shorthanded, when his pa dies like that?"

"I manage."

"Guess your ma helps out where she can?"

"My ma died of the fever."

"Well then," he said, "it's brothers and sisters what keeps you afloat?"

"Cut, clean, and haul myself, me and those ignorant mules over there."

"Make enough to get by?"

"Providing the weather holds, but then there's deer, opossum in a pinch."

"Guess the boats could use all the wood a man could cut?" Joshua said, dropping his head between his arms.

"Wood don't come easy."

Joshua stuck his hands into his back pockets and looked down the river.

"I better be getting back to the boat to help get the steam up. Captain said come on board for your money."

Caleb struggled to keep pace with Joshua's long stride as he followed him up the gangplank. He stopped at the top to say good-bye, and that's when he saw her, standing at the stern, her parasol twisting on her shoulder, the smell of her perfume like honeysuckle on a summer morning. About her neck was a fleur-de-lis, carved of rosewood, banded in gold, lying in splendor between the white mounds of her breasts. The black of her hair shimmered from the water's reflection as she leaned over the railing to watch the men at work. Never in Caleb's wildest dreams had he imagined that such beauty could exist.

"Fine-looking woman, ain't she?" Joshua said.

Black smoke poured from the stack as the bushing was tested, the engine's power evident in the green churn of water.

"She's beautiful," Caleb said.

"That's Joan Monnet, daughter of a big-shot railroad man. They say she's on her way to marry herself a lieutenant, and ain't the likes for woodcutters to be gawking at."

"Or boiler hands either, I'm thinking," Caleb said.

"It's a point, I suppose, though a poor one."

"Good luck, Joshua. Ain't every day I meet a hero in the making."

"Same to you, Woodcutter," he said with a wave of his hand.

After collecting his pay from the captain, Caleb made his way down the gangplank. He hesitated for a moment at the bottom to consider a last look up, but then she would not be there, that much he knew, such being the way of visions and dreams.

Chapter 3

That night, Caleb slept hard, dreaming of parasols, of yellow honeysuckle, of slack bushings and walnut wood. When something awakened him, he sat upright, gasping for air. So black was the night about him that his head whirled. He searched the darkness for the window, for the moon's reflection, or for a single star.

A man alone knows the margins of solitude, and Caleb knew that he was no longer alone. Should he call out, order them away with bravado, or be silent, let them take what they wanted in the hope they would leave him unharmed? But if they were there to kill him, to take his pay or to slit his throat for flour and sugar, what then? Even now he had no notion where his father's rifle was or even if it was loaded. Perhaps it was Baud, some trouble at home, or perhaps it was his imagination gone wild or a dream he couldn't stop. He'd heard of such things, of men going mad in their isolation.

Slipping from bed, he found the wall with his hand and edged along it in the darkness. If he couldn't see them, then they couldn't see him, at least that was his hope, his single plan for escape. It was then that the moon slid from behind a cloud, its ivory light against the windowpane, and he froze, pushing himself into the shadows.

A glint of light refracted from the blade of his father's axe, which leaned against the wall, there by the fireplace where it was kept. In his panic, he'd forgotten it altogether.

The handle was secure in his grip when the door creaked, and a sliver of moonlight fell across the floor. The figure cast a shadow, a murderer there to kill him in his sleep. With his heart stilled, Caleb raised the axe above his head and waited. There were few men better with an axe, and if he must, he would destroy this enemy. The shadow moved, then stopped, then moved again.

Certain now that he must attack with advantage, Caleb yelled, a war whoop, a scream of such passion that a chill raced down his own spine as he charged across the room, axe poised above his head.

The shadow, too, screamed, fear-struck at the lunatic thing descending from the night, and had it not been for the chair, Caleb's plan would have been executed without flaw. Instead, a blinding pain shot up from his toe and set off lights behind his eyes.

"Yeow!" he screamed, falling to the floor, his axe skidding against the wall.

"Don't kill me! Don't kill me!" the voice cried out from the black.

Caleb searched out the axe. Bluffing, he said, "Put down your gun, or I'll shoot you where you stand."

"I ain't standing," the voice said, "and I ain't got a gun."

There was something in the voice that Caleb recognized. "Who are you?"

"I ain't never been so lost," the voice said, "and now I'm dead."

"Who are you, and what are you doing in my cabin?"

"Oh, lordy, don't shoot," the voice answered.

Caleb, axe in hand, crawled over to the fireplace. With a match from the mantel jar he lit the lantern, holding it over his head. A man was curled on the floor, soaked to the skin, his hands covering his head.

"If it ain't Joshua Hart," Caleb said, "come back to rob me."

Joshua looked up at him through wet hair. "Woodcutter?"

Setting the lantern down on the mantel, Caleb straightened the chair and sat down, laying his axe across his lap. Even now his toe throbbed like a bad tooth, and he rubbed at the pain crawling up his leg.

"Guess you come back to kill me, take my walnut money, and buy yourself a time in Louisville?"

Joshua pushed his hair back from his eyes and said, "You going to cut my head off, Caleb?"

"I ain't decided yet."

"I ain't no thief, Caleb. I swear I ain't."

"What you call sneaking in my house, a visit? A invite to a box lunch or Sunday chicken dinner?"

Sitting up, Joshua rubbed at the weariness on his face. There was mud on his clothes, and one shoe was missing. A scratch ran the length of his cheek, and an eye was swollen into a dark slit.

"It ain't that way at all, Caleb. I got throwed off the *Belle* and damn near drowned when the paddle wheel sucked me under. I ain't never been so scared in my life, swimming in the dark, not knowing if I was going up or down."

"Throwed off?"

"Like a cat in a tow sack," he said, shaking against the cold. "Got in a poker game with them colored boys down in the boiler room. Guess they figured I was cheating, because first thing I know I'm spouting water and praying for shore. I been walking in these trees ever since, lost as I ever been lost, until I came upon this cabin. Didn't look like no one lived here, so I just thought to come in, take a nap until morning, you know, figure out where I was and what to do next."

"Never thought to knock, I suppose?"

"It ain't much of a cabin, Caleb, you have to admit. No offense."

Caleb set his axe aside and examined his bruised toe. Even in the dim light, he could see the damage was considerable.

"Still, a man ought knock or take the consequences, that's what I say."

Standing up, Joshua wrapped his arms about himself.

"You ain't going to chop off my head, are you, Caleb?"

"Well, much as I'd like to, it's a bloody affair, and the cleanup just ain't worth it."

Joshua's gaze shifted to the door, then back toward Caleb. "You think maybe I could stay the night?"

"How am I to know you won't murder me in my bed, come skulking up and run me through with a knife or a pitchfork?"

Rubbing his hands up and down his arms, Joshua shook his head.

"I swear I won't, Caleb. You can chain me to that door if you want. I ain't never murdered nobody in my life. I ain't even cheated at poker."

"Well, all right, but just for tonight. Wash up that river mud, though, because it's a stink in this rude cabin of mine, and there's some biscuits in the larder. Throw that blanket there on the floor for the night."

When he'd finished washing up, Joshua took a biscuit and sat down on his blanket. After chewing a while, he said, "It's a mighty hard biscuit, Caleb."

"Well, I ain't got the knack of biscuit making yet," he said, pulling up his covers.

"Tastes like copper, too."

"Goddang it, Joshua, you don't like my cooking, just put it back."

"Sorry, Caleb. I didn't mean no offense."

"Just go to sleep," he said, turning over, "before I throw you back in the Ohio."

Morning broke cold, with a sharp wind howling through every crack in the cabin, and there wasn't any shortage of cracks, the chinking having long since loosened between the logs. Shivering, Caleb slipped on his britches and examined his stubbed toe. Wincing, he worked his foot into the boot and waited for the throbbing to subside. Maybe he ought to just cut it off and be done with it, given its sad history.

Joshua curled small and half frozen under his blanket, the stink of river mud emanating from his clothes. Even though Caleb was determined to be angry with Joshua's intrusion, the prospect of having company about was exciting.

The dawn light fell across Joshua's face. Sitting up, he squinted into its glare.

"Lordy, but what it's cold," he said.

Caleb was perched on the side of his bed. "Well, build a fire, unless it's a inconvenience. There's firewood cut out there on the porch."

Hopping on one foot and then the other, Joshua started the fire, backing up to it in the hope of a little heat. A downdraft puffed smoke from the chimney, filling the cabin with its pungent smell, but soon flames were licking high.

"Oh, that *does* feel good," Joshua said, holding his palms to the flames. "What's for breakfast?"

"Biscuits," Caleb said.

"Biscuits?"

"Yes, biscuits."

"I still got a biscuit," Joshua said, pointing to his stomach. "It ain't moved one iota all night."

Caleb poured two coffees and took his place by the window. It was his favorite breakfast spot, because from there he could see the river, as well as the stable, and when the leaves fell, his father's grave would be visible at the top of the hill.

"Just dunk it in that coffee," he said. "Loosens it up." Taking a sip from his cup, he checked to see if Ben and Sophie were waiting for their feed yet. "Guess you'll be moving on to Louisville on the next steamer, then?"

Joshua dunked his biscuit and chewed in earnest before speaking.

"Fact is, those colored boys took my money before they escorted me into the river. Guess I'd have to walk to Louisville, providing something don't come up."

"You could swim," Caleb said. "It's downstream all the way."

Chewing, Joshua looked over at him. "It ain't easy swimming with a belly full of rocks," he said.

"I been thinking," Caleb said, "given you're here, and given I'm shorthanded, that maybe you could help me cut wood, least through the winter. Since it's my team and wagon, and my cabin, poor as it may be, I'd take two-thirds and you one-third of every load cut. Come spring, you'd have enough to move on."

Joshua walked to the window and looked down on the river.

"It's a fine offer, Caleb, but I figured to be in Fort Leavenworth by winter earning my sergeant's stripes."

"Well, suit yourself," he said.

Outside, the wind howled, and a blast of chilled air swept under the cabin door. Steam from Joshua's cup fogged on the glass pane, shrinking away against the cold.

"Course, spring would be soon enough, I suppose, though I ain't had much experience cutting wood."

"I need a loader," Caleb said, dropping his empty cup into the dishpan. "Bending over to pick up wood don't take all that much experience or brains either one."

Sipping on his coffee, Joshua thought it over. "Reckon it's better than swimming to Louisville," he said.

"Good then. Now, there's dry clothes in that trunk, and we'll fix up a bunk there next to the fireplace. The work's one-third to two-thirds right down the line. When you're finished dressing, come help me catch up the belly bands on these blame mules."

As the season deepened into autumn, they worked their wood, rising at dawn, falling weary into their bunks as the sunsets gave way to night. Soon, leaves cascaded from the treetops and covered the forest floor, whispering and crunching underfoot as the wood was cut and loaded. The smell of earth was about them, the quiet and promise of autumn.

The work was hard, but Joshua kept pace. Considering his frail build, he was tough and could put in a day's work. Of course, there was his endless talk of the army, his annoying swagger, and his bent for stretching the truth, but for the most part it was harmless, and they soon were fast friends. In the main, Caleb was glad for the company and the end of his loneliness.

Their stash of money grew with each trip to the dock. They bought supplies and hid the remaining cash away for safekeeping under Ben's feed trough. Still, Caleb's discontent mounted with the passing days and with the promise of winter. Sometimes at night he dreamed of the girl on the *Belle*, her fleur-de-lis against the whiteness of her skin, her hair as black as a raven's plume. His heart pounding, he would sit upright in his bed, a fire smoldering deep and unquenchable within him.

Climbing into the wagon, Caleb leaned back against the freshly cut wood. Reaching into his coat pocket, he retrieved the late-season pears he'd picked that morning and tossed one to Joshua.

"Ain't a biscuit, is it?" Joshua asked, pushing back his hat.

"It's a pear, your majesty," Caleb said, taking a bite.

Sitting down on the wagon bed, Joshua polished the pear against his shirt.

"Lordy, I wished I was in Leavenworth," he said, looking up into the trees. "I'd be a sergeant by now, what with stripes up my arm like a spring rainbow. Most likely be a hero, too, a mean son of a bitch, just like ole Sheridan, parading up and down main street for everybody to see."

"And maybe you'd have a arrow up your bum, from hiding your head in the sand."

"Maybe you'd kiss it then," Joshua said, grinning.

"Maybe I'd say a prayer and bury it for pity's sake," Caleb said, flipping the core of his pear into the leaves.

"I'd look fine in them blue uniforms, Caleb. Ain't a woman made what can resist a army uniform. Take a hero like myself, built like ole Ben here, if you know what I mean, just makes a man damn tempting to the opposite sex."

Caleb pulled his knees into his arms and rubbed at the ache in his foot.

"It's your power of reasoning that's in common with Ben, Joshua, and your smell, maybe the lilt of your ears, too, come to think on it."

"Well, when I get in the army, you'll see."

Taking off his hat, Caleb ran his fingers through his hair. Even under the autumn sun, woodcutting was hot work. "There's something I been wondering, Joshua."

"What's that?"

Reaching for his honing stone, Caleb worked at the burr that had developed on the axe blade from the morning's work. "Why you ain't wrote home? Won't your kin be wondering if you're dead or alive?"

Shrugging, Joshua studied the half-eaten pear. "It's different for me, Caleb, and ain't likely you'd understand."

"Understand what?" he asked, tossing away the core.

"My pa's a son of a bitch," he said, "not a Sheridan son of a bitch, but a selfish, no-good son of a bitch. Oh, it weren't the whippings, though there were plenty of those, but the other no-good stuff that made you hate him and hope him dead."

"Sometimes everyone feels that way, Joshua. It's just part of growing up, I'm thinking."

"It ain't a sometime hate with my pa," he said, tucking his hands into his pockets and kicking at a stone, "but a full-time hate, for a full-time son of a bitch, and I don't know I'll ever go back, not alive at least."

"What could he have done so bad?"

"Like none of us kids could eat until he was finished, until he put down his napkin and pushed back his chair. Course, by then there wasn't but gristle and bitter greens left, or cold gravy, or bits of meat he'd done stacked with his fork on the side of his plate. 'Eat your food, boy,' he'd say. 'I earned that food hard, and it ain't to be wasted. Eat it all or, by God, come tomorrow you'll do without.' Sometimes I sat in that chair just looking, just looking for the longest while at that food until both my legs gone dead as stumps hanging off that chair."

"It's a tough thing for a young'un," Caleb said.

"The next day I'd go without food just like he said. Go to bed with my belly growling like a trapped coon, but at least I didn't have to eat gristle and greens or listen about how hard a living he made."

"What about your ma?"

"My ma never raised a hand to me," he said, pausing, turning his back as if to listen for a steamer coming downriver, "but she never raised one to protect me either. It's a wonder to live like that."

"Guess I had no right asking," Caleb said, resting the axe on his shoulder.

"It got worse later on," Joshua said, shrugging.

"It did?"

"Yup. I got throwed in the Ohio River and left to eat copper biscuits with a wild man."

"Come on," Caleb said, grinning, "if we don't get this wood cut, neither one of us will be eating anything."

The days grew short and colder as they worked away the weeks into winter, but even with less daylight, they cut and stacked a load a day, their skills more polished, their confidence more certain. At night they sat about the fire and talked of the army, of wood, and of their savings under the trough, but most of what they talked about was their own virility and the glory and mystery of women.

At what point Caleb fell in love with Joshua's dream he wasn't certain, but what he came to know was that he, too, wanted to join the army, to wear the uniform, to be a hero and mean Sheridan son of a bitch just like Joshua. The more they talked, the more convinced Caleb was of the possibility, and the more his own world shrank about him.

Winter fell sudden, snow whipping through the trees like stinging white sand. On bad days they built a fire in the woods, pulling off their gloves to warm their fingers against the flames before returning to work. Standing hour after hour, Ben and Sophie suffered the most, snow gathering in their ears and clinging to their eyebrows like wet pearls.

At night they built their fire high and hot in the cabin and again when they left for work in the mornings, because it was firewood they could most afford. Sometimes at night, the coals would still be warm, no small luxury in the bitter cold as they returned from work.

It was on such a day that they made their way back to the cabin, a fresh-cut cord of pecan stacked and ready on the dock behind them. Come morning, they would meet the *Belle* and sell their wares for what the market would bear. Ben and Sophie picked up their pace in anticipation of corn and the dry of their stable. Orange streaks bolted from the horizon and into the blue of the sky as the sun dropped. Pulling up his collar against the wind, Joshua rode in silence, his hands tucked into the sleeves of his coat for warmth.

The smell of smoke from the cabin lifted their spirits as they pulled up the draw. Caleb leaned forward and snapped the reins to hurry them along. The day had been long, and his muscles ached.

"Whoa, Ben. Whoa, Sophie," he said, pulling up.

"What's the matter?" Joshua asked.

"There," he said, pointing to the sky. "Looks like the whole blame woods is on fire."

"Oh hell! It's the cabin, Caleb. She's burning to the ground."

"Giddup!" Caleb yelled, popping the reins.

As they rounded the corner into the clearing, Caleb's heart sank. Flames roared from the chimney and licked at the windowpanes. The cabin creaked, tired and defeated against the terrible heat that churned within her.

"Get the feed buckets from the stable," Caleb yelled, jumping from the wagon. "We'll carry water up from the creek."

Standing on the wagon seat, Joshua just shook his head.

"It's too late, Caleb," he said. "It's a chimney fire, and there ain't no putting her out now."

Falling to his knees in the snow, Caleb watched as the cabin groaned and a wall surrendered to the flames. Heat burned against his face and dried the tears that ran down his cheeks.

"I failed to clean that chimney, Joshua," he said. "My pa would have tanned my hide for such a thing. Now everything I owned is gone. I don't even have a clean shirt to put on. It's all gone."

The cabin gave way with a sigh, collapsing inward into the fire as it flared in a grand finale against the darkening sky.

Putting his hand on Caleb's shoulder, Joshua comforted him.

"It ain't all gone, Caleb. We got our stash in the stable, and you still got ole Ben and Sophie here. It's just a cabin gone, that's all, and a damn poor one at that."

That night they slept in the stable. Smoke from the charred remains of the cabin hung heavy in the air as they prepared their beds. They shivered under saddle blankets and pulled hay about themselves to ward against the bitterly cold wind that swept into the stable. Ben and Sophie leaned against one another for warmth and wondered at the invasion of their privacy.

Snow fell, great white flakes that dipped from the black sky and blanketed the woods. Even as the night grew silent, Caleb lay awake. It wasn't much of a cabin, like Joshua said, a small loss in the scheme of things, but it was all he'd had, all he'd ever known, all he'd ever been. Now there was naught but his father's axe and team and the apprehension of an uncertain future.

Morning broke clear, the sun sparkling cold across the frozen woods. Ben's and Sophie's breaths rose in a cloud as they awaited their feed.

"Goddang it," Joshua said from beneath the hay.

"What's the matter?" Caleb asked, sitting up.

"There's a chicken standing on my chest."

"Well, catch her up," Caleb said. "I can't leave them here for the coyotes to eat, anyway."

When Joshua grabbed her leg, the chicken squawked in alarm. "What am I supposed to do now?" he asked, gathering her into his arms.

"There's a wire cage over there," Caleb said. "I'll catch up the others while they're still roosting."

When they were all caught and placed in the cage, they loaded it into the back of the wagon. Then they loaded the remaining sacks of corn and an old harness that Caleb's dad had hung on a nail for repairs.

"What you going to do with all this?" Joshua asked, rubbing his hands against the cold.

"Take them over to Baud's. Maybe he'll stake us some blankets and grub until we get a chance to buy supplies."

After they'd harnessed the team, they hooked them up to the wagon and built a small fire in the stable. They cooked eggs in the bottom of a feed bucket, eating them with their fingers and without the benefit of salt or grease.

"That was awful," Caleb said, wiping at his mouth.

"Better than copper biscuits," Joshua said, "though not much, I admit."

Caleb wiped his hands on his pants and squared his hat.

"Better get over to Baud's before he goes to work."

They climbed up on the wagon seat, turned up their collars, and hunkered down against the cold. A circle of ash lay beneath the snow where the cabin had once stood, and curls of smoke still rose into the cold morning air. The stone steps his father had built for the front porch stood forlorn.

At the big maple tree, Caleb pulled up at his father's grave for a moment, the cypress cross gray and drab against the snow.

"Where do we go from Baud's?" Joshua asked.

"I been thinking on it," Caleb said, reining Ben and Sophie about and into the woods.

Blowing on his hands, Joshua waited. "Well?"

"I figure to join the army, too," he said. "If it's mean sons of bitches they want, then who better than me?"

"It's a rare man what sees his own nature," Joshua said, grinning. "But I don't figure we got enough money for both of us, Caleb. It's a fair way to Kansas from here."

Caleb leaned into his elbows and studied Ben's rump as they made their way through the snow.

"We can work our way downriver," he said. "Cut wood, sleep in the wagon, sell to the steamers at the fuel stops. Once we get to Louisville, we should have enough money for train tickets to Kansas."

"We'll join the army, by god," Joshua said, clapping his hands, "mean sons of bitches that we are."

Standing at his door, Baud buttoned his neck collar and reached for his coat.

"That's a real shame, Caleb," he said. "Near burned this ole nest down myself one time. Those chimneys start huffing, there ain't no stopping them. Climbed that roof like I was sixteen, what with a bucket of water in both hands, and got her doused. It was close, though, and my back hurt for a month afterward."

"This here's Joshua," Caleb said, climbing down from the wagon. "He's my new cutting partner. We was hoping to trade out some goods, Baud, what with these chickens, my half of the raft, too. There's a load of pecan down on the dock. I figure it's worth a gun, if you got one to give. My pa's burned up in the fire."

Baud stepped out on the porch. "Won't you be needing that raft come spring?"

"Me and Joshua here's joining up with the cavalry, Baud. It's heroes they looking for, and we figure to fit the bill."

Baud reached for his makings and rolled a cigarette, touching it off with a match. He blew smoke into the cold morning air. "That a fact?"

"Yes, it is. If you'll stake us a little grub and some blankets what we don't freeze, we figure to cut wood down to Louisville and catch a train up to Leavenworth."

"You boys get your peckers hung off a teepee pole, you ain't careful," he said, looking up through a cloud of smoke. "I hear them Indians save 'em up for souvenirs, that's what I hear."

"If it's peckers they're looking for, they could do a lot better than ole Joshua here," Caleb said.

"Well, maybe so," Baud said, picking a piece of tobacco off his tongue, "but a man's pecker is a mighty dear sacrifice, no matter how humble."

"You figure to help us, Baud?" Caleb asked.

"I guess we could scare up some flour and lard, Caleb, a little coffee, too. I got an old pistol and half a box of shells, but I ain't got no rifle. There's a couple of wool blankets, if you don't mind the itch and a hole or two."

"That will do fine, Baud, and feel free to take them timbers out our stable if you've a notion. I turned that ole milk cow out. She's near dry, anyway. Catch her up if you want."

Dark-eyed children watched from behind the door, giggling as they fought for position while Caleb and Joshua waited for Baud to return.

Sliding a tow sack into the back of the wagon, Baud dusted his hands before handing Caleb the old pistol.

"Guess that's it, Caleb," he said. "Don't suppose you boys would change your mind? I'd be glad to put you up while you built a new cabin."

Climbing into the wagon, Caleb reached down and shook Baud's hand.

"It's time I got out of these woods, Baud. They started closing in to where I can't stand it no more."

Kids watched on from the doorway, their heads like cord wood. Baud looked back at them. "Yes sir," he said. "That's the way of it as I recall."

"You check on my pa's grave now and again, Baud? A man's grave ought not be forgot."

"I'll see to it," he said.

"So long, Baud," Caleb said, tipping his hat.

"So long, boys," Baud said, turning back to his cabin.

The wheels of the wagon crunched in the snow as they made their way through the trees. Sophie shook her head against the harness, her breath rising into the cold. Looking back over his shoulder, Joshua watched as Baud's cabin disappeared behind them.

"You know the way to Louisville, don't you?" Joshua asked.

"I ain't never been out of this valley," Caleb said, "not in my whole life."

"How we going to get to Louisville, Caleb, if we don't even know the way?"

"Same as the *Belle*, Joshua," he said, pointing to the snow-covered banks of the Ohio below them, "by following that water wherever she goes."

Chapter 4

That night, Caleb and Joshua made camp in a draw. A small creek twisted through the trees and slipped unnoticed into the great expanse of the Ohio below. So slow had been their progress that day that Ben and Sophie were anxious to return to the stable for the night.

Come feed time, neither would eat, Ben tipping the feed bucket over with his nose. Braying, he pawed at the ground, his mouth twisted and his yellow teeth flashing at the humiliation of being staked out. Sophie, too, lay back her ears and swished her tail. Threats from Caleb were to little avail.

Digging through the tow sack for the first time, Caleb lay out the goods Baud had provided. The fare was simple but generous: beans, lard, salt, and flour. There was an old coffee pot, an iron Dutch oven, a mason jar filled with matches, some loaves, and half a pound cake slathered with butter.

"Look it here," he said, showing Joshua the contents. "Guess we'd have starved hadn't been for ole Baud taking care of us."

As the sun dropped away, the night fell clear and cold, and stars blinked on. Soon the night sky shimmered with lights. A steamboat's whistle rose somewhere in the distance. Joshua moved his feet in close to the fire, propping up on his elbow.

"How long you figure to Louisville, Caleb?"

"Depends on the cutting along the way. I aim to take the easy wood as we go and try not to top off a load too soon. There ought to be docking stops now and again where we can sell our wood, get supplies if we need. What with the money we have saved away, we should be okay."

After Joshua had gone to sleep, Caleb checked their money stash in the jockey box, counting the bills in the firelight before returning it. It was going to take some doing to get them to Leavenworth even with the extra. He climbed into his bedroll and pulled the covers up against the cold, lying sleepless as the moon tracked its way through the night.

The next morning, they followed the Ohio as planned, losing hours in the river's endless meandering. But at least they were secure in the way and knew that, sooner or later, the river would deliver them to Louisville.

As the sun set that day, the winds died away, and their spirits rose. The river turned southwesterly, mounting and swelling in its seaward flow. And when smoke rose above the treetops, they pulled up to listen and could hear the distant chug of a riverboat engine.

"She's not moving," Caleb said. "She's tied up at shore. Let's get on over there with our wood."

Joshua nodded his agreement. "And then a hot fire and some food," he said.

"And a little more money for the jockey box."

It was a steamer, just as they'd thought, a small freighter working the shore for whatever it could scavenge. A wagon was pulled up near the dock, and the captain was talking to a bearded man with a jug in his hand. The captain took the jug and handed it to one of his men before coming toward them.

"What is it you boys are looking for?" he asked.

"Have firewood for sale, Captain."

"I'm not interested in buying green wood," he said.

"It's hardwood, cured, and a bargain at five dollars a cord."

The captain looked the wood over. "Appears green to me," he said. "Three dollars and my men will unload it."

"That's a five-dollar cord, Captain. Maybe six."

"Three dollars or pack it on to Louisville yourself," he said.

Caleb looked at Joshua, who shrugged and turned up his palms. "Three it is then," he said.

The captain counted out the money and went to get hands for unloading the wood. Caleb was putting the money away when the bearded man drove by with his wagon, tipping his hat as he rumbled past.

That night, they camped not far from the river. After the fire was built, they set soup to boiling over the coals. Caleb went to the wagon for salt. The moon was bright, and the river shimmered below in the valley. In that moment, he sensed someone watching, someone in the shadows. A tingle ran up his spine.

"Who is it there?" he asked.

A man stepped out of the darkness. He had a beard, and his hat was cocked over an eye. It was then that Caleb remembered him as the man he'd seen talking to the captain earlier.

"Name's Lee Horn," he said.

"What is it you want?" Caleb asked.

"Something smells mighty good," he said.

"You traveling alone?"

"Alone, for certain," he said.

Joshua, who had been tending the fire, heard their voices. "Who is it, Caleb?"

"Says his name is Lee Horn, and he's smelling our soup." He turned. "I figure there's enough for three. You're welcome to stay. Come on over to the fire."

"That's mighty kind of you," he said. "I'll tend my horses first if you don't mind."

When he'd finished with the horses, Lee Horn joined them at the fire, standing up close for warmth. He had the look of hard times about him, of a man living by the day. Caleb poured soup into tin cups and cut the bread Baud had provided, passing the food around.

"It's a tad thin," he said. "But it's hot."

"I favor thin soup," Lee Horn said, sipping at the rim of his cup. "What you boys doing out here in the middle of nowhere?"

"We're headed to Kansas," Joshua said.

Lee Horn looked up, pointing his chin. "It's a mighty long road to Kansas."

"We'll be buying tickets on the train when we get to Louisville," Caleb said.

"Tickets, you say?"

"Joshua and me been cutting wood along the way, selling it out to the steamers."

"That's right smart of you boys," Lee Horn said. "By the time you get there, you figure to have enough saved up, do you?"

"That's right," Caleb said. "We got a good start at it already."

"And what's in Kansas, I wonder? You boys got kin waiting?"

"We got no kin waiting," Joshua said. "We will be joining up with the cavalry at Leavenworth. Going to fight Indians with ole Sheridan."

Lee Horn looked over the top of his cup. "I never knew a tougher man myself than ole Sheridan."

"You knew Sheridan?" Caleb asked.

"Fought with him at Missionary Ridge," he said.

"You kill many men in the war?" Joshua asked.

"Right many, until I got shot my own self," he said.

"You got shot?"

"Gut shot," he said. "Most men would have died, they said."

Joshua leaned in. "Did it hurt, being gut shot, I mean?"

Lee Horn set his cup aside and reached for a stick to poke at the fire. "No more than the burning fires of hell," he said.

"I don't figure on it myself," Joshua said. "I'll be keeping my head down all the way."

Lee Horn stood and stretched his arms over his head. "No one figures on getting gut shot, do they. Well, if you boys don't mind, I'll be settling in for the night. That wagon has me beat. I'll be thanking you boys for the soup. It was mighty satisfying."

Caleb awoke at sunrise, pulling the covers over his ears. The fire smoldered, and frost covered the ground. Joshua was curled up for warmth, his bare feet sticking out from under his blanket. Caleb sat up and rubbed the sleep from his eyes. His heart ticked up when he realized that Lee Horn's wagon was missing.

"Joshua," he said.

Joshua groaned and turned onto his side. "It's too early, Caleb. The sun ain't even broke."

"Joshua, Lee Horn's wagon is gone."

"Good riddance if you ask me," he said, turning over again.

Caleb pulled his britches on. "Come on, Joshua."

"Stoke the fire up first, Caleb," he said. "It's awful cold."

Caleb walked to the edge of the camp, and his fears were proven. "It's been opened," he said.

Joshua got up, hanging his blanket over his shoulders, and joined Caleb. "What's opened?"

"The jockey box," he said. "It's been jimmied, and he's taken the money."

Joshua danced from one foot to the other against the chill. "That was every penny we had," he said. "We can't buy tickets with no money."

Caleb slammed the lid shut on the jockey box. "It's my fault," he said. "I shouldn't have trusted him that way, telling him about our money. I should have known better."

"I would have done the same, Caleb. How was you to know?"

"What we going to do now?" Caleb said.

"We could go back," Joshua said. "Or we could go on to Louis-ville, I guess, or we could stay here and die of starvation. What do you think?"

Caleb shrugged. "One way is as broke as the other," he said. "We just as well go on to Louisville and figure it out from there."

Chapter 5

Louisville spread out before them in the valley below, a stirring and live thing growing from the bend of the Ohio. Smoke rose from a thousand chimneys, gray columns drifting away in the wind. The last color of fall fluttered in the treetops as the leaves surrendered to the inevitability of winter. Climbing down from the wagon, Caleb turned his back to the cold and blew into his hands.

"I ain't never seen so many people in one place, Joshua," he said.

"Like a chicken yard, ain't it?" Joshua said, joining Caleb at his side. "All scratching for the same bug in the same piece of ground."

Water gathered in Caleb's eyes, and his body shriveled at the clamor below.

"I ain't never felt so small," he said, "like I wasn't no more than a drop of water."

"Well, you ain't," Joshua said, "and high time you found it out, just like the rest of us."

"I ain't no yeller drop, least," Caleb said.

"Come on, I'm near starved, Caleb. Maybe we can find something for supper, a side of sugar-cured bacon and a fresh cabbage."

"That dab of change in your pocket ain't going to buy a side of bacon and a cabbage," Caleb said.

"Taters?"

"Nope."

"A cabbage, then, for soup?"

"Turnips, I figure."

"Turnips? Lordy," he said, shaking his head, "I'd as soon eat a fresh cow pie."

"If we spend every cent comes our way, we ain't never going to get to Leavenworth," Caleb said, climbing back onto the wagon.

"Maybe we can find work," Joshua said, dropping into the wagon seat and stuffing his hands into his pockets. "I sure wish I could've kilt ole Lee Horn for the dirty, thieving son of a bitch he is."

"Well, there ought to be plenty of work," Caleb said, "what with so many people running about doing nothing."

Snapping the reins, he pulled Ben and Sophie onto the well-worn trail that led into the Ohio valley below. Both boys fell silent as they plodded along, neither willing to acknowledge that it wasn't hunger that twisted in their stomachs but the uncertainty of this strange new world.

Soon the trail widened into a road that followed the bank of the river, piers jutting and broken like imperfect teeth, the smell of green churning from the river bottom, the prattle of voices and laughter from every aspect. Dogs, with their tails curled like desert scorpions, yapped from under wagons, deranged and furious at their presence.

From all sides, children played in the dirt, indifferent to the cold and to the dust that matted their hair and clogged their eyes. All the while, Ben and Sophie pranced at the rein, white-eyed with fear at the possibilities about them.

Black men bottom-fished from the banks of the river, their eyes yellowed with age, their cane poles bent, their corks bobbing and dancing against the cold wind. The smell of smoke and brown sugar, of savory hams and bacon sides, of corn whiskey and tobacco, of perfumes and lotions incalculable in degree, breached the evening. From the doorways, women's laughter pealed like bronze bells.

The sun yielded, fuming and orange, as Caleb and Joshua bought food at the open market—turnips, a bacon rind for flavoring, and enough coffee for morning dawn. Even then their money was gone, but a few cents left between them, and they drew down in silence as they searched for a place to sleep.

Night descended as they led Sophie and Ben down the narrow path that wound to the shore of the river. The wind failed to drop with the clearing of the night, the flames of their campfire flapping like sheets as they set the Dutch oven to heat. After peeling the turnips, Caleb rendered the bacon rind while Joshua lay out their bedrolls in the lee of a wash.

Pulling up close to the fire, they waited then, against the friendless night, against their burning hunger and the loneliness within them that neither could acknowledge.

Stirring the turnips, Caleb waited for the water to boil away, for the glaze to thicken and shine as his father had taught him, and for the brown, no more than a touch on the tips. After serving them up, he took the last of the bread from the breadbox, dried now to hard pan, and topped it with the fried pork rind.

Like ancient cavemen they clung to their fire as they ate, fat glistening on their lips as they chewed at the rinds and watched the sliver of a moon slip overhead.

"I never had such good turnips, Caleb," Joshua said, setting down his cup. "Fact is, I never had good turnips at all, far as I can remember."

"Thanks," Caleb said. "It's a poor soul what can't relish the delicacy and bitters of a fine turnip."

A fiddle wailed in the distance, its dispirited voice fading on the shifting winds, and laughter rose in its place, derisive and scornful from the streets. Lamps winked from the blackness as boats rounded the bend of the river, one upon the other like fireflies on a June night.

"I've been thinking," Joshua said, cleaning his cup.

"It's a blessed sign," Caleb said, wiping the grease from his lips with the sleeve of his shirt.

"I've been thinking about ole Lee Horn," he said, "about him stealing our money like that. I've been thinking about it over and over like it was caught up in my head."

"It's best not to think on it, Joshua. What's done is done, and there ain't no changing it."

"Times like this I wish there was a hell," he said.

"Don't wish it too hard, Joshua, for fear it be true. Now, let's go to bed while I got the strength left to get there."

Neither slept but little, covers pulled about their ears against the cold, the howling wind, the trees bent and weeping against its fury. Lying awake, Caleb listened to the distant whistle of a steamboat, its sweet and sad voice, and he thought of the girl with the parasol, smelled her perfume in the wind.

Sometime before dawn, clouds swept in like an armada of raven ships, and the night was black. When the dawn broke at last, snow fell, blanketing the world in a bitter, white shroud.

Caleb made the coffee, holding the cup between his shivering hands for heat. Donning his clothes, Joshua shivered against the morning chill. His coat hung loose about his thinning frame, and his nose was large in the breaking light. Sparrows hunkered in the branches above him, balls of fluff against the cold.

Joining Caleb, Joshua warmed at the fire before filling his cup from the pot.

"I'm near starved to death," he said.

"Well, who ain't?"

"Maybe there's some turnips left?"

"There ain't no turnips left, Joshua. You took care of the turnips last night."

"Lordy," he said, "my stomach's squeaking like a dry wagon hub."

"Teach you to complain about my biscuits, won't it?"

"What we going to do today, Caleb?"

"Get work," he said, sipping at his coffee, "or shrivel up on this blame riverbank like a beached catfish, either one."

"What kind of work?"

Looking up through the steam of his cup, Caleb shrugged. "How do I know what kind of work, Joshua. I ain't never lived in no city before."

Sniffing, Joshua took a drink of his coffee. "You don't have to be so dang cantankerous, Caleb."

"Just work, that's all. I'll head north, you south. We'll meet back here tonight."

"You think we ought to separate, Caleb?"

Finishing his coffee, Caleb tossed the dregs into the fire and waited for them to hiss away. "It won't do no good to follow each other around all day, will it?"

He put his cup away and snugged his hat down over his ears. When Joshua stepped out of the woods, his shirttail hung out from the back of his coat, and there was snow on the seat of his pants.

"Lordy," he said, buckling his pants, "squatting in a snowbank is a bitter task, ain't it?"

"There's fescue running up that draw where the wind blew off the snow, Joshua. Why don't you graze out Ben and Sophie for a couple hours, and then take them down to the river for water. Soon as we get some money coming in, we'll buy a sack of crimped oats. Until then, they'll just have to make do."

"Jeez, Caleb, why do I have to be the one stays with the mules?"

"'Cause I'm smarter and more apt to find work amongst civilized folks, that's why," Caleb said. "I'll see you come dark, Joshua."

Even in the cold, the streets spilled with people, their endless chatter, their shrill laughter and incessant commotion, like blue jays and bull snakes in a tree, Caleb thought.

By noon he'd stopped at a half dozen places, met with naught but indifferent shrugs and grunts of maligned shopkeepers, and his nerves were fairly well set to edge.

Realizing that he was weak with hunger, he lifted a green apple at the market and squeezed himself between the limestone walls of two buildings to escape the cold and take a moment's peace. From the ledge above, pigeons watched with beaded eyes, warbling and dancing in protest at his intrusion. Pitching his spent core at them, he headed out for a final sweep down the riverfront.

So close to the river was the Beer Bucket Inn that the waterline still marked the slat door from the last spring flood. Pushing it open, Caleb waited for his eyes to adjust to the darkness. The smell of tobacco and urine hung in the darkness, and a fiddle squawked off-key from somewhere in the depths. Rows of pine slab tables stretched the length of the enormous room. Kerosene lanterns, with smoked and oily chimneys, flickered like fading sentinels in a storm. The bartender leaned forward, a dirty towel draped over his shoulder.

"What will it be?" he said, without looking up.

"I'm needing work," Caleb said.

Peering up through heavy brows, he took the towel from his shoulder and wiped the bar in a mindless circle.

"You ain't buying beer?"

"I'm a good hand at hard work, Mister."

"Ever tend bar?"

"No, sir."

"Good," he said, straightening up, "'cause I don't want some poke in here thinking to get my job."

"No, sir. I wouldn't be thinking that."

"It's beer we sell in here, kid, buckets of it, like the sign says. Come sundown, every river rat in Kentucky comes in for his swill and whatever else he can find or steal. I need boys to carry them buckets of beer and keep shut in the process. You up to that?"

Looking about the room, Caleb nodded.

"Yes, sir, I can fell a tree in seven swings, so I reckon I could carry buckets all right."

"I ain't never hired no gimp before."

"It ain't much of a gimp, sir, and don't slow me down in the least."

"Well, it's night work, and ain't for the faint of heart. They that come ain't church deacons looking for the gates of heaven. It's twenty-five cents at the end of the day, and any breakage is yours. Supper's at midnight, if the crowd's died down. Sometimes it is, and sometimes it ain't. Mind your own business. Mind it to a fault. Trouble breaks out, which it's apt to do, Jude breaks the bones around here and don't want no interference from sissy boys come down out of the hills, hear?"

"Yes, sir. I ain't looking for nothing like that."

"Then that's good," he said, pushing up the corners of his mustache. "You come back here at six o'clock."

"Yes, sir. I'll be here."

"And wash off some of that river stink in the meantime."

Caleb exited into the sunlight and covered his eyes against the glare as he calculated its position. There was no time to go back to the wagon to tell Joshua of his luck. He'd just have to wait.

At the river's edge, he cleaned himself as best he could in the cold water, digging the dried manure with a stick from the shank of his shoes and combing back his hair with his fingers. He took refuge from the wind behind a cotton bale, holding his face to the warmth of the sun, and closed his eyes to wait for six o'clock.

When he opened the door at the Beer Bucket Inn, it was as if the whole of the riverfront was waiting there. The lanterns were turned high, their greasy and close smell hanging in the air. Men drank and waited for the buckets of beer, foam drying in their beards. Women drooped about their necks, laughing, shrill and uncertain of their welcome, their great breasts ebbing from the tops of their filthy dresses.

From up front, a fiddler scratched out a dirge, a blind fiddler with milky eyes that rolled ungoverned and useless in their sockets. His knee bounced to the aimless beat, and rings of sweat gathered under his arms.

There was little room to walk among the tables as Caleb made his way to the bar. Catching the saloonkeeper's attention, he leaned over the glasses so that he might be heard.

"I'm here, sir, to work."

The saloonkeeper retrieved two buckets from under the bar.

"Fill these at the pump there, boy. It's a quarter a bucket, and bring back the empties for refilling. You keep that beer coming and that money to home."

"Yes, sir."

"It's a sad day when someone cheats the Beer Bucket, boy. You see that man yonder? Well, that's Jude, and Jude don't care what he hurts, so long as the wait's short. You understand what I'm saying?"

An immense figure was perched on a three-legged stool at the far end of the bar, his huge hands opened in his lap, inert cannons waiting for some horrific spark. Pig bristle vaulted from his balding head, and gristle gathered in rolls at the base of his neck. Scanning the crowd, he searched for the slightest signs of distress, a cougar at prey, taut and centered and irrevocable. The eyes saw but motion, focused and remorseless in their intent. Thick lips were pursed and drawn down, as if sewn and gathered by rawhide, and covered the black stumps in his mouth. Powerful shoulders sloped from somewhere high on his neck, from somewhere under the small ears buried under folds of skin. A leather belt was buckled about his waist, its band soiled from sweat and rub. Even in the yellow of the lamplight, his skin was white, as white as eggshell, from the darkness of his work and the shame of his soul.

"Yes, sir," Caleb said, taking his buckets and stepping into the pump line with the other boys.

So as the night passed, he worked, his shoes slick with spittle and foam, his arms aching, his fingers tender and bursting from wet. No sooner would he arrive with his beer than yet another would cry out "Boy, boy!" or bang his pipe against an empty bucket. Women, smelling of sour and babies, taunted him as he passed, slipping their hands up his leg as he leaned over a table or bent for a bucket, slapping their buttocks, laughing, strident and coarse as the calluses on their hands, pinching red welts on the backs of his arms.

When a sailor's chair slid back, and his voice rose, Jude moved from his perch like a great white bear, eyes trained, and the sailor fell silent, turning back to his beer with resignation.

By midnight, Caleb's legs trembled, and there was a fire in his ankle. He dreaded the thought of collapse and death beneath the raucous crowd and prayed that they would soon leave. But they did not leave, except in a slow and painful dribble as the night passed. Not until two in the morning did the last man stumble out the door.

Like starved prisoners, the bucket boys lined up along the wall, delivering up their coins to the barkeep, save the single quarter earned. Jude watched on from the end of the bar, lord of discipline and all things evil.

After a meal of cheese and stale bread, Caleb was done at last, and he stepped out into a cold and still fog. More certain of his sense of direction than his knowledge of streets, he struck due west, missing the path the first time around, backtracking, missing it again in the heavy fog. Finding it at last, he worked his way down, picking his way through the vapor. Steamboats blew their whistles from the river, obscure and shrouded in the night, and he followed their sound.

The camp was dark, the fire long since extinguished by mist and neglect. Caleb undressed, his foot throbbing, and slipped under the cold and damp covers. From across the way, Joshua stirred. "Caleb?"

"Yes."

"You find work?"

"It's work, all right, Joshua. You?"

"No."

"You try?"

"Down at the docks. They told me that coloreds work for half the pay and twice as hard. Told me to move on, or they'd send me to the bottom of the Ohio."

"Well, you'll try again tomorrow."

"Caleb?"

"What?"

"Did you bring food?"

"We'll buy flour and lard in the morning, Joshua."

"Night, Caleb."

"Night."

Mist gathered in Caleb's hair and clung to his eyebrows as he tried to sleep. Ben stomped his hoof beyond the trees, a discreet welcome back. And as Caleb drifted into sleep, he thought of home, and of Baud, riding tall and true and black through the woods. He thought of his father and the sound of his voice, the fulsome blows of his axe settling like pools inside his chest. He thought of the girl standing on the deck, and the fleur-de-lis about her neck, the wash of her breasts as she leaned from the rail.

By the time he awoke the following morning, his foot had swollen to twice its girth and throbbed with each beat of his heart. The quarter he'd earned bought a small sack of flour, lard, a quarter pound of coffee, and a half dozen chicken necks. After making biscuits, Caleb dredged the necks in flour and put them to fry in the Dutch oven. They shined the bones clean and sucked the marrow from their centers, like coyotes at a kill.

There was no money left for oats for the mules, so that afternoon, while Caleb slept in the wash, Joshua grazed them out on the fescue. It was to become a ritual that filled the following days. Each evening, Caleb rose from his bed like a corpse from the grave and made his way to the Beer Bucket Inn. Each night, he brought back his money, which was then spent to buy food and supplies for yet another day in the camp, and each day, his ankle worsened from the hours and the burden of the buckets.

"We're getting nowhere," Joshua complained, "no closer to Leavenworth, no closer to nothing, except the dead of winter and our own bleached bones."

Throwing his coffee into the fire, Caleb stood, his face flushed.

"This ain't no marriage, Joshua. You don't like it here, just move on to where you favor."

Joshua turned his back, crossed his arms, and walked to the edge of the camp. After some time, he said, "I'll go to the docks again today, but the whole thing's useless, and those blame mules are mighty poor company, I tell you."

That night, Caleb trudged to the Beer Bucket Inn, his foot stiffened from the cold and the hours on his feet. It was Friday night again and a hard shift ahead, the populace dead-bent, as usual, on drinking Louisville dry.

Standing at the bar, Caleb waited for his buckets.

"That gimp of yours ain't getting no better," the barkeep said. "Now, I ain't a man to push, but you're moving slower every night. You got to hold your own around here, boy, or I'll find someone what will. That's just the way of the world."

"The swelling was better on rising this morning," Caleb said, "and better every day, far as I know."

"See to it you earn your pay," he said, turning back to his bar.

By dark, the Beer Bucket Inn was awash with customers, the fiddler with his unmerciful tune, the women with their chaffed elbows and prickly legs, their breaths of onion and eggs. As the night wore on, Caleb labored under the buckets, the smell of swill, of mold and hops, and he tried not to think of his foot afire in the confines of his boot.

By midnight, the crowd showed little sign of lessening. When they broke into a song of "Rye Whiskey," clapping at their own absurdity, Caleb's stomach knotted with weariness.

Jude watched on at the end of the bar, alert for movement or change, for any shift of posture or turn of voice. Like a viper, no emotion registered in those eyes, black lagoons in the whiteness of his face, no uncertainty or distraction in the singularity of his mission.

The night grew late, the beer flowed, an inebriate and stinking river, and the crowd danced for no tomorrow, bellies fuming and fermenting with brew, the empty laughter, the swagger, the talk a crescendo, a stew of tasteless and banal commerce.

It was the sound of the man's voice, discordant and pitched with anger, that caused the fiddler to fall silent, his murky eyes rolling into the darkness of his lids. Moving to the end of the bar, Caleb set his buckets down, sensing danger, thick and suffocating in the crowded room. Jude stood, his face the white of a shark's belly, the serpentine slit of his eyes, the smallest lift at the corner of his mouth.

The man was young, his face flushed with anger, and he rolled his sleeves tight over his biceps as he glared at the man across the table. With cocked hat, he looked about. There was sweat on the furrow of his lip and in the thin of his beard.

"It's a whuppin' I aim to give you," he said, "for your dirty hands under the table."

The woman at his side giggled, pushing her breasts at the crowd, basking in the sudden attention. "It ain't nothing, Hatch," she said, pulling at his arm. "He's just feeling good, that's all."

By then Jude had reached the table, poised and silent from behind, a stalking cougar, invisible even to those in his midst. He never spoke or made a sound, the enormity of his presence and certainty of his cruelty turning the young man about. Sweat dripped from his brow and ran down his cheek, and a quiver jerked at the edge of his lip.

"Mind your business, monkey man," he said to Jude, dread

manifest in the crack of his voice and in the liquid that rushed his bowels.

Jude struck, not with passion or anger but with predatory instinct, the swift and irrevocable intent to kill. His huge hands clapped the ears of his prey, a thundering and sickening pop that stilled the drunken jeers. Blood trickled from the young man's lobes, droplets the color of wine, and into the stubble of his beard. The woman's screams fell unheard on his busted drums, and his eyes widened in disbelief at the white pain that surged through his brain.

Wounded and lost, he grabbed at Jude's great neck, to strangle the evil that had befallen him, but even so, Jude delivered a staggering blow into his uplifted face. He dropped to his knees and slumped, his arms about Jude's ankles, an invocation, a prayer for mercy. A brow dangled from its mooring, and an eye seeped, loosened and bloodied in its socket. Ivory slivers of cheekbone hung from the blood that gathered on his chin and coagulated in the corners of his mouth. The second blow silenced him, and he slid into the filth of the barroom floor.

The woman screamed again, a piercing scream, her arms trembling above her head. Jude shoved in her nose with the heel of his hand, and she, too, fell in silence. Looking neither this way nor that, Jude dragged them from the room by their arms, like deer slaughtered, a blood slick trailing from their feet.

Jude took up his place at the end of the bar, the blind fiddler sounded his bow, and the crowd drank once more, and laughed, and danced again into the night.

When Caleb got back to camp, Joshua was hunkered over the fire, a blanket pulled about his shoulders. The fire was well stoked and warm against the evening. He pulled up a stump, took off his boot, and rubbed at the swelling in his ankle. After considerable silence, he fished out the night's earnings from his pocket.

"Joshua," he said, handing him the quarter, "I ain't going back to the Beer Bucket, not for no quarter or for a hundred quarters.

In the morning, I'm going home. Woodcutting ain't much of a living, I admit, especially what with no cabin left, but fighting Indians for Sheridan was just a dream, a boy's dream, that's all. You and me both knowed it all along."

Firelight flickered across Joshua's face, and the moon broke overhead, big as a melon now, with its ivory light flooding the Ohio valley.

Joshua fished something from his hatband and handed it to Caleb.

"What is it?" Caleb asked.

"Tickets to Kansas City," he said, looking away, "for the price of a wagon, two old mules, and a wore-out pistol."

Chapter 6

Fog from the Missouri hung over Fort Leavenworth like a gray shroud and muffled the trumpeter's tattoo. As Caleb and Joshua made their way back to the gate, the barracks' lights dimmed behind them, winking away one after the other in the quieting evening. Horses whickered from the stables, a hundred stalls, and the smell of hay and corn drifted in from the evening feed. A stone guardhouse rose into the fog across the compound, foreboding in its gravity and silence. The smell of smoke rose from dozens of chimneys and hung still and heavy in the air.

At the fort gate, the guard leaned from the lantern light.

"Where you boys headed?" he asked.

"They're sending us on to Fort Riley," Caleb said, holding up the chits for him to see, "two tickets to Junction City on the Kansas Pacific Railroad and meal tickets to boot."

"It's a posh life, ain't it," Joshua said, "tickets on Uncle Sam, three squares a day, and fine new uniforms awaiting?"

Shifting his rifle to the other shoulder, the guard pushed back his hat. Moisture gathered on the brim and in the thick of his mustache.

"Oh, it's a dandy life," he said, "home away from home, ain't it.

Say, ain't Riley where Custer's mustering the Seventh?"

"Sure is," Joshua said. "We're joining up there. I guess they knowed real Indian fighters when they saw them, didn't they?"

The guard leaned his rifle against the wall and took out a twist, filling his jaw, giving it a roll before speaking.

"Why, I can see that myself," he said, spitting into the dirt between his legs. "General Custer will be mighty pleased to see you boys come help save him from the Indians and all. Wouldn't surprise me if he didn't invite you to supper for a chat, plan the war out and such as that."

"Aw, we don't know all that much about planning wars," Joshua said, "least not yet, though we did have a set-to getting here from Kentucky, didn't we, Caleb?"

"It's a fearsome pair you make, all right," the guard said, picking his rifle back up.

"We best be going," Caleb said to Joshua. "It's a fair walk to Junction City if we miss our train."

"You boys tell the general I said hey," the guard said.

As they made their way back to town, Caleb retrieved his axe from where he'd hidden it at the base of a rock fence. It was good in his hands, its weight and set comforting after the reserve and cold of Leavenworth.

"You going to carry that fool axe all the way to Riley?" Joshua asked.

"Maybe I just will," Caleb said. "It's got us this far, ain't it."

Below, they could see the lights of the city, and the lonesome whistle of a train sounded from down the valley. The ride from Louisville was alive, still, in Caleb's bones, the power and thrust of the engine as they'd charged through the countryside. With each mile his confidence had waned, drowned in the vast distances and speeds. But in those moments when he was tempted to go back, the smell of the Beer Bucket Inn and Jude's soundless vigil came back to him like a black dream.

"You think that guard was pulling our leg?" Joshua asked.

"About Custer and all?"

"Don't figure a general would be deliberating with privates what just enlisted," Caleb said, "even ones of particular intelligence."

"Especially ones what ain't kilt a man?"

Turning his axe on his shoulder, Caleb looked over at Joshua.

"Maybe when you kilt a hundred men, maybe then, or stormed a thousand strongholds or took a dozen arrows in your gizzard, maybe then a general would invite you to supper or for a smoke so's you could talk about the war."

"Well, maybe so," Joshua said, his voice trailing. "But killing a hundret could take some doing."

It was not until morning that their train was to arrive, so Caleb and Joshua took up seats near the woodstove in the little depot, dozing in its warmth, but at midnight, the operator invited them out. He blew out his lantern, locked the door behind them, and disappeared into the darkness.

Curling onto the wooden benches outside, they pulled their coats about their ears to wait for morning, but during the night, the fog turned to drizzle, then to sleet that chattered against the boardwalk and set them to shivering. They took refuge in an empty freight car that smelled of horse manure and awaited the coming dawn like chattel to market.

The train arrived with its whistle screaming. Half frozen and smelling of barn, they presented their tickets to the conductor, who in turn escorted them to the back of the car where other men were gathered for the final leg to Fort Riley. As the sun broke in the morning, the train chugged from the station, its engine wheezing and rumbling and struggling into the vastness of the prairie.

They fell silent and watched as civilization disappeared behind them. None spoke of his fears, even in his communion, each harboring his uncertainty at the choices he'd made. The prairie rolled into the sky about them, swelling and ebbing and swallowing them in its immensity. Haze drifted in its valleys, a blue and aimless smoke, and at times great herds of antelope watched motionless as they passed, the flick of a tail, or turn of an ear, or lift of a hoof.

When a pale river twisted through the valley ahead, the train banked, giving full view of the cars.

"Look at that," Caleb said, pointing to the car behind the engine.

"It ain't got but one big window," Joshua said, "with a curtain on it, too."

"It's a private car," the blond boy sitting next to Joshua said. "They say it's Monnet, big shot with the Kansas Pacific on his way to the railhead at Fort Harker. They say his daughter's with him, though I ain't seen her."

"With a whole car to hisself?" Joshua asked.

Taking out his makings, the boy rolled a cigarette and stuck it in the corner of his mouth. "His own private cook, too, least that's what they say."

"Lordy," Joshua said, taking another look. "I'd like to have my own cook right this very minute. I'd have him fry up some chicken, maybe a side helping of mashed taters and gravy, a slice of sourdough slathered in butter, ice-cold lemonade, and half a cherry pie for finishing."

"You ain't going to have no cook of your own," Caleb said, "now or never, or clean socks either, far as that goes."

"Well, if I had a cook, and he cooked up copper biscuits, I'd have him shot right off," Joshua said, "then I'd toss his body in the river without so much as a word to mark his passing. That's what I say."

When the train stopped for water, they all got off to stretch and to see what place had befallen them. A tower leaned into the blue sky, water dripping from between its weathered cedar boards. Starlings gathered on its top, darting down, one after the other in turn, to drink from the muddy puddle at its base. Down the track, a shack stood empty, its window clouded and gray, its chimney blackened and cold. The hopeless door sagged and squeaked against the prairie wind.

"Lordy," Joshua said, shaking his head, "it's the end of the world, ain't it, what with no place to eat or bury the dead. What we supposed to do with these meal chits, I wonder, cook them up in a black pot?"

Caleb looked down the platform, the smell of the air like sun-dried sheets. Beyond the slow chug of the train, the wind hummed its haunting refrain.

"Maybe we was supposed to eat before we left," he said, "or maybe it's some kind of army joke what played on recruits, or maybe it's just mean-spirited sons of bitches all the way 'round for all I know."

"I'm apt to be wasted dead away by the time I get to Riley," Joshua said.

When Caleb turned again, he saw her, standing at the steps of the private car, a parasol hooked over an arm, a fleur-de-lis about her neck. She held a gloved hand over her eyes and scanned the horizon, her gaze falling on Caleb for the briefest moment, and his heart stilled.

"Joshua," he said, "ain't that the girl who was on the *Belle?*"

"I'll be shot if it ain't," Joshua said, "all the way from Kentucky, too."

"Going west for her lieutenant, I suppose," Caleb said.

"Well, she ain't been following us from the Beer Bucket Inn, that's for sure."

"That must be her pa's private car, and this here his railroad."

"Well, it don't matter one way or the other, does it. It's the scraps from their table you'll be having, if you have anything at all. I'm thinking you spent too many years in the woods to know much about the world, Caleb. That girl just as well be the Queen of England, far as it matters for the likes of us. It's a world you and me ain't ever going to know, and that's just the way it is."

When Caleb turned back for a second look, she was lifting her skirt to step into the privileged world of the car. Her perfume lingered in the scrubbed air of the prairie.

He didn't see her again, not at the second water stop, where he walked the full length of the train in the hope of catching a glimpse, or at the station when they pulled in, or while they were loaded into a military ambulance for the last trek to Riley. As the wagon rumbled away, Caleb watched the car for as long as he could see it, its draped window flashing in the brightness of the afternoon sun.

There were no walls, no blockhouses, no gates at Fort Riley, just stone buildings arranged in a square, all facing the compound in both private and public matters. Some were as houses, officers' quarters, elegant and clean, while the enlisted barracks rose from the prairie like cold and detached mausoleums. Board walkways stretched their length, trussed and strutted for the endless goings of soldiers. Chimneys abounded, the smell of wood smoke thick and pungent.

Dust from the trampled parade ground gathered in their wheels and in their eyes as the wagon pulled to a stop. Turning, the driver wiped the water from the end of his nose and examined his sad cargo.

"All right, girls," he said, "this here's Riley. The corporal here will take you for your blanket and tick mattress issue. It's a blanket each and one tick between you. It's back to back, ain't it, and keeping to your own side. First thing, come morning, the Officer of the Day will see you to the surgeon. If you're well enough to be kilt in a proper military way, then you'll be sworn in, God help you, and took to your first sergeant, a kind and understanding man dedicated to the brotherhood of the Seventh Cavalry. Course, if you're too sickly or too lunatic to serve in the Seventh, you'll be turned out forthwith, and it's a free ride back to Junction City right here on this spot."

"Sir," Joshua said, "do we get to eat supper?"

"Meals in the army are morning and noon, boy. Supper is

coffee and bread, if there's any left over, and there ain't none left over today. Course, you kilt something out hunting, then that's extra, ain't it, and you can share it all around. Some buy from the sutler's store, but it's twice the price and mighty poor practice for a career man. There's many a soldier lost his pay and his stripes at the sutler's check, ain't he."

"Will we meet Custer soon?" Joshua asked.

"Soon enough, I suspect, and it's 'General Custer' or 'sir' to the likes of girlies like yourselves, 'less you want to be bucked and gagged and chained to the flagpole for the rest of your miserable lives."

That night they slept in an empty barracks where they were separated from the other soldiers. Still under construction, the room was without stove or lamps or anything beyond the bare bunks and their own unwelcome presence. As they climbed into bed, the night grew cold, and their loneliness mounted within the room's desperate vacancy.

Caleb lay awake, his axe secured under the tick. Back to back to Joshua, he listened to the sentry on the deck, the clack of his boots on the wooden planks, the pendular turn and pause of his watch. Pulling the blanket about his neck, he closed his eyes to await the morning.

Reveille sat them upright, like a blade in the soft bellies of their dreams. Shivering, they climbed from the warmth of their bunks and donned their clothes, their breaths rising into the cold of the room.

"Lordy," Joshua said, tying his boots, "I hope we get to eat some breakfast while I can still walk."

An officer stepped into the doorway. Black gloves were tucked into his belt, and a saber hung at his side. His hat was squared, and there was authority in the way he cocked his chin. A corporal stood at his side, feet apart, hands clasped behind his back. The room fell silent with uncertainty.

"I'm Lieutenant Clay," he said, "Officer of the Day, and this is

Corporal Brinehart. Soon as the mess is cleared, he'll take you down for breakfast. After that, you'll receive your physical at the post hospital, then whereupon the quartermaster will issue your clothing and a carbine. It's government property, gentlemen, and not to be lost, damaged, or destroyed, but to be taken care of with the loving care of a mother for her child. To do otherwise will cost you dearly both in pain and pay, I assure you."

Stepping into the room, he looked into each of their faces. "Now, I'm going to ask this question just once," he said, "and you are to answer it with consideration, not just for yourself but for the good of your country and your fellow soldier." Pausing, he studied the shine of his boots for a moment. "Is there anyone here who's in trouble with the law? If so, then step forward, and you'll be sent on your way without question. However, if I find out later that you failed to own up, it will be an unpleasant day all the way around." There was the smell of soap and cologne about him as he walked the line of men. He waited at the end with his back to them. "Anyone care to step forward?"

When there was no answer, he turned to Corporal Brinehart, who yet stood with his hands behind his back.

"It's Christians everyone, Corporal, so take them to breakfast." The lieutenant stepped into the doorway and turned for a last look at the pathetic lot that shivered at the ends of the bunks. "Check them for head lice. The surgeon says another infestation, and he'll burn the fort to the ground with the lot of us in it."

"Yes, sir," Corporal Brinehart said, snapping a salute.

Breakfast was fried grits and molasses, sugar-cured ham, pinto beans, two slices of sourdough bread, and a slab of yellow onion, all served up with the blackest coffee Caleb had ever tasted. No soldiers other than them were there, all having mustered for stable call in the pitch of dark. So they ate alone, like strangers in the land, but the stove burned hot in the center of the mess and drove the chill from their bodies and the misgivings from their minds.

In fact, for the first time since leaving Louisville, Caleb sensed the adventure and possibility of a soldier's life and was more certain than ever of his decision. In the distance, the soldiers' horses whinnied as they were led onto the hardpack of the parade ground. Maybe Joshua was right, after all. Maybe they would be Indian fighters and heroes to the last.

"Now, this here's bread," Joshua said, mopping up his plate and looking over at Caleb.

After breakfast, Corporal Brinehart lined them up at the door for a lice check, parting their hair with his fingers, searching for nits like some strange, blond chimpanzee.

"Well," he said, reaching the end of the line, "there ain't no lice, Lord knows why. I've seen cleaner hair under a mule's tail."

They marched to the post hospital and waited in line once more to take their turn with the surgeon. The morning sun fell against the rock wall and warmed them despite the chill day. The American flag flapped in the wind, mounted on a pole smack in the middle of the fort, the highest pole Caleb had ever seen, and crows scolded from its height, cawing at all who dared enter their territory.

When Joshua exited the surgeon's office, there was a smile on his face.

"It's a soldier of the Seventh Cavalry I'm to be," he said, slapping Caleb on the shoulder, "and a mean Sheridan son of a bitch."

"Caleb Justin," the corporal called from the door.

"Yes, sir."

"Step it up. The surgeon is waiting."

"Yes, sir."

"Good luck," Joshua said.

Shelves rose to the ceiling of the surgery, laden with jars of all variety, and the room reeked of camphor and the stink of sick. The surgeon sat behind his desk, his mouth hidden beneath a walrus mustache, and he entered some vital piece of information into his notebook. On the wall behind him was a single shelf of books and a chart of the digestive tract outlined in red. Without looking up, he pointed to the table.

"Sit there."

"Yes, sir."

"And take off your clothes."

"Sir?"

"Everything but your drawers."

"Yes, sir."

"And hang them over that chair."

Slipping out of his clothes, Caleb draped them over the back of the chair. A tree limb had torn out the leg of his drawers, and they now hung down to his knee like an old dishrag.

The surgeon took his stethoscope from about his neck and hooked its tips into his ears with practiced skill. First he listened to Caleb's chest, then to his back, thumping him from time to time as if testing the ripe of a watermelon.

"Now take off your drawers and lift your sack."

"Sir?"

"For all I know you're a girlie," he said. "Besides, I can't check for hernias through your drawers. There. Now cough."

"I ain't got to cough, sir."

"Cough anyway. It's an order."

"Yes, sir," Caleb said, and coughed.

When he finished probing, the surgeon picked up his notebook and made an entry.

"Am I in the Seventh Cavalry now, sir?"

"Well, you don't have a hernia, and you aren't a girl, least not a pretty one. I want you to put your feet together, Mr. Justin, and stand up straight. That's it. Now, walk to that desk. Now, come back." After another entry into his notes, he looked up. "How long you had that gimp, son?"

"Oh, that? Why, that ain't nothing, sir," Caleb said. "A tree was felled on my leg and busted it up some, but it healed right up."

"I see. Sit up on this table for me."

The surgeon pulled up a stool and examined Caleb's foot, turning it first one way, then the other. Caleb studied the bald spot on the back of the surgeon's head, a few gray hairs sprouting from the brown of his scalp, and wondered if someday he, too, might have such a spot.

"It's healed up just fine," Caleb said.

"Does it hurt when you walk?" the surgeon asked, looking up through his brows.

"Oh, no, sir. It don't never hurt, walking or sitting neither one."

He twisted the ends of his mustache and studied his notes, working Caleb's foot once more, turning it to the side as far as it would go.

"It's healed back crooked," he said. "Didn't anyone set that foot?"

"No, sir. There wasn't no one around, except Baud, and Baud ain't much one for fretting over things."

"Well, you've lost the orbicular movement just here, see."

"I reckon it's a movement I don't need all that much, sir, 'cause I can stay up with the best of them. And I'm strong, too, just ask anyone. Why, I can fell a tree in a dozen licks. I'd make a good soldier, sir. I know I would."

Closing his notebook, the surgeon walked to the window and looked out on the compound. "I don't doubt you'd make a good soldier, Mr. Justin, but I'm afraid that's not going to happen."

"I don't understand, sir."

"The army can't take you, not with a bum foot. On a hard march, it would give out soon enough, and there you'd be, wouldn't you, a burden on your fellow soldiers. I think you're man enough to see how that just wouldn't work."

Heat rose into Caleb's neck, his head whirling at the words. He was dirty and unworthy, a burden to his fellow soldiers. At that moment, he wished that he could hide, could cover his ragged drawers and his bum foot from the excellence everywhere about him.

"I come all the way from Kentucky," he said.

"I'm sorry, Mr. Justin. There's nothing I can do. It's the way of things."

He walked to his desk and picked up a form, scratching his signature at the bottom. "Take this to headquarters," he said, handing it to Caleb. "They'll issue a chit to get you back to Leavenworth. From there, you're on your own." Walking to the window, he looked out again, his back to Caleb. "I know you're disappointed, but I just may have done you a favor. This is a desperate life, son, one to drain the humanity from your very bones. Now, get on out of here."

When Joshua spotted Caleb, he waved his hat.

"Hey, soldier," he called, "how'd it go?"

Caleb ducked his head and moved away from the line of men who still waited their turn to see the surgeon. He was a stranger now, an outcast, and needed to be as far from their presence as possible.

"I didn't get in," he said.

"Didn't get in?"

"No."

Joshua looked around, as if someone might be listening, before sticking his hat back on his head.

"What do you mean, Caleb?"

"Just what I said, goddang it, Joshua. You deft or something? They ain't letting me in on account of this bum foot."

"But, hell, Caleb, we came all the way from Kentucky together. They got to let you in now."

"So long, Joshua," he said, shaking his hand. "I got little doubt you'll be a mean Sheridan son of a bitch when it comes to it."

"What you going to do, Caleb?" he called after him.

"I don't know," he said, without looking back.

As he walked across the compound, the eyes of Joshua, and of every man, bore down, and his heart beat a solitary cadence in his chest. He retrieved his axe at the barracks and made his way to the waiting wagon. From behind in the compound, the

sergeant barked an order, the first of many to come in a world
Caleb would never know. A chasm opened within him, a boundless void of darkness and despair.

The driver said little on the return ride to Junction City, having
long since known the pain of rejection on such men. For this,
Caleb was thankful. The wind drove at their backs, taking its
due, and darkness fell as complete and bleak as Caleb's own
life, but it was not until he stood at the tracks, his eyes tearing
in the cold as the wagon pulled away, that he remembered the
chit for his return trip to Leavenworth.

Caleb appraised his situation as he huddled from the wind.
He had no money, no promise, no hope. There was no one to
care, no one to know or to grieve. Even Jude, silent and white at
the end of the Beer Bucket bar, existed more in his retribution
than Caleb now did in his meager severance.

The moon edged into the sky, casting its light on the polished
rails of the track, shafts of ivory driving into the darkness. To the
east was Leavenworth and the emptiness he'd left behind. To the
west was Fort Harker, the railhead, the perils of the unknown.

He despaired as the singular sweep of a train's light broke
down track, the engine rumbling under his feet as she pulled
the final grade into the station. He stepped into the shadows
and waited as she slowed to a stop, as she hissed and groaned
like an ancient and angry beast. Behind her were a dozen cars
loaded with ties, rails, and kegs of spikes.

Minutes passed as the rail hands filled the boiler with water,
checked the bushings and the oilers and the fuel. The engine
sighed with impatience and blew steam into the cold night air
as she waited for the engineer to pick up his orders from the
operator, for the fireman to pee on the far side of the tracks, and,
at last, for the brakeman's signal swing.

When she pulled from the station, sparks spewed from beneath
her colossal drive wheels. Her horn wailed for the night and for
the onerous trip ahead as she labored west into the prairie. The

fireman stoked her boiler, his face red against her fiery belly, and he knew that she was a fine engine, this ole girl.

But in the darkness of the boxcar, Caleb Justin shivered behind a spike keg, against the wind, and the loneliness, and the uncertainty of tomorrow.

Chapter 7

T he train had slowed to a crawl, and for the first time since leaving Junction City, Caleb chanced a look out of the door. The orange of sunrise seeped through the clouds and spread across the horizon. A vast herd of buffalo swarmed about the train, their backs a brown and churning sea. Their bovine breaths, smelling of earth and grass, rose into the cold of dawn. Enormous bulls pawed and pranced, or butted heads as they battled for favor, their flanks trembling with power and excitement, while the cows looked on, or grazed with indifference, or groomed themselves with startling black tongues.

So absorbed was Caleb in the buffalo that he failed to see the riders. Stepping back into the darkness of the car, he watched them race full out across the plain, a half dozen or fewer, and soldiers to the last by the looks of them. The train whistle blew, and he jumped, startled by its shrillness. Chills raced down his spine. When he looked again, the soldiers were gone, their dust still drifting along the top of the ridge.

The train picked up speed, and as the buffalo disappeared behind, an expanse of grass opened into the distance, the color of cinnamon as it swelled and ebbed like a thing alive, a thing haunted and inconsolable in its immensity. Haze curled in the basins, pardoned from the ceaseless winds above.

Moving his axe to his side, Caleb lay down, closing his eyes to sleep, but the hunger prevailed, twisting and cold, and he wondered instead of home, of the trees with their green and their abundance, of the gentle rains and river fogs. And he wondered of Joshua, too, of his saber and boots and badges of honor, and he wondered of the girl with her fleur-de-lis, of her ebony hair and smell of honeysuckle.

He slept but for a short while, the squeal of brakes, the running jolt of cars sitting him upright in the darkness. Grabbing his axe, he made for the exit, knowing too well the risk of delay. He gauged the speed before tossing out his axe and leaping into the banks of grass below.

He waited for the cars to pass. And when the caboose wobbled by, he turned onto his back to warm his face in the sun. A sparrow fluttered to the ground, searching for gizzard pebbles, flitting away in alarm when it spotted him in the grass. The last clack of the wheels disappeared in the distance; he rose, found his axe where it had fallen, and struck out down the track.

He'd walked but a short way when he saw Fort Harker, perched atop a grassy knoll overlooking the valley below. A shallow stream wound along its bottom. Boxcars, with doors slid open, lined a siding within feet of the fort. The buildings, unassuming in number and size, were built of mustard-colored stone, the same as layered in the hills beyond. The most prominent was the guard-house, apparent in its austerity and its bars. It was a simple square structure two stories high. Boardwalks stretched the length of both levels, with connecting steps to permit outside access to all the cells. A guard paced the perimeter, his rifle couched on his shoulder, and from somewhere within the compound, camp dogs barked. Caleb knew that to go closer, he must declare his presence.

Unprepared for that just yet, he crouched in the grass. What was he to do now?

What had he been thinking when he'd boarded that train? Why hadn't he just gone back to Fort Riley and collected his chit for Leavenworth? He could have worked the rivers homeward from there. At least in Kentucky he knew how to survive, how to cut wood for the steamers and make his way. Here there was naught but rejection, and defeat, and the unrelenting wind.

Hunger gnawed at his stomach, not a cold hunger now but a hot hunger, like a burning ember, and even as it burned, the day cooled in the waning light. He turned to make his way to the stream below. With his axe, he could cut wood for a fire, make a camp, take time to think. After all, trains ran both ways, and there was time yet to do what he must.

The stream was a muddied and stale trickle, but he drank anyway, to quench the ember still burning within him. Shivering from the icy water, he worked his way downstream until he was secured from view of the fort. A cottonwood, struck by lightning, lay across the stream, its limbs seasoned and perfect for a fire. He chopped his wood, taking comfort in the thrust and power of his skill. Afterward, he stacked the logs as a windbreak, spreading dry grass at the base for his bed. It wasn't much of a shelter to be sure, but better than the draft and dark of the boxcar.

When he'd finished, he searched for driftwood in the bends of the stream, for kindling to start his fire and to feed the coals against the morning cold. An owl swooped from a draw, a swish of wings in the evening shadows. That's when Caleb spotted the garden, furrows against the slope of the hill, and his heart leaped with joy, a five-toothed cultivator pitched on its side, a stack of gallon peach cans, stakes, a shovel with broken handle, a ball of twine half-buried in the dirt. There were rows of onions with shriveled tops, beets, turnips, and a dozen hills of pumpkins. Using the broken spade, he dug out a large onion, a turnip, a handful of beets with their smell of earth and mold, and put them into a peach can.

By the time he got back to camp, night had fallen, stars spiraling and winking in the infinite sky. He started his fire using grass from his bed, blowing the flame into life with care so as not to waste his matches, adding kindling until flames rose warm and bright against his face.

With his pocketknife, he peeled the onion, the turnip, a few beets for sweetening, and sliced them into the peach can. He placed the can into the coals and waited for the vegetables to brown, stirring them with the blade of his knife, the aroma of onion an elixir, a celebration and ceremony, and when they were at last cooked, he spooned them into his mouth with his fingers. Even without salt, they were delicious, warm and filling, and the red of beet dripped like blood from his chin.

Afterward, he stoked the fire higher, banking it with a log against the wind. Placing his axe within reach, he curled onto his bed. Taps drifted down the valley from the distant fort, and his heart shriveled with loneliness and doubt. Turning onto his side, he closed his eyes, the firelight flickering and warm through his lids. "Now I must decide," he said, "what I am to do." But no answer came as taps died away, as the fire crackled in the deepening cold, and he slept at last in this untamed land.

It was as if waking underwater, his lungs bursting for want of air, that blinding and certain panic from the depths of sleep. He struggled against the hands about his throat and battled back to consciousness, clawing at his murderer's eyes, his ears, his brimming, wet mouth. A giant was upon him, towering and fierce and with blinding strength. To die at the hands of a stranger was an unacceptable thing, an implausible thing, and even as lights flashed in Caleb's eyes, and his lungs decayed to sludge, and saliva drooled down his beet-stained chin, he did not die.

At what point he found the axe lying at his side he could not know. Perhaps it was no more than an instinctual spark deep in his brain, that final and compelling need to survive, but there it was in his hand. With what strength remained, he brought it broadside into the giant's head. Like a felled tree, the giant leaned, first this way, then that, as if testing the disposition and attitude of his pitch before collapsing full tilt upon the ground.

Caleb gasped and crawled to his knees, spitting blood into the dirt between his arms. When once again he could breathe, he took up his axe, prepared to finish the job if it came to that. The giant lay sprawled against the wood stack, a knot swelling from above his ear. He wore the uniform of a soldier, but his clothes were blackened and dirty. Groaning, he lifted his head and shook away the fog.

"Who are you?" Caleb asked, his axe at the ready.

The giant focused in on Caleb, his hand against his ear.

"I'm thinking I could ask the same thing," he said.

"Suppose you could, but it's me who's got the axe," Caleb said, "and the notion to use it."

"It's a point," the giant said. "My name's Jim Ferric."

"You a soldier?"

"Well, I ain't no potentate, or president, or a angel of God, as you can see."

"It's a son of a bitch that you are, then," Caleb said. "Maybe I'll shorten up your legs with this here axe so's we can have a closer match."

"I'm the blacksmith up to Fort Harker," he said, "and a soldier in the making, you might say."

The morning sun broke through the trees, and a curl of smoke twisted from Caleb's cold campfire. He could see in the light that he'd been lucky to escape the clutches of a man such as this, with his bull neck, his powerful shoulders and rippling strong arms. A thick, red beard curled from the square of his jaw and into his collar. There was a look of confidence in his eye, coming, no doubt, from a lifetime of physical advantage.

"I got just one question," Caleb said.

"There ain't nobody got just *one* question."

"Why did you try to kill me?"

Jim brushed off his pants and looked up toward the fort. He was younger than Caleb had thought, and there was a faded place on his sleeve where chevrons had once been sewn.

"You'd be dead as a carp this very minute, buster, had I that notion."

"When a man has his hands around my throat, I figure he's out to kill me," Caleb said.

"I was just choking you down some so's I could carry you back up to the fort, that's all."

"I ain't done no harm to you or anyone else," Caleb said.

"Ain't you one of them deserters took out of here yesterday with army mules in tow?"

Hooking his axe over his shoulder, Caleb walked to the other side of the campfire.

"I ain't no such thing," he said. "I'm a woodcutter, that's all, come up out of Kentucky."

"I'll be dogged," he said, pushing back his hat, revealing the line of black coal dust that had gathered there. "Hell, I thought you was one of them deserters, and I was aiming to pick myself up a extra month's pay."

"You get paid for bringing in deserters?"

"It's a standing offer by the commander, yes sir, one month's pay, dead or alive or anywheres in between."

"Well, I ain't no deserter and don't take to having my neck squeezed off."

Jim shrugged and nodded, like a kid caught out of hand. "I guess maybe you ain't at that. I guess you ain't no more than a beet thief, that's all."

"A beet thief? What are you talking about? I ain't even heard of no beet thief before."

"What's that red all about your mouth then, if you ain't no beet thief? I suppose you been eating raw buffalo out with the wolves or stealing chickens, biting off their heads and such."

"You better watch what you say, Jim Ferric, or I might just take off your head with this here axe."

"Well, for your information, them beets is military property. You're lucky I don't take you for a stay in the guardhouse."

"You just try," Caleb said, brandishing his axe.

"Well," he said, rubbing at his head, "I doubt the army will miss a few beets. Maybe I shouldn't have jumped you like that, not knowing if you was one of them thieving deserters or not."

"You near scared the life out of me," Caleb said, lowering his axe. "I thought a grizzly bear had hold of me, sure."

"Sorry, Mister," he said, holding out his hand.

"Name's Caleb, Caleb Justin."

"I come to take the shears off that cultivator back there in the garden, so they can be sharpened back at the shop," he said.

"Sorry about the beets, and the turnips, too," Caleb said, "but I was near starved down."

"Man would have to be starved to eat the likes of beets and turnips," he said, "or at gunpoint, either one. Listen, I brought lunch in my saddlebag, hardtack, jerk, and a little coffee. I'd as soon have it for breakfast. You be interested?"

"Ain't you had breakfast already?"

He rubbed his great stomach and grinned. "It don't know breakfast from high noon, does it; besides, I could use a little help with them shears later on."

"Jim Ferric, you got yourself a deal."

While Jim retrieved his horse, Caleb built up the fire. The morning was cold, but the wind had died away overnight, a blessing indeed, and soon the fire crackled in the morning stillness.

Jim exited the trees, leading the biggest bay horse Caleb had ever seen, with hooves of a draft and a great trembling chest. A white blaze ran the length of its enormous head.

"Takes a big 'un to carry the likes of me," Jim said, unloading the food from his saddlebag.

Soon the aroma of coffee filled the camp. Caleb's belly growled in anticipation of real food, and he was not to be disappointed. Never had hardtack and jerk tasted so good. Washing the last of it down with coffee, he looked over at Jim, who had been watching him with curiosity through the smoke of the campfire.

"I had a coon hound eat my glove one time," he said, "'fore he realized it weren't a rabbit."

"Sorry," Caleb said, wiping his mouth with his sleeve. "I left you nothing at all. It's been a while since I had a decent meal. Most times I ain't such a pig."

"I'm just proud there's someone what eats like me," he said. "Sort of takes the lonesome out of it, don't it."

Taking a twist from his pocket, he filled his jaw, tucking it back.

"What are you doing out here, Caleb? You don't even have a rifle to hunt with, or to fight off Cheyenne, or to kill a deserter, all what as soon leave you dead as not. It ain't a place to be alone and unarmed, no sir, no place at all."

Anxious to share his misery with someone else, Caleb told him the story, told him of the death of his father, of Joshua, of how the cabin burned and everything he owned in it, and of their decision to join up with Sheridan. He told how he'd lost his mules and pistol, and how he'd been rejected because he was a no-account gimp, and how he'd hopped the work train west out of Junction City with no thought or care of what might happen next.

When he finished, he stood, and knew how ridiculous the story sounded.

"Why, that's the most fool thing I ever heard," Jim said, spitting into the fire. "Why didn't you go back home?"

"I reckon I don't know the answer to that," Caleb said.

"It's a fool thing being out here without a carbine. Why, it's a fool thing being out here even with a carbine, even with a twelve pounder and a spit fire Gatling, come to think on it."

"I suppose I know it," Caleb said, leaning back against a tree, "but here I am."

"Well, come on, then. Let's go get them shears off."

All morning they worked at the rusted bolts, and when the shears were at last loosened, they placed them in a sack Jim had brought along to hang off his saddle horn.

When a rabbit poked up in the pumpkin patch, Jim shot it through the head. They dressed it out and threaded it on a spit they rigged from a piece of strap iron taken off the cultivator. Then they threaded on a couple of onions out of the garden and salted them with salt from a tobacco sack Jim kept in his saddlebag. After that, they roasted up the whole thing over the fire until it was brown and juice sizzled into the coals, and the most marvelous smells filled the draw.

"You can give me my half now, if you don't mind," Jim said.

As the afternoon sun fell warm on their backs, they ate the roasted rabbit, grease shining on their chins and their fingers, and when they were finished, they lay down in the garden rows for a rest, not rising until the sun edged low in the sky.

Jim sat up, crossed his legs, and leaned forward on his elbows.

"It's getting late," he said. "If I don't get back, they'll be sending a detachment out to look for me."

"Be dark soon enough," Caleb said.

"You can't stay at the fort, Caleb. The commander wouldn't be having it."

"I know."

"It's just army rules. Even contract teamsters have to camp off the compound."

"I understand."

"And I can't give you my carbine. It's against regulations. A soldier caught without his carbine is in for guardhouse time, or worse. "

"A soldier needs his carbine, all right."

"So, where do you figure to stay?"

"I'm thinking in my camp, until I get things figured out."

Jim stood and brushed the dirt from the seat of his pants.

"Follow me," he said, "I got something I want to show you."

They walked to the far end of the garden, where they entered a stand of sumac that ran thick up the draw. Out in the middle, Jim stopped, looked around, and scraped at the dirt with his foot.

"There," he said, pointing.

Half-covered with dirt was a door made from barrel slats and with the words TURNHAM & ARTHUR SALT PORK still visible in red paint.

"What is it?" Caleb asked.

Jim threw back the door and looked into the darkness. The smell of stale potatoes and vegetables rose from the entrance.

"Was to be a root cellar," he said, "but they hit yeller rock and couldn't get it deep enough to hold off the freeze. We dug a new one up at the fort."

Jim stopped to let his eyes adjust before leading the way in.

"It's mighty dark down here," Caleb said.

"It's dry, ain't it, and there's a table across the back for taters and winter squash. It will make a fine bed up off the ground and out of the wind. Best of all, it's hidden from view, cuts down on visitors, Cheyenne, and black bear what might squeeze off your neck."

"You figure it's all right, Jim?"

"She's been abandoned, hasn't she; besides, the garden's near petered out for the season. The cook's helper might be down for a few of those root vegetables along, or pumpkins for pie, but he ain't all that smart and little enough to worry about. Just keep your eye out. Course, there's a work crew at the railhead a few miles west. They might take you in, if you was to favor it."

"I ain't much for strangers at the moment, Jim."

"Then come on. I'll walk back with you."

At the camp, Jim untied a bundle from behind his saddle and tossed it to Caleb.

"It's a sack coat," he said, "what help ward off the chill. I figure I can get by without it for a spell."

"You coming tomorrow?" Caleb asked.

He mounted up and looked down on Caleb from the height of the immense bay. "Most likely, to put those shears back on. I'd clean up this camp if I was you, cover them ashes, and your tracks, too, best you can. Them Cheyenne can read signs in the pitch of dark, and there's mighty little they fear. Sometimes at night they bark and hoot and call out signals just beyond the fort. Last week one rode up on the hill there in broad daylight, dropped his pants, and bore his ass to the whole of the company whilst they stood inspection. So keep that axe to the handy," he said, rubbing the side of his head. "It's a unpleasant sight what them Indians can do to a man, things you can't imagine."

With his hands stuck in his pockets, Caleb watched Jim ride from view.

"I'll be careful," he said to himself.

After covering the ashes, he scattered the remaining firewood into the brush, wiping out his tracks with a cottonwood branch. By then, an orange moon, big as a wagon wheel, bulged on the horizon. Somewhere up the draw, a coyote barked. He hoped it wasn't a Cheyenne like Jim had said.

Shaking it off, he made his way along the streambed to the garden, the temperature dropping about him, his breath rising into the night. He picked his way through the sumac to the root cellar as the moon climbed overhead, farther away now, a cold and ivory button in the tar-black sky.

He left the cellar door open and lay down on the table, the smell of sunless dank and gloom, and he wished for the comfort of a fire. He thought about what Jim had said, about the Indians and the deserters and the perils of being unarmed, but decided not to chance it. Pulling the sack coat over him, he steeled himself against the cold, against the mustiness and loneliness of his crypt, and when the moon popped into view through the doorway, ivory light cast across the floor, he knew that hope would out, that tomorrow would come, and that Caleb Justin would endure.

When he awoke, a spider suspended on a silver thread bounced just inches from his face. Startled by Caleb's sudden movement, it scaled upward, disappearing into the cracks of the ceiling. Caleb sat upright, his heart thumping with uncertainty as he struggled to orient himself, to remember where he was.

He rubbed the sleep from his eyes and climbed his way out of the root cellar and into the morning sunrise. A fog hung low in the valley, obscuring the stream and the trunks of the trees that grew in sparse clumps down its length. From the top of a large cottonwood, a sparrow hawk watched him with apparent indifference.

Slipping on Jim's coat, Caleb picked up his axe and worked his way down to the streambed, moving west away from the fort to scout out his surroundings and in the hope of finding something to eat. The coat hung to his knees and drooped from his shoulders, a pathetic sight, of that he was certain.

Trees were scarce at best, hardwoods of walnut, pecan, a few mulberry, an occasional cedar with its pungent and oily smell. Nearer the water, cottonwood reigned, dotted with willow from out of the backwash and mud. Compared to Kentucky, it was no wood at all, and what was there was of poor quality and size. A man would have a far walk indeed for even the least of loads.

By late morning, he'd found an ancient pecan growing from the bank of the stream, its fruit spread about its trunk. So profuse was the bounty that even the squirrels had abandoned their hoarding, leaving the remainder behind to rot.

With a rock and the broad side of his axe, he cracked the nuts, picking the fruit from the crushed shells with a stick, their smell of mold and bark and fresh-turned earth, placing them in his hat until it brimmed with golden meats. He ate the pecans in a sunny spot handfuls at a time, while high up in the tree, the squirrels scolded his audacity.

By the time he got back to the garden, Jim was there, putting the shears back on the cultivator.

"Howdy," Caleb called from a distance so as not to alarm him.

"Well, if it ain't the woodcutter," Jim said, laying down his wrench. "I reckon the grizzlies didn't get you last night, after all."

The black of coal was on Jim's face and in the crevices of his hands, and the smell of coal oil was strong about his clothes. A tobacco cud protruded from his cheek, the corners of his mouth stained brown.

"It's a mighty ignorant grizzly take on a man with a axe," Caleb said.

"It's the smell of a real man on that coat what scares them off."

"It's a smell to be feared, all right," Caleb said.

"You eat breakfast?"

"I ate with the squirrels."

"Why, ain't that nice."

"It was a brighter conversation than some I've had."

Jim leaned under the cultivator and set his wrench on a nut.

"Get hold of these things whilst I tighten them up, then I got something I want to show you."

When they'd finished reattaching the shears, they dragged the cultivator to a tree, securing it around the trunk with a chain and lock Jim had brought from the shop.

"We'll just leave her here for the winter," he said. "Deserters and woodcutters ain't big on stealing cultivators, too much work in it, I figure."

"So what you got to show me now," Caleb asked, "a Indian bearing his ass up on the hill, I reckon?"

"Maybe I won't show you at all," Jim said, "given the coarseness of your ways."

"All right, I'm sorry. So what is it?"

"In them trees just there."

Tied under an elm was a wagon and a team of army mules, and in the back were two wooden crates.

"That your team of mules, Jim?"

"No, sir, I'm thinking that team is yours."

Caleb looked up into Jim's big face and shrugged. "I don't understand."

"It's 'cause you hail from Kentucky most likely, or from talking to squirrels, either one."

"Where did they come from, Jim?"

Hanging his big arm over Caleb's shoulder, Jim looked at the team with pride. "Well, sir, them's army mules, scheduled for the soap factory back to Kansas City. Being on the wrong side of ten, the army don't want them no more, so I worked a deal in exchange for a bowie I forged out of a hoof rasp. And that wagon there was dragged off to the fort dump with a broken axle, left there by one of them slickers traveling the Santa Fe Trail, I reckon. She's a Spring Wagon from Concord, and with bois d'arc wood changed out on her wheels. There ain't none better for prairie traveling, I can tell you."

"But the broken axle?"

"Fort Harker's got the finest blacksmith this side of the Missouri, they say, and he's forged up that axle good as new, hasn't he." He untied the reins and handed them to Caleb. "Thing is, I talked to the first sergeant about you, and he talked to the commander, and they decided that having a woodcutter for the fort might just be a good thing, freeing up the men for more military duties, like marching around the compound all day with logs on their shoulders, or brushing their horses until there ain't no hair left on 'em, 'cept the fuzz under their chins."

"But I can't pay for these."

"Course you can't, and the army can't pay you either, since you don't have a government contract, and ain't likely to get one, but you can trade out goods, can't you. It's a army tradition, you see. Keep track of the cords cut, and they'll give you credit against them at the quartermaster's. You can swap out oats for your mules and such or anything else what comes, I suppose. Every building up there's got to have wood for burning, one way or the other. It won't take much for you to live, a few staples to get by, 'cause the hunting's good in these parts, 'less you're a drinking man, then that's another story altogether, ain't it."

"I don't know what to say," Caleb said, rubbing the nose of one of the big army mules.

"Well, it's a far piece from one tree to the next in this country, so you'll earn your keep."

"I'm a fair woodcutter."

"The commander gave his permission for you to live down here as long as you don't set the prairie on fire or shit in the vegetable patch. Course, given army cooking, it might be an improvement anyways."

Letting the news soak in, Jim worked at his tobacco for a moment before commencing. "I figure that work crew at the railhead could use a little wood, too. Who's to say but what they might even come up with some cash on the deal, just in case you ever want to get a little something at the sutler's store."

"Thanks, Jim," Caleb said. "What you got coming out of all this, anyway?"

"Why, I figure to have my wood cut for my stove at the blacksmith shop, don't I. Forge heat shoots straight up the chimney, burning off your face whiskers in the process."

"I reckon wood for your stove could be arranged," Caleb said.

"And in the wagon bed there is a few supplies to get you by until you can get some credit built up. Them crates would make a fine table for a new soddie, too, I figure. Course, you'd have to stop digging holes with them squirrels and learn to eat like a human being."

He reached under the wagon seat, pulled out a rifle, and handed it to Caleb. "This here's a Spencer carbine I traded off the ordnance officer. It was run over by a freight wagon and suffered a broken trigger guard, and the firing pin was bent up too, but that ain't but child's play for a good blacksmith, though it does jam up from time to time. You take it and use it long as you want. Comes a day you leave, I'd like it back, 'cause I figure on getting out of this blistering hell some day and having a shop of my own, and this ole carbine would make a fine rabbit gun, wouldn't it. Oh, and there's a box of shells just there, so don't ask how I come about them, 'cause I ain't saying."

Walking around the mules, Caleb examined the harnesses and could see that they, too, had been salvaged and repaired by the resourceful Jim Ferric.

"You'll have a load first every day, Jim, if the whole fort goes without wood. That's a promise."

"It's a fine sentiment, Caleb, but you keep the commander happy first, 'cause if he ain't happy, it's a cold winter all around." Walking to the back of the wagon, he took out a chain with a leather-covered hasp attached to each end. "Put these side hobbles on your mules when you graze them out at night." He dug into his pocket, brought out an iron key, and handed it to Caleb. "Keep them hobbles locked, or the Cheyenne will have them stole before moonrise, and remember them mules is smooth-mouthed, the both of them, and will require a side of oats and a gentle hand if you expect to get them through the winter."

"They got names?"

"Course they got names. Whoever heard of mules without names, I wonder?" Pointing to the larger mule, he said, "This here one's named 'Mule One,' 'cause I got him first, didn't I."

"Then this would be 'Mule Two,'" Caleb said.

"Why, you're a tad smarter than I had figured," Jim said, spitting between the legs of Mule Two. "I got to be going, hear."

"You coming again tomorrow, Jim?"

"There's a keg of nails to forge up for the new shutters they're putting on the officer's quarters. The sentry caught Private Kidwell watching Lieutenant Bookerman's wife going to the chamber pot in the middle of the night. Turns out Lieutenant Bookerman isn't keen on that idea, so Private Kidwell's walking the log for the rest of his life, ain't he. Anyways, I might not get back for a while. When you get that wood cut, bring a load to the fort. Have the guard come get me, and I'll see you around the grounds." Climbing up on his bay, Jim turned about and kicked him into a trot. "You be careful, Woodcutter," he called back over his shoulder.

Back at the root cellar, Caleb hobbled Mule One and Mule Two. After turning them out to graze, he built a fire at the entrance of the cellar, the Spencer loaded at his side just in case.

He emptied the contents of a crate onto the ground and went through his spoils. There was a wool blanket, pockmarked from a thousand campfire embers and stamped with "U.S. Army" in huge blue letters; a frayed horsehair lariat; an old pot for boiling water; a cast iron frying pan with a triangle broken out of its side; a tin cup and plate; a spoon; a bundle of beeswax candles; an old skinning knife, with leather straps having been cut from a saddle cinch and hot riveted for a handle; and, lying in the bottom of the crate, a stack of outdated *Harper's Weekly* magazines, yellowed with age and bearing the wear of endless readings.

The other crate was packed with all variety of foods—sugar stored in a canvas bag against the damp, a can of black molasses, a sack of flour, a smaller sack of cornmeal, vinegar, ground cinnamon, a bag of dried beans, salt pork packed in bran, a tin of coffee, a tin of lard, a package of Preston & Merrill's Infallible Yeast Powder, and a bag of coarse salt, taken no doubt from the U.S. Army livery stable.

As the sun set and shadows stretched into the darkening prairie, he boiled water in the pot for corn mush, topped it with molasses, and ate it with a spoon, just like a normal human being. It was warm and sweet and satisfying in the evening cool. With the remaining water, he brewed a pot of black coffee and drank it from the hot lip of his new tin cup.

Afterward, he carried his supplies into the root cellar, turning up the crates for a table as Jim had suggested. He lit one of the candles and watched it dance and flicker against the ceiling. With his wool blanket about him, he read magazines until his eyes drooped in weariness. Sliding the Spencer within reach, he blew out the candle, the smell of wax smoke filling the tiny chamber.

Outside, the campfire flared in the wind, and even as it died away, Caleb slept, secure in tomorrow, in his work, and in his newfound friend.

Chapter 8

Caleb took up his lariat after breakfast and made his way into the frosty morning. Clouds, curdled and pink with dawn, filled the sky. Down at the creek, birds swooped in from their morning feed, blackening the treetops in turbulent clusters.

The tracks of Mule One and Mule Two were clear in the frost-covered grass, and Caleb soon spotted them grazing up the draw, not a hundred yards from where he'd turned them out. Resigned to their hobbles, they awaited his approach. He looped the lariat into a nose halter and slipped it over Mule One's head, scratching behind his ears, talking to him in reassuring tones. As he led him back to the root cellar, Mule Two fell in behind, her side hobble rattling like slave chains in the stillness of the morning.

He harnessed them to the wagon at the garden, rethreading Mule Two's hip strap through the loop and opening up Mule One's collar, which was tight even at the last buckle hole. By all appearances, it had been a good while since the harnesses had been used, the leather stiff from the salt and perspiration of past labors, signs of patches and repairs all too obvious.

When he'd finished harnessing the mules, he tied them under

the big elm and sharpened his axe with a sandstone dug from the garden. It lacked the grit and cut of his Arkansas sharpening stone at home, but it sufficed. Afterward, he cut a swath through the sumac wide enough to accommodate the wagon and the mules so that he could stack his wood near the cellar.

After that, he sliced off a piece of salt pork, wrapped it in a page of *Harper's Weekly*, and tucked it in his pocket. Wiping off the skinning knife, he slipped it under his belt, loaded rounds into the old Spencer, and made his way down to the wagon.

As he rode out of camp, the sun broke warm and bright above the trees, and the wind gathered up for its daily blow. He followed the stream west, looking for something other than the stringy cottonwood, which made for poor heat at best.

By noon he'd downed a cedar, with its maddening limbs scratching the hide from his arms, and an elm, with its core rotted away to sponge. He cut up a walnut from a steep bank at the creek and then had to tote the whole thing back up the bank a piece at a time. He was beginning to see why the army was so quick to strike a deal for a woodcutter. Jim had been right—he was going to earn his money in this country.

Starved, he found a windbreak and built a small fire of bark. Threading his salt pork onto a stick, he turned it against the coals until it browned, then wolfed it down, salt crust, green mold, and all, regretting that he hadn't brought more.

He worked the remainder of the afternoon with the steady and unhurried pace his father had taught him, searching and cutting and loading his wood, some so knurled from drought and heat that he wondered if it was worth cutting at all. When he was exhausted, he turned homeward with a thin load to his credit.

As the sun dropped low in the sky, he put on Jim's sack coat to ward off the chill and snapped the reins against the mules' rumps. They were old, as Jim had said, apparent in the hard pulls with their wheezing and snorting and farting, but they were full of heart and determination, and his respect for them grew.

He pulled up to let them blow at the top of the knoll overlooking the valley. Below, the craters of a prairie dog town stretched to the horizon, and beyond, the haze of the prairie faded into the blue of the sky like a vast ocean.

When the prairie dogs grew confident in his presence, they popped from their holes, first here, then there, then as far as he could see. With hands folded like a thousand priests, they watched his every movement. He clucked his tongue, and they barked back in an angry chorus before darting into their holes.

As Caleb approached the stand of cottonwood that grew along the streambed not far from the garden, he pulled up once more. Shoulder to shoulder in the highest limbs, silhouettes were lined against the evening light—not buzzards, as he first had thought, but wild turkey, lifting from the streambed with absurd flaps of their wings as they struggled to gain altitude to the roost.

He tied up the mules and checked to make certain the Spencer was loaded and ready, working his way from tree to tree, getting the final light between him and the roosting turkeys. Dropping to his knee, he leaned against the trunk of a cottonwood, bringing his site onto one of the shadowy figures high above him. He held his breath and settled in, squeezing off a shot. At first he thought he'd missed, and as sudden, the turkey spiraled from the tree, a free fall into the plum thicket just feet from where he stood.

By the time he got back to the cellar, night had fallen. A pack of coyotes yipped from the blackness, a frenzied and hot chase, falling silent as it had begun, and the hair crawled on the back of Caleb's neck as he checked the location of his Spencer.

Each time he reached for the trace lines, the mules shied and pranced, uncertain as to what approached them in the darkness. "Whoa," he said, "goddang it," and when he was finished, he put on the hobbles and turned them out to graze. He was going to have to get grain soon, as Jim had said, or the old mules would give out on him when the weather worsened.

Once his fire was built, he relaxed against its reassuring warmth and light. He dressed out the turkey with his skinning knife at the edge of his camp, a fat and healthy hen, tossing the guts and feathers into the darkness. Afterward, he rolled the pieces in cornmeal, sprinkled them with livery salt, and dropped them into a pan of smoking lard.

The aroma soon filled his tiny camp, and the fire drove away the darkness and uncertainty of the night, and when the turkey was finished, he ate from the pan with his fingers, the pieces hot and crispy and wonderful, a great feast of his own making, and the night was good.

Soon, when he had a full load cut, he would go to the fort and trade for grain for the mules, and maybe there would be enough left for something special, a jar of jam, or a side of bacon, which he liked to take while out cutting wood, because even just smoked, it was delicious and nourishing.

Anyway, for now, things were not so bad, because no matter how simple a man he might be, no matter how ignorant of private railroad cars and fancy doings, no matter how unfit for Sheridan's Seventh, at least he knew his purpose in this world. He was a woodcutter. This is what he was, what he did, and he did it better than anyone else.

That night he slept hard, exhausted from the work, the lateness of the hour, and the enormity of his meal. But in those hours before dawn when the moon rose in a cloudless sky, the cold deepened, and frost gathered in the stillness of the prairie. And in the darkness of the cellar, he lay with heart thumping, with the certainty that something had awakened him.

They came with the ferocity of the pack, fierce growls and snapping teeth as they tore at the discarded guts and feathers. A pup yelped, pinned under the snarl of an elder, and when there was no more, they circled the camp in search of spoils, marking their arrival with the foul and telling spray of their clan.

Reaching for his Spencer, Caleb brought it about, aiming it

at the moonlit doorway, to stop them if he could. She appeared even in that moment, a grand and ancient bitch, and when she lowered her head to peer into the blackness of the root cellar, moonlight cast in the yellow of her eyes. But Caleb could not shoot, seized by her command and beauty, and then she was gone, and once more the night was silent. But he was not to sleep again, until at last the dawn rose.

There was a full week's work stacked high behind him as he made his way to Fort Harker. Not since jumping from the boxcar had he seen any living human being, except for Jim Ferric. It was all long ago, and now that the fort was in sight, he squirmed in the wagon seat with uneasy anticipation.

The guard stepped forward, his rifle held across his front, his face reddened from the cold.

"State your business," he said.

"I'm Caleb Justin, woodcutter. Jim Ferric, the blacksmith, said the commander wanted stove wood traded out and that I was to come to the blacksmith shop when I was loaded."

"That a fact?"

"Yes, sir."

"You with that work crew up to the railhead?"

"No, sir. I'm by myself."

"No you ain't," he said.

"Yes, sir, 'cept for these here mules."

"You're cutting wood by yourself?"

"Yes, sir."

"Don't you know ole Red Nose and his warriors is running loose in them hills just looking for dumb woodcutters like you?"

"No, sir. I don't know Red Nose or anyone else, 'cept Jim Ferric."

"Hell, man, ever since ole Chivington kilt all them Cheyenne over at Sandcreek, them Indians been running all over hell looking to get even. Just last week a patrol found a wagon train straggler with his ears cut off. If that weren't enough, they scalped him, didn't they, and burnt up what was left in a sagebrush fire."

"I'm hid good," Caleb said, "and keep to the tree lines when I'm out cutting."

"Well, there ain't that many trees in Kansas, as you ought to know. I wouldn't ride out there by myself for all the wood in Missouri."

"A man does what he does," Caleb said.

Shifting his rifle, the guard rubbed the cold from his hands.

"Every soldier here would have lit out months ago, if he wasn't afeared, and there wouldn't be no Fort Harker at all, would there, which is what God intended from the first, I figure."

"You think you could direct me to the blacksmith shop?"

He pointed across the compound.

"Keep your wagon off the parade ground, or the commander will have me humping the rogue's march again."

Caleb clucked his tongue to bring about his mules and said, "I'll be careful."

Looking up from his anvil, Jim Ferric flashed a grin and wiped the sweat from his forehead with the back of his sleeve.

"Woodcutter," he said.

Caleb climbed down from the wagon and shook his hand. "It's good to see you, Jim. I brought in a cutting like what you said."

"That's a right fair load, Caleb," Jim said. "Sit down while I get some of this black off so's they don't set me up with ball and chain."

Holding his hands over the forge clinkers, Caleb waited while Jim washed the thick off his face in the rain barrel. It was a shop designed for hard use and for giants, the likes of which Jim Ferric most fit. The forge itself was made of the same mustard rock of the buildings and occupied a good quarter of the entire space. Leather bellows with handles of oak were attached to the back of the forge, and a chimney big enough for a man to stand in rose straight through the center of the roof. Within arm's length of the forge was a two hundred pound Mousehole anvil mounted atop a cottonwood stump. An iron rack encircled it with all manner of hammers, tongs, and fullers. An enormous floor mandrel for rounding up wagon wheels sat in the corner of the shop, and next to it was the biggest swage block Caleb had ever seen. In the far corner was a small wood-burning stove, with its stovepipe, suspended by ceiling wires, running into the forge chimney itself, and next to the door sat a barrel half-full of three-sided nails.

Drying off his beard, Jim pushed back his thinning red hair with his fingers and donned his hat.

"It's a fine shop," Caleb said. "I guess there ain't much a good smith couldn't make here, if he had a notion."

"I could forge you a new shirt, given sufficient time and the absence of army regulations," he said, grinning. "Come on, and I'll show you where the stoves are and where to stack out your wood. Once these boys know who you are, then it will be all right, won't it."

And so for the next hour they made the rounds—the barracks, the post hospital, the commissary, the bakery, and the sutler's store, where Caleb drooled over the jars of strawberry jam and luxuries untold. All buildings had wood stoves, some small, some big as a wagon bed, and all had need of Caleb's services. At the quartermaster storehouse, he was introduced with great care to Sergeant Wins, a man whose features were as weak as his handshake. Sergeant Wins would keep the unofficial record of his credits and dole out his subsistence. He was, it appeared, key to the whole scheme of things. So before they left, Caleb traded the entire load of wood for a side of bacon and a hundred pound sack of oats for the mules.

"Pick it up at the back door," Wins said with a flat voice, "and make certain you ask for me and nobody else."

From there, he and Jim walked the row of officer's quarters.

At the end of the row was the company commander's quarters, which looked a good deal like an English country house, had it been set anywhere but in the Kansas plains.

"Stack the wood there," Jim said, "by each outhouse, and contact the strikers if you have questions. Don't bother the commander or officers, Caleb. A man what stirs up a skunk has to live with the stink, don't he."

"Strikers?"

"Enlisted servants, paid by the officers."

"They've got servants?"

"Tucked in and kissed by angels, ain't they," Jim said.

At the guardhouse, they were shown into the entrance by way of the guard. The cells were packed with soldiers, men of all ages and ranks, their arms hanging through the bars as they watched on in silence. Each had a ball and chain as constant companion, the balls polished from the wear of their hands as they carried them about, like mothers with babes in their arms. Even with the stove lit, Caleb's breath rose in the chill.

"They don't cut that much wood for the stockade," the guard said, "just enough to keep the pots from freezing, 'cause they're stinking hell to get thawed up, ain't they."

At the end of the hallway was a single cell, isolated from the others and smaller in size. A young man sat in the corner on the floor, his hair in a single black braid down his back. There were pieces of red cloth wound into the braid, and his buckskin outfit was slick with wear and grease.

"Is that a Indian?" Caleb asked.

"Well, he ain't no Episcopalian, is he," the guard said. "That's Little River, one of the scouts here at Harker. Claims to be a scout, or some such, but you don't never know, do you. His English is better than mine, which ain't saying all that much. Claims he learned it off a female army nurse what lived with his tribe whilst they were all dying of the smallpox." Opening the door of the wood stove, the guard shoved in a piece of bois d'arc, pushing the door closed with his foot. "I'd as soon have my arms tore out as have the pox," he said.

"Why is he locked up?" Caleb asked, looking over at the Indian, who was watching him back through the bars of his cell, his eyes black as midnight.

"Got liquored up and rode his horse onto the commander's porch, leaving a big plop right up there for the Lord Jesus of Fort Harker to step in. Well, the commander was unhappy about a Indian riding onto his porch and leaving a plop at his front door, as you might imagine, so Little River here's taking a leave of absence for the time being."

"Why's he by hisself?"

"'Cause these upstanding soldiers here object to sleeping with a Indian, that's why, and that particular Indian don't take kind to objections. So, it's a bad situation all around, ain't it. Now, if you'll listen up and quit worrying about that Indian for a minute, I'll show you what's what."

"Sorry," Caleb said, looking over at Jim.

"This here's the wood box," he said, "and there's another upstairs. You ain't to come in here on your own. Just contact the guard, and he'll get one of these prisoners to help carry in the wood. If there's one thing we got around here, it's folks willing to come out of them cells for a spell."

"Okay," Caleb said, "and thanks."

After leaving the guardhouse, Caleb and Jim went back to the blacksmith shop, where Jim showed him a set of slap hinges he was making for the new root cellar door and a ring he was forging out of a hub nut.

"Army don't take to forgin' up personals," he said, "but a man's got to have something, don't he."

"I best be going, Jim. Once I get this wood delivered, I figure to swing over to the railhead and see if I can't drum up a little business. Anyway, I'm setting off my first batch right here, and to hell with the commander, I always say."

"Don't say it too loud," Jim said, "'cause he's a man with fearsome power, ain't he."

After Caleb made his deliveries to the commander's house, the quartermaster, and the commissary, he had but an armful of sticks left and decided to take them to the guardhouse. If anyone at Fort Harker could use a little extra firewood, it was those poor bastards under ball and chain and the freezing draft of the prison.

Much to Caleb's surprise, it was the Indian who was brought out to help unload the wood.

"He ain't half the trouble prizing out," the guard said, cradling his rifle across his arm, "being by hisself like he is."

The Indian said nothing as Caleb stacked wood on his outstretched arms. Even as his muscles rippled under the weight, he bore it without protest. They were close to the same age, Caleb guessed, and of the same slight build. Beyond that, they were worlds apart, as evidenced in the silence between them.

They had finished, and Caleb was stacking the last of the cedar into the wood box, when the guard motioned for Little River to move back to his cell.

"Thanks," Caleb said, looking up from the box.

"The white man carries the wood to his camp," Little River said, "but the Indian takes his camp to the wood so he doesn't have to carry it."

"It's a point," Caleb said, tossing in the last piece, "but the rabbit, which ain't even a human bein', has no need for either, does he?"

Little River lifted his chin and thought over the words for a moment before turning back to his cell.

From there, Caleb pulled the empty wagon about, making certain to stay off the parade grounds, and took the back road to the dock of the quartermaster storehouse. After loading in his oats, he wrapped the bacon side in a sack for keeping off the dust and slipped it under the wagon seat.

Sergeant Wins wrote figures into his book as he watched on from the dock.

"It's more wood we'll be needing soon," he said. "If you can't manage, then we'll just have to get someone what can, won't we." Slipping his notebook into his hip pocket, he leaned forward, his hand on his knee, and spit tobacco juice between Mule Two's ears. "Better feed this ole hinny 'fore the buzzards eat her right out of the harness," he said.

As Caleb approached the railhead camp, a soldier mounted on a sorrel rode down the track to meet him. He held his hat against the wind with one hand and the other up for Caleb to stop.

"Whoa," Caleb said, drawing up the reins.

"You got business with the railroad, Mister?" he asked.

"No, sir, given I ain't been there yet."

"What's your name?"

"Caleb Justin."

"I'm Corporal Fitz," he said, "with a detachment out of Harker, guarding this here work train against Indian depredations. I suggest you move on."

"I ain't a Indian," he said, "just a woodcutter come to see if the camp needs wood brought in. Jim Ferric, the blacksmith out of Harker's the one what sent me."

"Jim? Yeah, I know Jim," Fitz said, bringing about his horse. "Ole Jim's a fine blacksmith and a mighty poor soldier. Lost his corporal stripes when he set the cook on top of his stove. Lifted him right up under his arms like he weighed no more than a sack of sugar. You could hear that cook screaming all the way to Leavenworth. Course, he deserved it, didn't he, and he ain't sat down since either. Every time ole Jim comes in the commissary, that son of a bitch scrambles out the back door just as quick."

"Jim thought the railroad might pay a little cash money for firewood," Caleb said, "what cut and stacked for convenience."

"Well, Caleb Justin, do you know there's Cheyenne about what like to have your hair hanged off their teepee pole?"

"Yes, sir, but I'm armed, ain't I, working the trees and keeping out of sight."

"It's *your* hair, I reckon, and none of my say."

"You figure I could go in to camp and ask about the wood-cutting?"

"I suppose it would be all right," he said. "Those track boys keep a fire blazing day and night, to drive off the fiends and the fear in their hearts, I'm betting, but it don't, does it? Monnet's got his own stove up there in that private car of his, keeping hisself and that daughter all cozy, whilst the rest of us freeze off our balls in these saddles. But I reckon you could check with him, if you was of a mind."

Caleb's heart leaped at the possibility of seeing the girl again. "Ain't he the owner of the railroad?" he asked.

Slipping his carbine back into its scabbard, the soldier leaned forward on his saddle horn. "Ain't nobody owns a railroad, 'cept God, and He ain't got but a partner's share. Now, ole Monnet is a big shot, don't get me wrong, and one to be reckoned with. Got that daughter with him, too, a real looker, ain't she, waiting on her lieutenant fiancé to come out of Fort Larned and whisk her away."

"That's what I heard," Caleb said.

"Well, you just be careful where you let them eyeballs fall 'cause ole Monnet's got a pack of men working for him and willing to do anything what he takes a mind of. Say," he said, turning in his saddle, "ain't them army mules?"

"Salvaged out on account of their age," Caleb said, "and headed for the glue factory. Jim Ferric traded 'em right out of death's door. This here's Mule One, and this one here's Mule Two."

"Hell's bells," Fitz said, "I didn't know 'Mule Two' was a girl's name."

"Was all along, far as I know."

"Well, you take care, Woodcutter. I got to get back up there and protect them railroad boys, or they start crying to Monnet, and Monnet cries to the commander at Harker, and the commander makes life unfit for living, don't he."

"Thanks, Fitz," Caleb said.

The private car sat on a siding just yards from where the track stopped. An iron step hung from the doorway, but with cold welcome, as the curtains were pulled against the rudeness of the outside world. A hundred yards farther down, civilization itself ended, and men worked as ants, laying tie and rail into the wilderness ahead.

With trepidation, Caleb knocked on the car door. He stepped back and removed his hat to comb his fingers through his hair. Moments passed before the door opened and a man appeared. Dressed in coat and tie, he peered down from the height of the car, his glasses perched on the end of his nose, suspended there by some invisible will. Dark, intelligent eyes bore through Caleb.

"Yes?" he asked.

"Mr. Monnet?"

"That's right."

"My name is Caleb Justin. I'm the woodcutter for Fort Harker. I was wondering if you might be interested in having firewood cut and stacked for the work crew, or maybe even for yourself here at this car?"

Placing his finger in the center of his glasses, Monnet pushed them back up his nose, and his eyes rounded and grew under the magnification.

"This is the railroad, Mr. Justin," he said.

"Yes, sir."

"The railroad doesn't need anyone else to cut its wood. It's quite capable of cutting its own wood."

"Yes, sir. I can see that plain enough. Still, I work a sight cheaper than a high-paid rail hand, a man what should be laying track and shaping the course of America instead of cutting wood just to keep hisself warm at night. It's woodcutters what should be left to do their share, though a mighty small thing it is, sir."

Once again the glasses eased to the end of Monnet's nose, stopping just at its tip. "Don't blow smoke up my skirt, boy. It's been tried by the best."

"Yes, sir," Caleb said. "It's a mighty thin smoke, I admit."

Just as he turned to leave, the girl appeared at Monnet's shoulder, the hardness in his eyes softening with her touch.

"What is it, Papa?" she asked.

"It's nothing, Joan. This boy claims to be a woodcutter, that's all."

She lifted on tiptoes to see over Monnet's shoulder and asked, "A what?"

"A woodcutter."

A wisp of ebony hair fell across her face as she studied Caleb, the scent of her perfume exotic and sudden in the earthy confines of the camp.

"What does he want, I wonder?"

"To sell firewood to the railroad," Monnet said, stroking her hand with the tips of his fingers, the way one might stroke the nose of a spirited horse.

She hooked her chin on Papa's shoulder and leaned in, the emerald green of her eyes, the whiteness of her skin, the startling dimples that set Caleb's heart to tripping.

"Papa," she whispered, "is he hungry?"

Heat flushed in Caleb's face, and he turned away so that they would not see.

"How much do you charge for wood, Mr. Justin?" Monnet asked.

When Caleb turned back, he avoided the green eyes of the girl, who saw him for what he was—destitute and miserable and unworthy. "Five dollars a load," he said, "but it's earned wood, sir. You don't have a need, then I'll just be moving on."

"You're a might touchy for a man concerned about the course of America's future."

He looked back at his mules and paused before speaking, but when he did speak, he spoke to the girl who watched him from over her papa's shoulder.

"I carried wood for my pa ever since I was big enough to climb into a wagon, sir, and when I was strong enough to lift a axe, I cut kindling, sometimes no bigger than my finger, but I cut it right alongside, and when I was older, I cut two loads of hardwood a day, a rarity even for growed men, and when my pa died, I cut wood alone to make my way, cut it with my pa's axe, this axe right here, and in all that time I never asked for nothing what I didn't earn with my own two hands."

Monnet pushed his glasses up again, centering his attention on Caleb. "Two dollars a load then?"

"Three," Caleb said.

"All right, three dollars. Agreed?"

"Yes, sir. Agreed."

"Cash money on delivery from the paymaster in the end car there. I expect you not to interfere with the crew or take up my time, Mr. Justin, because as you pointed out, time is of the essence when building a railroad. The course of America depends on it. Now, if you'll excuse me."

And when Caleb looked again, both papa and daughter were gone, and the door to their private world was closed once more.

By the time Caleb rode into his camp, the cold sun was shimmering below the cottonwoods, and in their tops, wild turkey were gathered in the limbs once again, like black-robed priests huddling against the sharpening chill of evening. But tonight they would sleep undisturbed, because it was smoked bacon Caleb had on his mind.

He unharnessed the mules and fed them peach cans of oats in the dry, clean buffalo grass, sitting on his haunches to watch them eat, the grind of their teeth like drums in the hollowness of their skulls, and when they were hobbled out, he cooked the bacon, wrapping it in fried bread made of water and flour.

The night darkened, and a great weariness pressed in on him. It had been a busy day, a day fraught with people and words and difficult things, but now at least his way was made. All that remained was the promise that he work, that he cut wood and deliver, and these were but ordinary companions to a man such as he.

Climbing into his bunk, he pulled the blanket about him and listened to the fire, watched the frolic of shadows, and wondered if she might visit his door tonight, the coyote bitch with the eyes of yellow.

But fatigue washed over him, and soon he slept the flawless sleep of resolve and decision. Not until the wee hours did he stir in his dreams, and there from under the moon were the eyes, as he knew they would be, but not of yellow, or of savagery, or of valiance untamed, but the eyes of green, and of emerald, and of Papa's own daughter.

Chapter 9

For two weeks Caleb worked into the night, ranging ever farther from camp in pursuit of suitable firewood and plodding home in darkness, frozen, wearied, and half-mad from the eternal winds.

Twice he'd made deliveries to the fort and was short-changed both times by Sergeant Wins, who claimed the wood inferior, or shy, or too wet to burn. It was then that Caleb held back the best sticks of hardwood for the rail camp, stacking them next to the cellar until he could get a full cord saved. At least at the rail camp, he'd get cash money for his efforts.

On this day, Sergeant Wins leaned forward from the dock and spit tobacco juice on Mule Two's rump, wiping his mouth with his sleeve.

"It's trash, ain't it," he said, "and not worth the haul, if you ask me."

"The best there is, Sergeant, 'less you want it freighted in from Kentucky."

"Shy of hardwood, ain't it?"

"No, sir. It ain't."

Taking out his notebook, Sergeant Wins made his entry with a stub pencil.

"I'm docking you a third, 'cause nobody cheats the army. It's something woodcutters got to learn."

"It ain't the army being cheated, Sergeant."

"Well, now," he said, "you don't like army business, you can just sell it somewheres else, can't you. Maybe ole Red Nose would like a load or two. Why don't you just send up a smoke signal and see?"

Pulling his team about, Caleb didn't answer, because there was no answer. Wins was right. The army's business was all that bore between him and starvation at the moment.

There was no need to go by the blacksmith shop because Jim Ferric, according to the guard at the gate, had been assigned to a detachment of supply wagons sent to Riley, so after the best wood was delivered at the commander's house and the commissary, Caleb stopped at the guardhouse to finish out his load.

He knocked on the door and waited, his back against the wind that cut unheeded across the compound.

"What is it?" the guard asked through the crack in the door.

"I got some pretty good elm left," Caleb said. "Thought you boys could use a little."

"Could always use a little. Hang on," he said, closing the door. When he opened it again, a private shivered at his side. "Mooney here will help you load up the box. He's sprung come morning anyway, so don't figure he's apt to murder no woodcutter."

After the box was loaded, Caleb stoked the stove while the guard returned Mooney to his cell.

When the guard had resumed his post by the stove, Caleb asked, "Where's the Indian?"

"Little River?"

"Ain't but one I ever saw," Caleb said, "what with the red tails in his braid?"

"Done his time," the guard said, warming his hands to the fire. "Hopped on his pony and rode off without so much as a smooch or a wave. Guess the guardhouse wasn't to his liking, though I don't see living in a snowbank and eating dog as much improvement, myself."

"Living in a snowbank ain't so bad," Caleb said, buttoning his coat, "though I can't say about eating dog, least not yet. See you in a couple weeks."

With a sack of pinto beans and a twenty-five-pound bag of flour under the wagon seat, Caleb headed back to his camp. As he topped the hill above the garden, the sky darkened in the west, and the smell of moisture rode in on the wind. The prairie dogs watched from their mounds as he passed, reverence in the fold of their hands and the tilt of their heads.

By the time the mules were unharnessed, flakes of snow had gathered white on their backs. Caleb doubled their feed and tied them in the hollow behind the cellar, the one place sheltered from the bitter north wind.

He dug an onion from the garden and built a fire of hardwood, taken against his better judgment from the rail camp stash. With his skinning knife, he quartered the onion and cut up the last of the bacon, browning it in the pan. Adding water, pinto beans, salt, and a dash of vinegar, he snuggled the whole of it into the coals to simmer, and by the time the aroma wafted through the camp, snowflakes had thickened about him, gathering on his shoulders and the brim of his hat, filling the camp like silent but determined guests.

The beans were delicious, and he mopped the last of them from the bottom of his tin with a hunk of sourdough. To ward against the dropping temperatures, he donned Jim's sack coat and added wood to the fire. He settled back and listened to the sizzle of the flakes as they swept into the flames, vanishing to nowhere, just as they had come.

A coyote called from the blackness, of loneliness, of desolation, of questions unanswered, and Caleb's own doubts spilled within him. Rubbing at the stiffness in his foot, he thought of that day in the woods, of the tree with its terrible weight, and of his pa so still on the porch. He thought of the cabin, of Ben and Sophie, and of the window beyond which the Ohio twisted and flowed. He thought of the steamers struggling against the river, their whistles screaming against the impossible current, and of the smell of smoke, and of the fire, and the end of his life. That time was far away now, from a different world, a different life, one he could never reclaim or know again.

That night he stored kindling in the cellar to keep it dry for the morning fire. Slipping on a pair of extra socks, he pulled both Jim's sack coat and the woolen blanket over him, shivering against the bitterness of the night even still. Outside, the snow buried and quieted the valley in its softness, but for tomorrow, when the sun rose on the frozen world, he would load the wood for the railhead camp. With luck he would catch a glimpse of her, the girl with the fleur-de-lis and the eyes of green, making this night, this place and time, more bearable.

The next morning, he climbed from his bed, clapping his hands to warm them against the cold, his teeth chattering as he slipped on his stiff and frozen boots. Even in the cellar, his breath rose, freezing in his beard and the brows of his eyes.

He stepped outside with his arms full of kindling and squinted against the light, a morning locked in a shimmering sunrise. As far as he could see, drifts swelled and ebbed like a vast crystal ocean. Steam curled from the creek bed into the stillness, and tree limbs drooped under stacks of snow. High in the branches, blackbirds lifted and settled in joyous chatter, invulnerable to the piercing morning cold.

Once the kindling was blazing, Caleb knocked the snow from the sticks of wood, adding them with care so as not to douse his fire. While his coffee was simmering, he brushed the snow from the backs of the mules and rubbed them down with a flour sack. He doubled their feed once again to keep up their strength, talking to them as he fit their collars and harnesses and lines.

After breakfast, he loaded the wood, a prime load of walnut

and pecan, and struck out for the railhead camp. The going was slow under the pull of the drifts. He drew up on several occasions to let the mules blow and to walk the stiffness from his own frozen feet.

Two hours later, he smelled the rail camp fires, the unmistakable drift of smoke on the wind, and waited as Fitz rode out to meet him.

"'Lo, Woodcutter," Fitz said, hooking his reins over his saddle horn and stuffing his hands into the depths of his pockets. "Reckon it's a load you're bringing?"

"That it is, Fitz, hardwood and hot enough for driving the winter out of your bones."

Fitz's horse snorted and shook his head against the delay.

"Well, them girlies can use it, delicate what they are," Fitz said. "All sniffly and cold, ain't they. Stack it over there by the cook shack, and put Monnet's at the end of his car, just there by the coupling. Be careful you don't track things up, 'cause he's mighty particular about woodcutters mucking up his mansion, and it's likely to get me wrote up, although a stay in the guardhouse might be a relief after the backside of this here frozen horse."

"Thanks, Fitz."

Fitz pulled his hands from his pockets and held them against his face.

"Indians ain't big on fighting in the winter," he said, picking up his reins, "'cause it's cold, ain't it, and they got no fodder for them starved-out ponies of theirs, but there ain't nothing they like better than odds, such as a woodcutter wandering about like a jackrabbit in a snowbank."

"Once I get this wood delivered, I figure to hole up, Fitz. Take a grown badger to dig me out."

"See that you do," he said, bringing his horse about with a wave of his hand.

Tossing back the best pieces for Monnet, Caleb stacked the wood near the cook shack as Fitz had said. Even the railroad had surrendered to the sway of nature, the immense mule teams idled and left to their boundless feed of oats, the men freed to curse the cold and the misery of their camp as they played cards or dominoes about the fire.

He knocked on the door of Monnet's car and checked his feet for mud. Some time passed before the girl opened the door a crack.

"Yes?"

"Miss Monnet?" he asked, holding his hand to his eyes against the glare of the snow.

"What is it?"

"I'm the woodcutter here with a load of wood."

"Papa's gone on the work train," she said. "I suppose he's been delayed because of the snow."

"Yes, Miss, but I have a load of good hardwood what needs unloaded. You wouldn't want to be caught up short in this kind of weather."

"Oh, maybe you should," she said, pushing open the door. "The box is just there on the landing. Goodness, you're half frozen, aren't you?"

"Yes, Miss," he said, loading up his arms, stepping past and into her world, the smell of her perfume like an embrace in the crisp winter air. "It's fair open to the north pole, I reckon."

As he filled the box, she watched him, her presence a heat against him, and when he was finished, he brushed the snow away from the floor with his hat, so that Fitz wouldn't have to go to the guardhouse.

"I'm sorry," she said, holding her arms about her against the draft, "but I didn't get your name."

"It's Caleb Justin, Miss."

"Do I owe you something, Mr. Justin, for the wood?"

Emerald eyes pulled him in, weakened his knees, swept him into their depths, and he put his hand against the side of the car.

"No, Miss. Your pa arranged pay."

"Oh, yes, I remember now. Then you must come in," she said, pushing the hair back from her face, a black sheen against the white of her skin, "for some tea and to warm up for a moment."

"Oh, no, Miss," he said, looking down at his feet. "I ain't fit for coming in."

"Mr. Justin," she said, propping her hands onto her waist, "I insist, and I'm freezing out here. Now, you stoke my fire while I put on some tea."

He brushed the snow from the tops of his shoulders and checked his boots once more.

"Yes, Miss. I'll bring in some pecan. It's the hottest of all for a day like this."

The stove was small, its door of cast iron and silver, and took but a few sticks of wood. Backing up to it, he took in the room while she prepared tea. Scarlet drapes hung in folds about the window, the same as he'd seen that day at the siding, then again from the wagon as he rode off to Riley, sumptuous and rich, as he knew they must be, to hold at bay the discourteous world. A tucked and pleated leather couch sat under the window, a book opened over its arm, abandoned there at the woodcutter's knock, and all about was the opulence of carved mahogany, of brass lanterns, of marble stands and leather-bound documents. At the end of the car hung a picture of a steam engine, smoke churning from its stack as it labored up a mountain, and there to the side, a curtained berth, her lair and place of sleep, her warmth beneath the comforters, and the robes, and the crackle of her fire.

"It will be but a minute," she said. "You must take off your coat, or the heat will drive in the cold."

"Yes, Miss."

She sat down on the couch and placed a marker in the book before setting it aside.

"Now, Mr. Justin, tell me about yourself."

"There's sad little to tell, Miss."

"Well, then, I'll just have to wait, won't I, because I haven't had anyone to talk to for the longest time, and if someone doesn't talk to me soon, I'll surely go mad."

"I'm from Kentucky," he said.

"I see. Is that all?"

"Yes, Miss."

"Mr. Justin?"

"Yes, Miss?"

"Must you be so formal?"

"No, Miss."

"Good, then," she said, rising, pouring from the kettle with great care, as if in it were all that one might ever need. "And here's your tea."

Reaching for the cup, he sipped at its thin and delicate lip, its taste as exotic as the hand from which it had come.

"And you, Miss?"

"Me?"

"What brings you to a place such as this?"

She glanced up, her eyes pooling liquid green, and there was in them a wisdom he'd not noticed before. "Well," she said, sipping on her tea as she looked out the window, driblets of melted snow racing its surface, "I came out here to meet my fiancé, but things have not worked out. It seems Quartermaster Officer Forgan at Fort Larned died of a bursted appendix, a horrible death they said, and then they had no one who knew how things were to be done, so they commandeered my fiancé until a new officer could be assigned. It was just the worst luck."

"Suppose Officer Forgan would agree with that," Caleb said.

"So when Lieutenant Gillian returns, he's to put in for a transfer to Fort Leavenworth, and we will live there in the officer's quarters. They are quite adequate you know, and it's very important to one's career to be at Leavenworth, they say."

"I didn't know that, Miss," he said, taking another sip of the tea.

"Well, because that's where the most important people are, you know, for promotions, socializing, and the like. They say it's just extraordinary and with just everything provided."

"It's been hard for you then, the waiting and all?"

"Yes," she said, sighing. "I wouldn't have come all the way out here if Papa wasn't going to be here anyway, and it just seemed like a good plan. Then, of course, the army left me stranded here in the middle of nowhere. It's just been the most lonesome time, and Papa's always so busy." Taking another sip of tea, she set her cup down. "I don't suppose it matters that much, if we go to Leavenworth I mean, because Lieutenant Gillian will have an important job waiting for him on the railroad if he decides to get out. That's what Papa says."

Finishing his tea, Caleb set the cup down and slipped on his old coat.

"Thank you, Miss. I'm much warmer than I was."

She clasped her hands in front of her and smiled. "I'm sorry I talked so much, Mr. Justin, but it's just been so long, and it just came pouring out."

"I enjoyed the company, Miss, and the tea, too."

"Mr. Justin, do you read?"

"Just what's on hand, Miss. I got a whole stack of *Harper's Weekly* magazines back at the camp. They put me to bed near every night."

"Oh, dear, that won't do. Here, take this. It's a copy of *Bleak House*, and just everyone's reading it."

"I'd like that fine, Miss, but a book like this is in some danger in a camp like mine."

"Oh, Papa would never know, would he?"

"Thank you, Miss. I'll have another load of pecan soon enough if the weather doesn't drive me in."

Holding open the door, she handed him his hat. "Well, good-bye then, Mr. Justin."

"Good-bye, Miss," he said.

He stopped at the paymaster on his way out and collected his three dollars. The cash money felt good as he tucked it away into his pocket. First chance, he was going to the sutler's store to buy some of that strawberry jam.

After securing the book in a flour sack, he climbed up on the wagon and pulled his hat down over the sting in his ears. Fitz stood at the fire with the rail crew and tipped a salute as Caleb drove off into the frozen prairie.

Home bound and with an empty wagon, the mules picked up their pace, and the rail camp soon disappeared behind. But as the sun drew down, the sky cleared, the cold deepened, and the wagon wheels squeaked on the powdery snow. The orange light of sunset soon spilled across the frigid tundra, the absence of warmth in its retreat.

Pulling up the collar of Jim's sack coat, he barricaded himself against the cold and the emptiness within him. To have seen the girl in her world, to have stood at the divide, at that great chasm between them, had set him adrift and despondent.

He rode into the prairie dog town just north of his camp at sunset. "Whoa," he said, pulling up the team. It was impossible to see the mounds under the snow cover, and holes were dangerous for an unsuspecting animal. A broken leg could not be mended. He searched in vain for his friends, the little priests with their wisdom and cheer, but none was to be seen, none to greet him on his return trip home. It was a city emptied of life.

Turning about, he listened to the silence, to its vastness and measure. At first, he overlooked the streak of blood, so close was it to his feet, a smear of crimson across the snow.

"Whoa," he said to Mule One, who was prancing in anticipation of oats. "There's something here."

A buffalo carcass lay just in the shadows, its eyes frosted and dead. Both tongue and hump were cut away, as were steaks from the flank and rump. The large bones of the leg were crushed and splintered and picked clean of their marrow, sprinkles of pink still scattered about in the ice and snow. The buffalo had been taken in a hurry by someone hungry and cautious.

Mule One's eyes whitened as he peered around his blinders at the thing in the shadows, caught the gamy smell of death. Caleb reached for his Spencer and listened again, stared into the shadows for signs of movement. Dropping onto a knee, he studied the horses' tracks, small and unshod where they'd circled the prey, and then, there in the snow, the shaft of an arrow, splintered under the collapsed buffalo.

His hair tingled on the nape of his neck. A few hours earlier and it could have been him, butchered under the frenzied attack, dismembered and strewn and left for eternity.

He climbed onto his wagon and snapped the reins, pulling away, looking over his shoulder with trepidation, because this much he knew for certain, knew it with the certainty and finality of death: he was no longer alone.

Chapter 10

The winds ceased as night fell across Caleb's camp. By the time he'd fed the mules and lay in kindling for the morning, snow had fallen once more, great white flakes that gathered and stacked and muffled away the sounds of the night. Too weary to build a fire, he lit a candle and ate a cold supper under its wavering light.

Afterward, he cleaned his boots of snow, turning them upside down over sticks of kindling in the hope that by morning, they'd be dry. Checking the Spencer, he lay it at the head of his bed and leaned his axe against the cellar wall. It was not a night for visitors, not of man, or of beast, or for uninvited reveries, not in the heart of a Kansas blizzard.

But then this was not a rational time but a time of Lee Horns, of shameless men with brazen hearts, men who lived and died without reflection, men like the deserters, with nothing to lose, no rules or conscience to follow as they roamed unheeded through others' lives.

Once in bed, he shook the images away and opened *Bleak House*, to read under the yellow light of the candle, the smell of Joan Monnet's perfume still lingering in the pages of the book, and he read of the death of the sun, and of the streets of mud, and of the petulant England fog, and he knew that books such as these were of her world and not of his. Into the night he read, even into his weariness, and it was not until the candle quivered and died in a molten pool that he lay the book aside.

For two days it snowed without stop, so during the light, he fed oats to his mules, clearing the snow from under their bellies, leading them to the stream where he broke ice with his axe so that they could water. He cooked a pot of hot soup from the remaining salt pork, baked cornbread with lard and meal, and wished for eggs, for the comforting cluck of his chickens, now so far away.

When night came, he climbed into his bed once more to read under the pale light, until his eyes burned with fatigue, until the candles drowned away, until the book was finished and there was no more.

The next day, Jim Ferric waved from atop the hill, his huge profile unmistakable in the newborn sun. Caleb waved his hat and walked out to meet him, delighted to see him once more.

"Come to dig you out," Jim said, sliding down from his horse.

"Coffee's on," Caleb said, shaking his big hand.

"Coffee will do," he said.

Back at camp, Caleb poured coffee and pulled up a stump across from Jim.

"So," he said, "I hear you've been to Fort Riley?"

Jim sipped at his cup and let the steam warm his face before answering.

"They had to chip me off the wagon seat with a pickaxe when I got back. Course, I got a little time off for it, which accounts for my being here drinking your coffee and answering questions about where I been."

Looking out onto the prairie, Caleb shook his head.

"I never knew it could snow like this on the prairie, Jim."

"Oh, yes, sir," he said, "but it ain't but a picnic compared to summer heat. Just the thought of it makes me want to dig into one of these here snowbanks and never come up again."

"Well, maybe so, but it's a misery for a man needing to cut wood, I tell you. I'm running far behind as it is, what with the rail camp, and then with Wins cutting my load every chance he gets."

"Glad to hear you got the railroad work, Caleb."

"It's cash money, just like you thought, Jim, and mighty welcome."

Jim tossed the dregs from his cup into the snow and cut himself a chew, loading his jaw.

"Wins is a son of a bitch and not to be trusted if you ask me," he said. Spitting into the fire, he looked over at Caleb. "Every time someone holds him to bear, that lieutenant of his steps in to save his bacon."

"Lieutenant Gillian?"

Jim sharpened a stick into the fire with his pocketknife, the curls of wood twisting away in the coals.

"A son of a bitch in his own right," he said.

Rising, Caleb poured himself another cup of coffee, setting the pot out of the fire to cool.

"I've met his girl over at the rail camp," he said.

"A right pretty one, I hear tell," Jim said, working at the opposite end of his stick, "and with a rich daddy to boot."

"Right pretty," Caleb said. "She's figuring on going back to Leavenworth when they marry so's they can socialize and make promotion faster that way."

Tossing his stick into the fire, Jim closed his knife and rose to look down on the garden now buried beneath snowdrifts.

"The Indians have a hard time getting their horses through the winter, Caleb. It's the one time of the year they ain't up for a fight. The rumor at Fort Riley is that Sheridan's planning a big campaign for next winter, to drive the Indians south into the Territory. It's the last push and the end of the line for them if he pulls it off."

"You figure it's true, Jim?"

"I ain't but a ignorant blacksmith, but I do know that nothing stops the railroad. This army will do whatever it takes to keep it going, and it ain't likely Lieutenant Gillian or anyone else is going back to Leavenworth so's they can smooch up a general."

The sun broke, falling warm across Caleb's shoulders.

"I saw signs when I was riding in from the rail camp, Jim."

Turning, Jim studied him. "What kind of signs?"

"A kilt buffalo, hump and tongue cut out and with his bones all cracked up."

"Could have been them deserters," Jim said. "They've been tearing up the country. Stole a wagon right off a ox train, kilt two oxen in the doing, dragging the wagon master halfway to Fort Wallace with him screaming full of pear cactus the whole of the way."

"Them ponies weren't shod, Jim, and there was a broke arrow still under the carcass right where it was felled."

"You don't say."

"It's a fact."

Jim looked out over the garden again and said, "Maybe it's time you went on back to Kentucky, Caleb."

"I got no home left in Kentucky, Jim, just this here hole in the ground."

"Why, I'd say that's just a plumb crazy reason, if I wasn't in the same situation myself. Say," he said, turning, "why don't you and me go cut a little wood?"

"It's mighty deep snow out there, Jim."

"Sissy girl scairt of a little snow?" he asked, pushing his hat back from his big face and grinning.

Even empty, the wagon was a considerable pull out of the draw, the mules lunging chest deep against the drifts. Jumping down, Jim put his back to the wagon, and they soon pulled atop the plain. There, the snow was more shallow, having been swept clean by the wind.

"Maybe I'll just harness you up," Caleb said, snapping the reins. "You got more heft than either one of these here ole army mules."

"Why, it's a tempting offer," Jim said. "Better than blacksmithing for the cavalry, I figure, if it weren't for eating oats and having some woodcutter cuss my danged ear off all the time."

When they passed the prairie dog town, the population barked in alarm at the stranger in the wagon, dashing into their holes with indignation. Caleb pointed out the buffalo kill, little left now except a few polished bones and the faint pink of blood in the snow.

"It's Cheyenne, all right," Jim said, turning the broken shaft of the arrow between his fingers.

By noon they'd cut a good half load, all from a single old hackberry that twisted out of a rock outcrop not far from the stream. Even in the cold, sweat dripped from the ends of their noses as they worked. Cutting wood was a sight easier with someone to help, and Jim was a good hand. There was no doubting that as far as Caleb was concerned. What he lacked in skill with an axe he made up for in brute strength, perseverance, and a winning way.

At noon they built a fire from the hackberry limbs, and Caleb heated snow in the coffee pot, pitching in a handful of coffee grounds as it started to boil. Afterward, they ate leftover cornbread and jerked beef that Jim had brought with him from the fort.

The wagon groaned under the load as they worked their way back to camp that afternoon. The day cooled under the sunset, orange rays spraying into the icy sky.

As they approached the rise to the prairie dog town, the mules bore down against the load. Caleb stood, popping the reins. "Giddup," he yelled. "Ho! Ho!" At just that moment, the wagon tipped into a prairie dog hole, and Caleb spilled over the side as if shot, carbine, axe, and all. The mules stopped, twisting their necks at the unending mystery of man, and from above, Jim laughed, a great roaring laugh, and slapped his knee with glee.

"Goddang it," Caleb said, wiping the snow from his face and the front of his coat, but when he looked up, Jim was standing in the seat of the wagon, waving his hand for Caleb to be quiet. Dropping down, Jim gathered up his rifle and slid off the wagon, placing a finger over his mouth and pointing up the hill with another.

"I heard something," he said, whispering. "Get your carbine, and keep it quiet."

They labored their way to the summit on their hands and knees and peered over the top. Snow clung to their beards and the brows of their eyes, and their breaths steamed in the frigid cold. In the basin below, three men gathered about a campfire, their horses tied to the limbs of a mesquite that poked from under a snowbank. Two of the men wore the blue coats of cavalry, the other, squatting next to the fire, a buckskin coat and hair long, but both britches and hat marked him as cavalry as well.

"Who are they?" Caleb asked.

"It's them deserters, I figure, but that ain't the half of it," Jim said, pointing to the hill below them.

A dozen Indians just out of sight of the deserters gathered up like wasps preparing to attack. They were donned in buffalo robes and blankets against the cold. Their ponies were thin and gaunt from want of fodder, and their heads hung low with weariness.

The lead warrior gestured with his hand, and the others tied off their reins, stringing their bows, orchestrated and skilled and lethal.

"What we going to do?" Caleb asked, his heart thumping in his chest.

"There ain't nothing to do," Jim said, turning onto his back, "'cept pray they don't come over this hill, 'cause we can't kill them or outrun them neither one."

The leader threw his blanket to the side and worked his way up the hill. At the top, he looked back at the waiting warriors and then stood, exposing himself to the soldiers below, daring them against the lowering light of sunset.

Just then the man in the buckskin stood.

"It's a goddang Indian, boys!" he shouted, pointing to the warrior, who now limped across the rim of the hill like a bird wounded and unable to fly.

"It's a trick," Caleb said, his voice trembling at the prospect of what was about to happen.

"Let's get him," one of the deserters cried out, mounting his horse, the others following suit as they yelped up the hill in excitement at their luck and the odds before them.

By now the warrior had dropped below the rim, fatigued and disheartened, his leg dragging, a wounded and pitiful animal.

Whooping and hollering from behind, the deserters pursued their prey, their horses racing, wide-eyed and frenzied with spur-bloodied sides. As they topped the hill, the waiting warriors attacked, and the evening was seized with the whine of bowstrings and the thud of shanked and mortal arrows. Throughout the valley, the screams of the deserters rose as they clutched at their saddle horns, their bodies bristling with arrows. Stunned and dying, they rode like children at play, round and round, all fall down, their blue coats seeping with blood, their heads bobbing against the pitch and scream of their wounded horses.

And as their mounts tumbled, kicking and pitiful, on their sides, the soldiers crumpled like discarded ragdolls, but even then the warriors did not stop, circling again and again, casting spears attached to their wrists with leather thongs, to thrust and to retrieve from the lifeless bodies, over and over like some mindless and horrible refrain.

Others fired yet more arrows into the red smears across the snow as they circled on their ponies, now white-eyed with the smell of gore and death and blood. And when they were exhausted and could fire no more, they leaped from their ponies, stripping their victims of their clothes, their bodies shriveled and impotent in death, and with their knives they opened their bellies and cast out the entrails, and with bloodied hands carved great wounds in the thighs, and buttocks, and calves, and sawed away patches of scalp, lifting them high to bleed in the white innocence of the snow.

Caleb and Jim lay waiting, their hearts stilled and frozen, until there was no more, until at last the warriors rode away, satiated and victorious, their war calls lingering long after they'd disappeared beyond the white swell of the prairie.

Rising, Jim dusted away the snow from his front.

"Caleb," he said, "there's a lesson to be learned from this."

"What's that?" Caleb asked, unsticking his tongue from the roof of his mouth.

"Don't never chase a Cheyenne warrior over a hill," he said, 'less you're damn certain what's on the other side."

"It's a point," Caleb said, "and one I ain't apt to forget."

It was dark when they reached camp, and by the time the wood was unloaded, the stars had filled the cold blackness of the sky. After blowing into his hands to warm them, Jim untied his horse.

"I best be on my way, Caleb," he said, swinging into the saddle.

"Ain't you spending the night, Jim? It's a far ride to the fort and a cold one to boot."

"It's those danged coyotes,'" Jim said, looking back the way they'd come. "By morning there won't be enough left to know if them boys was deserters or kilt buffalo."

"You ain't going back there?"

"It's a sure bet I am," he said, reining his horse about. "There're three months' pay out there, and I aim to have it."

That night Caleb built his fire hot and high and sat with his back to the cellar door. From the night there came the yip and snarl of coyotes, Caleb's scalp tightening in the certainty and horror of their feed. Tomorrow, as Jim had said, there would be little left, pieces of hair, bits of clothing, the trace of pink in the snow.

But it was not this alone that caused him to reach for the Spencer, to lay it across his lap, because when he and Jim had ridden from the bloody basin, he had still not been certain, had not told of what he'd seen.

But now, alone in the solitude of this star-filled night, he could see him, clear now in his mind, the warrior with his limp, with his cunning at the rim of the hill, with the red bits of cloth turned into the braid of his hair.

Chapter 11

Within a few days the snow passed, as it is wont to do on the prairie, the winds shifting warm and dry from the desert. Caleb took advantage by working long hours laying in wood next to his cellar.

But as the weeks passed, the best cutting grew scarce, forcing him ever farther from camp. Even though these were long and lonely times, his love for the prairie germinated from the tiniest seed, grew from the smallest capitulation to its serenity, to a full-blown celebration of its expanse and mystery. In the prairie's isolation, he found peace; in its bleakness, a determination and will to survive; and in its cruelty, courage beyond all that he'd known.

Trips to the fort were infrequent, driven in part by the scarcity of wood, in the other part by his disdain for Sergeant Wins, who without fail managed to rob him of his due. "Might as well burn prairie grass," he'd say, "as this here tender," or "green as buffalo shit, ain't it, boy," or "wet to the core," or "the load's short," or "too much dirt," or "burns in a stink." Whatever it was, Caleb knew with the certainty of sunrise that he would ride away with less than what he'd had coming.

On the other hand, Jim Ferric was forever the bright spot on those trips, bringing him the news, news that settled and pooled in such a place as Fort Harker, an important juncture for the never-ending stream of strangers rumbling down the Santa Fe Trail.

It never failed that Jim had something or other to give him, a loaf of bread from the bakery, a knife he'd forged from a mule shoe, a jar of strawberry jam traded out of the sutler's store. "It ain't but fair," he'd say, "what with you helping out capturing them deserters and all." Then he'd laugh, that big belly laugh that came from down deep in his humanity.

Caleb put together a fine load of walnut and loaded it for a trip to the rail camp. Not since Joan Monnet had loaned him the book had he been able to see her. Once, she was sick with the fever, they said, and could not be disturbed. Another time, the private car was gone, having been pulled back to Leavenworth for inspection and supplies, and Caleb was left to unload the wood at the siding. Each time the camp was farther away and the trail more difficult. Soon he would no longer be able to follow in the wagon, to keep pace across the rugged terrain. In any case, with the coming of spring, his livelihood was bound to dry up.

As he rode past the prairie dog town, the prairie dogs bobbed their heads in recognition and flitted their tails like Chinese fans. The smell of spring was in the air, and the south wind was laden with moisture and warmth. Every chance, Mule One and Mule Two worked at the tiny shoots of grass in anticipation of better times.

Fitz sat on a pile of ties and examined his carbine, now strung about his feet in a dozen pieces. When he looked up and saw Caleb, he waved his hat for him to approach.

"It's been a while, Woodcutter," he said, holding his carbine against the sun to peer down its barrel.

"Hello, Fitz. Thought I'd bring this load of walnut before you boys get all the way to Mexico."

Fitz snapped the parts of his carbine back together one by one and squinted up into the sun.

"I'm afeared you're a tad late, Woodcutter."

"What do you mean?" Caleb asked, slipping down from the wagon.

"Monnet's gone back to Saint Louis, ain't he, and left that pretty daughter of his at Fort Harker."

"Fort Harker?"

"Yup, that's the one. Left her with the commander's wife, living in splendor, or as near to it as you can come at Fort Harker. Guess she's going to wait there for her intended hisself."

Snubbing his mules up to a tie, Caleb sat down next to Fitz.

"What am I supposed to do with all this wood, Fitz? It's a hell of a climb through them hills."

"Well, sir, I figure the paymaster would take it off your hands this time, if he was here, but he ain't, so I figure you'll just have to carry it on back or dump it best you can. It's coming up spring, Woodcutter. How long you aim on selling wood where wood ain't needed no more?"

"Long as they buy it," Caleb said.

Fitz set his carbine to the side and looked at him from under his hat. "Yes, sir, that's what I thought, and as long as that pretty girl was around."

"I hadn't noticed," Caleb said, "except in passing."

Standing, Fitz slid his carbine into the scabbard on his saddle before mounting up. "Woodcutter, my boy," he said, "there ain't nothing what endures more than a season and a quick spit in this here hell hole, that includes winter, Monnet, and this here railroad camp."

"Yes, sir," Caleb said, waiting for his point.

"Just something I noticed in passing," he said, reining about his mount.

It was nigh on midnight by the time Caleb left to go back to his camp, the wagon still loaded with walnut, and it was high noon by the time he'd pulled out once more for Fort Harker with the same walnut load.

Leaning over the loading dock, Sergeant Wins cleared his jaw onto Mule Two's rump.

"It's a bit wormy, ain't it," he said.

"No, sir, it ain't."

"You can't sell wormy wood to the army, boy, and expect a full load trade; 'sides, it's coming up spring, and we ain't going to need much more sorry wood, one way or the other." He wet the end of his stub pencil and made his entry into his book. "Now, I got your tally right here. You just sign off and pick up your goods on the way out."

"It's short a quarter load, Sergeant, and this here's prime walnut."

"It's wormy," he said, "and ought go in the river, hadn't I such a charitable heart."

Gritting his teeth, Caleb turned into the wind to cool the heat from his face.

"Is that all?" he asked.

"Take this over to the commander's quarters and make sure these here mules don't leave no plops behind. The commander hates plops on his yard and would have me humping the rogue's march for it."

It was a fine load of walnut, and Caleb stacked it with care, watching the back door the whole time for a glimpse of Joan Monnet. Stalling, he cleaned up the bark and then cleaned again in the hope that she might appear. He turned to leave just as she stepped from the door.

"Hello," she said, wisps of her hair feathering in the wind, catching for a moment in the corner of her mouth, as if in a caress.

"Miss," he said, tipping his hat. "I heard you'd moved to Fort Harker. I was hoping I might catch you."

"Oh?"

"To return the book you lent me out at the rail camp."

"Oh, yes," she said, her eyes like melted puddles of jade, "I'd forgotten altogether."

"Here it is, Miss," he said, taking the flour sack from under the seat. "I kept it best I could."

"Did you enjoy it, Mr. . . ."

"Caleb Justin, Miss."

"Now I remember, Mr. Justin. Did you find it to your liking?"

"Didn't sleep for three days, Miss, and near froze in the process."

"Yes," she said, her eyes smiling, "that's the way of it. I'm afraid I have no more books to offer, they having gone the way of my papa's library."

"It's all right, Miss. With no more wood to cut, I'll likely need be moving on anyway."

She sat on the steps and pulled her knees into her arms, the alabaster turn of her ankles, and she studied him with a steady and genuine gaze.

"But where will you go?"

"I don't know just yet, Miss, but it's a big country for sure."

"Yes," she said, "it is a big country. It turns out I'll not be going to Leavenworth as I had planned either."

"Oh, Miss?"

"Lieutenant Gillian, my fiancé, is being assigned to Fort Dodge. The army is expanding the Quartermaster Division to take on additional supplies out of Fort Larned. It seems that they can't do without him there."

"Well, Miss, it's the way of the army to change things up."

"We're to be married in Fort Dodge in the fall," she said, pausing, "and without my papa's attendance." Looking into the prairie, she pushed the hair from her face and sighed. "Oh, well, I do hope Fort Dodge is better than Fort Harker."

"It's bound to be, Miss."

She laughed, and her laugh lit him up, warmed him from the inside out, and he thought for just a moment how lucky a man was Lieutenant Gillian.

"Well, Mr. Justin, best of luck to you, and do be careful. The commander says it's more dangerous with each passing day and that soon something must be done."

"Yes, Miss," he said, climbing onto his wagon, "and thanks for the book. It was a wonder and world far from my own."

"Good-bye, Mr. Justin," she said, leaning forward onto her elbows, the dark folds of her hair falling about her face.

"Good-bye, Miss," he said, turning the mules about, looking once over his shoulder to see if she was still there, still watching him pass with regret in her heart, but she was gone, and there was naught left but the squeak of his wheels and the emptiness inside him.

On chance of seeing Jim, he swung by the blacksmith shop and found him laboring over his anvil, his face streaked with coal dust and sweat.

"Climb down, Woodcutter," he said, "and hold this flattie for me."

Caleb dropped from the wagon and held the flat hammer against the hot iron while Jim struck it with solid and flawless blows, the metal spreading and shaping beneath as malleable as bread dough.

"Wins shorted me again," Caleb said, while Jim examined the iron against the light from the door.

Jim placed the metal back into the forge and pumped at the bellows.

"If it ain't red, it ain't hot," he said, ignoring Caleb's comment.

"Said my walnut was wormy and it being the best wood I ever cut."

Taking the iron from the fire, Jim worked it with sharp, short strokes.

"Caleb," he said, "Sergeant Wins takes his off the top, bringing up them tallies for his own purposes, and others, too, I figure. It's the way of things, and every man here knows it."

"He's been thieving me all winter," Caleb said, "and I'm dog sick of it."

Putting his iron back in, Jim pumped at the bellows once

more, pulling out the iron when it was shimmering and white as snow. Sparks showered across the shop when he struck it with his hammer.

"Sometimes a man don't get his justice when he has it coming, Caleb, but he gets it sooner or later, that much I'm sure of."

"As long as I can witness it, Jim, that's all I ask."

"Yes, sir," he said, "I suppose I can understand that."

"I got to figure on what to do now that winter's near gone."

"Well, sir," he said, striking the iron, dropping a beat against the anvil with his hammer before striking it again, "the bakery's in need of wood year 'round, but the guardhouse boys take care of that."

"I could cut through the summer, if I didn't starve out in the doing," Caleb said.

Sliding the piece into a trough of water, Jim waited as the steam boiled into the air, the smell of metal and rust filling the shop.

"Things are heating up out here, Caleb. Red Nose and Black Kettle are mighty burned up about that Sand Creek raid. They lost a hell of a lot of people, what with them standing under a white flag the whole of the time, just so's ole Chivington could go home with blood on his hands. Them Cheyenne plan on leveling it out some, I'm thinking.

"Here's the thing I'm telling you," he said, taking out a plug of tobacco and picking pocket lint off its end, "they don't care if you're a soldier or a woodcutter either one. They'll gut you out as quick, leaving you for the coyotes, just like them deserters. It's a mighty poor way to die, my friend, and there ain't no bounty for me dragging your carcass back to the fort, neither."

"Maybe I could catch a work train to Leavenworth," Caleb said, "given that's how I got out here in the first place."

Bunching up his coals with the fire rake, Jim gave a couple of pumps on the bellows, and sparks raced up the chimney.

"It's past time, ain't it. I heard at Fort Riley that General Custer's headed this way and that something's in the works. Trouble and

Custer is poured from the same mold, and God help anyone who gets in his way."

"Fort Riley? That's where my friend Joshua joined up to fight with Sheridan."

"Well, he's apt to get his chance," he said.

"I best be on my way, Jim, 'fore it gets dark on me."

"Over yonder is a hasp I forged up out of the commander's old door hinge. You put it on the inside of that tater cellar and drop a stob through it at night. Least you won't get scalped whilst you sleep."

"Thanks, Jim."

"And right there by the door is a fire poker I worked up so's you won't singe off your eyebrows every time you stir up your fire. Now don't you go catching no work trains without me knowing."

"I'll drop by for certain, Jim."

As Caleb pulled around to the quartermaster storehouse, the wind slid in from the north, spinning and swirling from across the compound. Mule One and Mule Two stepped out with renewed energy at the prospect of picking up oats.

Sergeant Wins swung open the storehouse door, his jaw set and obstinate as usual.

"What is it?" he asked.

"Oats," Caleb said, "and a wool blanket, maybe a can of lard, if you ain't shorted me out of it."

"It ain't all day I got for you to be making up your mind."

"Oats and a blanket," Caleb said.

Wins dropped the sack of oats into the wagon bed when he returned and tossed the army blanket onto the seat next to Caleb. Moth holes big as coffee cups were eaten from its center, and it reeked of horse manure and stable straw.

"This here's a old blanket," Caleb said.

"Better than freezing to death in a tater cellar, ain't it?"

"I want a new one, Wins."

"It's 'Sergeant Wins' to you, Woodcutter, and I suggest you ride on out of here 'fore I take it back altogether."

Wins leaned over the side of the dock, chewed for a moment, and then spit an amber wad of tobacco direct into Mule Two's ear. Flopping her head from side to side, she rattled her harness and then her ear drooped over as if broken.

Caleb stood, Jim Ferric's new fire poker there in his hand, and he brought it across Sergeant Wins's ear, tearing it away from his skull. Blood oozed from its mooring, still white with surprise, and raced into the thickness of his beard.

A bellow rose from within Wins, a howl of disbelief that his ear now drooped rootless from the side of his head. Screaming, he leaped from the dock, as a stalking cougar might leap from rocky heights, spilling Caleb into the dust of the compound.

Caleb's lungs emptied, gasped for air from beneath Wins, the mules rearing, their feet striking the ground with their immense weight and lethal hooves.

Pinned, Caleb was unable to ward off Wins's staggering blows, the sickening crack of his ribs, like the snap of kindling, and the dazzling pain, and the bile that rose bitter in his throat. But from within him was a reserve, a strength honed and robust from hours at the axe. Reaching into that stock of power, he lifted Wins away, throwing him against the wagon wheel.

Wins shook his head and then pulled himself up by the wheel's spokes. In desperation, he searched for his enemy, his eyes dimmed and confused. Caleb struck again, this time a stunning and final blow, and waited as he crumbled unconscious at his feet.

He took the tally book from Wins's pocket and then tossed the soiled blanket into the dirt beside him. As he pulled away, the smell of warm bread drifted from the post bakery, and he was as hungry as he'd ever been in his life.

When they passed the commander's house, Mule Two hesitated, lifting her tail, and Caleb pulled up. After bobbing her head to loosen the reins, she plopped a salutation of her own making on the red rock path that twisted from the compound to the commander's front door.

Caleb looked about to make certain no one was watching, took out Sergeant Wins's tally book, and dropped it center of the steaming plop. With all the bad luck and suffering in the world, there was little sense in passing up such a rare opportunity.

The following week was without event, the weather warmer with each day. There was no need to cut wood now, so Caleb spent his time hunting wild turkey and exploring the meandering stream. Not since the deserters had there been signs of Indians, and no reason to believe they were about, but even so, it was a rare occasion that he left his Spencer beyond immediate reach.

Caleb awoke to a fine spring morning and listened to the robins as they stretched fat worms out of the soft earth of the garden. He cooked his breakfast and fed the last of the oats to Mule One and Mule Two before hobbling them out to graze. With a little luck, they could get by on what oats were left and the green shoots that sprang from the clumps of dead winter grass. Even though it was now thin and short of nourishment, the grass would improve with the sun-filled days.

Now more than ever, it was clear to Caleb that he would have to move on. Fort Harker was enemy territory and with little left except the likelihood of a beating from Wins and his cronies if they caught him alone. It was not the moving so much that he minded, but even now, his dilemma remained unchanged. To go home was to face the emptiness of his past. To go forward was to risk his life in a land fraught with uncertainty and danger.

He poured himself a last cup of coffee and leaned back against the cellar door. He closed his eyes to warm his face in the morning sun. It had been a winter of winters, one he'd never forget, and he was attached now to this hard land, even to this dark and curious home of his.

When he opened his eyes again, a figure was standing in the shadow of the tree where the cultivator was chained. Caleb's heart ticked up a beat as he reached for his weapon.

"'Lo, there, Woodcutter," the figure called out.

There was a familiarity in his voice, in the tilt of his head and the dangle of his long arms. Caleb dropped his carbine to his side, his finger on the trigger.

"State your business, stranger," he said.

"Mind if I come into camp?"

"If you come as a friend, and with your hands where I can see them."

When the figure stepped from the shadows, the blue of his uniform was unmistakable, and there was a grin from under the shade of his hat.

"You got any copper biscuits cooking, Woodcutter?" he asked.

"Joshua Hart? Is that you? Well, I'll be hanged. What you doing out here?"

"Hunting antelope and Indians with General Custer, what you think?"

"Sit down, Joshua," he said, shaking his hand. "I'll pour you a cup of coffee."

Taking off his hat, Joshua pulled up a stump and waited while Caleb poured the coffee. He was older than Caleb remembered, seasoned, the innocence gone from his face.

"I ain't got long," he said, taking the cup. "We're headed for Fort Wallace soon."

"How did you know I was here, Joshua?"

He sipped at his coffee and wrinkled up his nose.

"Smelt this here coffee clean from Fort Riley," he said. "What you make it from?"

"Prairie dog droppings," Caleb said.

"Mighty poor droppings, ain't they. Anyway, that smithy at

Harker put me onto you. Said to tell you that Sergeant Wins ain't hearing like he ought and that he's humping the rogue's march for plopping on the commander's garden path. Said you'd know what he was talking about, all right."

"Maybe so and maybe not," Caleb said. "Guess you're a mean Sheridan son of a bitch now, Joshua, just like we talked about, strutting around in that uniform and all?"

He set his cup down, leaned forward chin in hand, and studied the fire.

"It ain't like I thought at all, Caleb. Custer is crazy as a treed bobcat, tearing up everything what comes in his way. Hunts all day long, don't he, what with them scouts and them hounds of his."

"Hounds?"

"Shot his horse between the ears whilst chasing a buffalo full speed across the prairie, didn't he, and we had to pick him up in a wagon and carry him back, and there ain't no end to the bugling." Joshua threw his hands up in frustration. "Why, he bugles when we get up in the morning and when we go to bed at night. He bugles to stop and then to go, when we're doing a number one and again for number two, when we eat and when we don't eat, when we stand or sit or fall over dead from bugling. There ain't nothing on God's earth what don't get bugled at before the day's out, and there ain't a Indian or living creature in Kansas what doesn't know we are on our way three days before we get there."

Squinting into the sun, Caleb studied his old friend's face.

"Guess this gimp leg of mine ain't so bad after all?"

"I'd trade my horse for it this very minute. Ole Autie Custer will march twenty mile without so much as a rest, leaving his own men to chance if they drop behind or come up sick. God help the horse with split hoof or what falls out from thirst, 'cause it's his end right there on the spot, and his rider can walk or stay either one. It's crazy as crazy, riding in circles day on end, looking for heaven knows what, just riding in circles like mules at a sorghum mill."

"Would you like some more coffee, Joshua?"

"No, thanks, Caleb. My stomach ain't fit up for prairie dog droppings just yet."

"So where do you go from here?" Caleb asked, raking out his fire with Jim's new poker.

"Most likely in a circle," he said, "though some say there's a big campaign in the works to drive the Indians south to the Territory come winter. Some say the Seventh Cavalry's going to do the driving. Maybe we'll just bugle them to death, Caleb, bugle them 'til they can't stand it no more, 'til they shoot themselves right out of the saddle. Then we can go home, I reckon. It's the only thing makes sense anymore."

"It's a mighty poor business, Joshua."

Putting his hat back on, Joshua gave it some thought before looking over at Caleb. "That's enough about Custer, I'm thinking, 'cause there ain't no end far as I can see. What about you, Caleb?"

"I've been faring," he said, "cutting wood for Fort Harker and the railhead camp."

"Ain't you afraid you'll get scalped out here by yourself?"

"Them Cheyenne ain't interested in no woodcutter, Joshua, what with the Seventh Cavalry for pickins'. Besides, I got my Spencer here and a stob for my door at night."

"Seems mighty thin to me, Caleb. Why don't you go on back to Kentucky? I sure as hell would, 'cept I'd get my head branded or kicked around the compound until I wished I was dead, or hanged off a cottonwood somewhere."

Standing, Caleb slipped his hands into his pockets and looked out into the prairie. "Guess you know better than most what I got back in Kentucky."

"Reckon so. Look it here, Caleb," he said, showing his sleeve. "Got myself a stripe. Course, it don't mean spit, 'cept more work and a extra cussing from time to time."

"Right good job, Joshua. Why don't you stay a while? There's a turkey roost not far from here, and we could go hunting."

"I'd like that fine, Caleb, but I've got to get back. Custer finds out I'm gone, and I won't ever see daylight again."

Walking with him to where his horse was tied, Caleb waited while Joshua looped his reins over the saddle horn and mounted up. Joshua shook Caleb's hand, his grip firm and certain.

"You be careful, Caleb."

"Thanks, Joshua. I'm glad that dream came true. You made it so, and out of no more than grit and hard work. Most men don't."

"Thanks," he said, flashing him a smile. "You think about going on home, Caleb. There's Baud, ain't there, and you could always rebuild that cabin."

"Take care," Caleb said, waving as Joshua rode up the creek bottom.

That night, the moon rose in the warm sky and cast a thousand shadows under its glow. He gathered his bedding from the cellar, placed it by the fire, and lay on his back. He thought of Joshua and of what they had been through. He studied the sky and the boundless stars, the winks and sputters of light so mysterious and unattainable, and he wondered of his own being, of his own existence in such a vast and unknowable place.

From beyond the cellar, Mule One whinnied, as he was wont to do at end of day, and Caleb rolled onto his side to doze against the final flutter of firelight. She came to him then, in veiled and extravagant reverie, as luxurious and lush as her own sweet laugh. She touched him with fingers as cool as polished marble, her fragrance that of spring honeysuckle.

As his sleep deepened, the fire ashened to gray, and the prairie was silent, not the silence of day's end, or of order, or of rest and peace, but the silence of fear and foreboding misfortune. Sitting upright, Caleb peered into the darkness, his heart stilled. From all about they watched with furious black eyes, with war paint glistening, with evil bows drawn in retribution.

Chapter 12

The last thing Caleb remembered was the blinding light that exploded in his head. When he awoke, the smell of burning flesh was sweet and strong, a hand smoldering in the coals of his campfire. A stab of pain jolted him into consciousness, and he realized that his hand was in the fire. Rocking in agony, he held the blistered appendage against his chest and struggled to focus through blood-caked eyes.

In the breaking dawn the warriors rummaged through his things, tucking them away or casting them with disdain about the camp clearing. Here and there a yelp pierced the quiet, like an assenting wolf at the chase, first from the confines of his cellar, then from the garden below, then from beyond where Mule One and Mule Two were hobbled out to graze.

Caleb tried to stand, but a foot shoved him down, its suffocating weight against his throat.

"Stay," the voice said, a voice from somewhere out of Caleb's past.

And so he lay prostrate beneath his enemy's moccasin, the smell of earth and despair, the rippling yelps of his attackers, the squeals of Mule One and Mule Two as they kicked out their lives below.

When all had been pillaged, and there was no more, the warriors gathered about his fire, the morning sun sprinkling warm through the trees. His captor jerked him upright by the hair of the head, and Caleb peered back through bloodied eyes, shriveling with fear at what must lie ahead. The sun broke full and bright then, and he saw him, the bits of red cloth in his braids, his father's axe there in his hand.

"Little River," Caleb said in a whisper.

"Shut up," Little River said, "or you will die before another breath is taken."

From across the campfire, a warrior drew his knife, his muscles quivering with hatred. Little River spoke to him, his tone calm but decided. The warrior argued, his eyes narrowing, spittle spraying from tightened lips. Little River's voice was angry, and their eyes locked in that uncertain moment. Sheathing his knife, the warrior spun about, mounting his paint and riding away.

Through his cracked and swollen lips, Caleb asked, "What is it?"

Little River shoved him aside and spoke. "You are not to ask questions, Woodcutter. I have claimed you as my property. From this point on you will do what I say. It is my claim that keeps you alive. Red Nose has much hatred and wants your hair for his teepee pole. On a another day, I might have given it to him."

Turning to the others, Little River barked out an order, tossing them the axe, and two of the warriors scrambled down the hill to where Mule One and Mule Two lay slaughtered and quiet. They returned within moments, the hobble still secured about the severed shin bones of the mules. From Caleb's pocket they retrieved the key, fastening the hobbles about his wrists, and returned the key and axe to Little River.

"My mules," Caleb said, the smell of their blood still strong on the hobble.

"Old and toothless," Little River said, "and too tough to eat. That horse over there is mine. I stole it myself from Fort Harker when I got out of your guardhouse. Ride it, but do not fall behind,

Woodcutter, because I will kill you when you are of no use to me. This I promise you."

The sun rose high in the spring morning as they rode from the valley that twisted below Fort Harker, Caleb at the rear, the hobbles heavy and unforgiving about his wrists. Ahead, the warriors rode with unerring certainty through the maze of ravines. Behind the column of warriors, Caleb struggled to keep up, convinced of Little River's promise to kill him the first time he fell behind. They exited the valley and rode onto the great breadth of the plains. Caleb glanced over his shoulder for a last glimpse of what he might never see again.

In the distance Fort Harker was little more than a pile of stone tossed up on the horizon, but it was where she was, the last place he'd heard her voice or looked into the green of her eyes. A spiral of smoke rose from the chimney of the blacksmith shop and into the thin blue sky, a sign and a farewell from his friend and comrade.

Caleb lowered his head and drove on into the dust of his enemy. Once, in his cellar on a long winter night, he'd despaired, certain that his life could be no bleaker or more desolate. He'd been wrong.

The drive into the prairie was without pause or rest, and by high noon, Caleb's wrists seeped from the weight and swing of the hobble. The burn on his hand soon crusted black with dust, and his fingers curled into useless and unfeeling claws. Riding bareback took its toll, the endless pummeling from the horse's back, the salt and sweat blistering his thighs and backside.

Once, the warriors stopped for water, drinking in silence from a clear spring hidden beneath a rock overhang, its only signature a throaty gurgle and the faint green of moss among the rocks. When they were finished, they watered their horses and then rode on, giving Caleb no water, leaving him to face the day with cracked and peeling lips.

As evening fell across the prairie, sunset flared into the sky, bolts of oranges and reds, pink, clabbered clouds boiling upward. Red Nose pulled up, lowering his hand to silence the band. Even then Caleb did not see the antelope, still as dawn in the persimmons below. Red Nose brought about his bow in silence, aimed, and fired, the arrow entering and exiting with finality, the antelope toppling, uncertain even in that moment of its imminent death.

Sliding from his mount, Little River unsheathed his knife, tossing it up to Caleb.

"Go dress the kill," he said, "and then bring firewood."

Caleb slid down, bearing on the horse's mane against the weight of the hobble. He was grateful to get off his horse.

"My axe," he said, "for the wood."

Reaching for the axe, Little River examined its keen blade.

"Here," he said, handing it to Caleb. "It would be foolish, Wood-cutter, to think you can escape. I'll send an arrow between your shoulder blades before you reach the next hill.

"I can't work with these on my wrists," he said, holding up his arms.

Little River reached for the key and unlocked the hobbles. "Fasten them to a leg," he said. "That should do."

First, Caleb gutted the antelope, opening the cavity under the razor edge of Little River's knife, the antelope still warm from life, its smell of wild and blood, its grass-matted eyes watching him as he worked. When he finished skinning it out, he cut away the large portions of meat and wrapped them in the hide.

After that, he worked his way into the trees, looking for downed wood, something dry and ready for fire. The hobbles caught in the limbs at every step or gathered up vines, or spun off the swing of his axe, or tore the thin flesh from the top of his foot. Little River watched him from above as the others talked and laughed and made fine jokes among themselves.

As Caleb loaded wood into his arms, he spotted the water, no more than a puddle in a cradle of roots, green and smelling of slime. Taking a chance, he dropped to all fours, drinking with abandon from the foul pool. Little River rose, watched him for a moment, and then turned his back to talk with the others.

After Caleb built the fire, Little River chained him at the edge of camp, locking one end of the hobble around a mesquite limb. He did not speak or acknowledge Caleb even then, no more than the mules who had once borne the same chains Caleb bore now.

As darkness fell, the antelope was cooked on sticks over the fire, charcoal scraped onto the meat for salt. The warriors ate in silence, grease shining on their fingers from the flames of Caleb's fire, but no meat was brought him, his stomach cramping from the tainted water and the lack of food.

The night turned chill, and the fire was fed, its flames licking into the darkness, and the warriors circled the camp, dancing to their chant, an incantation of gods and of things that Caleb could not know. As the night drew down, he trembled, desperate from the cold, from the darkness and distance of this place, from the loneliness and despair of his bondage.

They danced through the night, the beat of their feet like the beat of a hundred hearts, their spirits as one as they circled the fire, and from the shadows Caleb lay shivering and forlorn in an alien land.

When exhausted at last, they slept, scattered about the grass like bedded buffalo, and Little River rose from his place, a dark and invincible shadow, and made his way to where Caleb quivered at the end of his hobble.

"Here," he said, from the darkness, "meat and water for the hunger and a blanket for the cold. Tomorrow you must do better, Woodcutter, or I will kill you for the buzzards. You ride like an old woman."

"Riding ain't the way of a woodcutter," he said.

"You are with the Cheyenne now. We are of the horse, of one and of the same. If you cannot ride, then you cannot be of my property, and I must kill you. It is the way of things."

"Tomorrow I will ride better. This food will make me strong again." When Caleb looked up to thank him, he was gone into the night.

Dawn broke cold and still beyond a drifting fog. Somewhere in its depths, crows bickered over the antelope's entrails. Shivering beneath his blanket, Caleb awoke to the bleakness of his circumstance. He worked his fingers back to life and rubbed at his swollen ankle beneath the hobble. He wondered of the coming day, of its demands, of its dangers and peril. By night the crows may well quarrel over his own discarded bones.

Voices drifted down from the ridge, muffled and unintelligible in the fog, and he held his breath, listening, turning his ear into the morning thickness. But it was useless, the voices failing under the sound of hooves as the horses rode away.

Little River came at last with his mount in tow, but without food or water or morning greeting. Caleb drew himself onto his horse, his legs burning with the familiarity of its back, and soon they rode hard into the depths of the prairie. The old blisters filled once more, broke, and filled again, ruined and bloody wounds from the relentless ride.

Throughout the day they drove on, and when sunset fell at last, Caleb marveled that he still lived. The sky erupted with color as the sun set, and in the valley below, a small buffalo herd grazed with heads lowered, their tails switching in contentment.

The warriors slid from their horses and dropped into the grass, signing with exact hand gestures. Caleb waited, holding his hobbles from clinking. Without game, there would be no supper, certainly not for a captive, of that much he was certain.

It was Red Nose who took the lead once more, working his way to the ridge, his movements rippling the grass no more than the silent and invisible winds. When he took aim, Caleb saw it for the first time, the gleaming blue of a new cavalry carbine. The report startled Caleb's horse, his muscles quivering beneath him, and the buffalo cow dropped to her knees before toppling into the grass.

Little River unlocked Caleb's hobbles and handed him the knife, and then the axe. "Take the hump, tongue, and liver, Woodcutter, then bring wood for the fire." Nodding, Caleb slipped the knife into his belt and stiffened his legs against the weakness in his knees. Little River locked his gaze on Caleb and pointed his chin to the prairie. "You would have to ride a day to be out of my sight," he said.

Rubbing at his ankle, Caleb shrugged. "Then why the hobbles, Little River?"

"A cut muscle would do as well if you wish," he said, turning about.

So huge was the cow that Caleb struggled to turn her head, her tongue, big as his forearm, quivering in his hands as he cut it away. The hump alone was enough for a feast, and he struggled to carry it back to camp. Returning, he opened her belly, steam rising into the evening, and took her great liver, its feral smell of blood and heat.

There was majesty in this animal's death—he could feel it in the powerful, stilled heart, in the unrelenting black eyes and battle-scarred horns. As he lifted its liver into the sunset, blood dripped from his elbows, and he knew there was honor here, something noble, and worthy, and hallowed.

By the time wood was gathered, a moonless night had covered them in darkness. Without a word, Little River hobbled Caleb once more about his ankle and with blessed space between flesh and iron.

The warriors gathered about the fire and waited as Red Nose sliced the liver, passing the raw pieces about, eating in silence, in communion and accord, before roasting the slabs of hump over the coals.

Afterward, Little River brought a piece of the meat to Caleb, and a drink of water from a horn that smelled of earth and sweat, and dropped the blanket at Caleb's feet. "You rode better today, Woodcutter, more like a girl than an old woman."

"Thanks," Caleb said, chewing on the meat.

"Perhaps I'll not kill you right away," Little River said.

"I ain't sure that's good news," Caleb said, wiping at his mouth with his sleeve, "given the condition of my rear end."

"It's necessary to feel your horse," he said, "here, between your legs, to know what he's thinking."

"He's thinking to kill me before you do with that scrawny back of his."

"Tomorrow we will come to our camp," he said, turning about.

A wind rode in from the west, and the warriors' fire crackled with its arrival. In it was the warmth and promise of spring. It was with relief that Caleb stretched out on the ground. Soon the ride would end. But even as he drifted off, a whiskey bottle was produced and passed among the warriors. Tipping it against the yellow firelight, they drank. They drank with an urgency and gravity that caused Caleb's stomach to twist, and he lifted on an elbow to listen.

The warriors' laughter rose, strident and boisterous in the night, and he knew that things could turn dangerous. The Beer Bucket Inn had taught him well the perils of alcohol. Drawing himself down, he waited, praying that they would forget him in their drunkenness. They danced, yelped, laughed, and darted through the fire, the intoxicated beat of their drum like a dying and erratic pulse.

What caused the argument Caleb didn't know, but one warrior pushed the other, and then again, angry and loud. In an instant, a stick of firewood came down with a sickening thud, and one of the warriors dropped, his head feathers fluttering in the evening breeze. But the dancing neither stopped nor slowed as the drums beat on into the night.

Dawn broke and they rode once more, ever deeper into the heart of the prairie. None spoke of the night before or acknowledged the warrior's face, now split and swollen and seeping with blood.

As if from nowhere, the camp appeared, teepees twisting through a ravine below. Children played at the camp's edge, and women worked at buffalo hides or stirred the steaming pots of soup. The warriors sounded their arrival, and all came running, a great fuss being made. The women looked at Caleb from under their hands, and the children grinned with curiosity. Little River spoke, pointing at Caleb, and the others nodded in approval of this fine acquisition.

That night Little River hobbled him under a lean-to made of cottonwood limbs and sage brush where animals were butchered. Charred bits of meat, still smelling of smoke, clung to its limbs, and the ground was clotted black with blood. A young child brought him soup in a bowl, and Caleb ate without inspection, drinking it down as a man starving.

The drums beat from the camp, and the cries of celebration filled the night. Shivering, he curled into the corner of his hut, a man forfeited and lost in the land of his enemy. He could remember only the name "Woodcutter," his real name lost somewhere in the past, and a loneliness emptied him of all that he was or had ever been, bereft now even of tears to console him in his desolation.

That night the winds dropped away, breathless and dark with secrets, and a cloud bank blotted out the moon. A rush of cold wind swept from the night, and dirt swirled into Caleb's hut, stinging his injured ankles and stripping raw the last of his hope. Lightning flashed, and the night was fixed in its brilliance. When thunder rolled through the valley, rain began to fall, wet, cold, and relentless. All night it rained, Caleb trembling with cold and abdication, his hut stinking with the slaughter of the past, and when morning came, he cursed the rise of the sun and of yet another day.

Chapter 13

Late that morning Little River came from the camp. Rested and smelling of bear grease, he stooped under the muddied lean-to.

"There is the horse, a travois, and the axe," he said. "Each morning you are to bring wood for the fires. When you have finished, you will be given food and then hides to clean. When the hunting party goes out, you will ride to prepare our camp. Make yourself useful, Woodcutter. It is the thing that keeps you alive."

"How am I to walk with the hobble padlocked to my leg?"

"The same as your guardhouse prisoners with ball and chain," he said. "It is the one thing of use that I learned from your people."

So each day Caleb rose and waited for Little River, and each day he made his way into the prairie in search of wood. After practice and considerable determination, he learned to mount his horse with the hobble cradled in his arm, but even so, with the travois to be dragged behind, it was little faster than walking. The hobble was an anchor and a burden to both his body and his soul, and he carried it wherever he went, like a babe in the arms. It soon shone from wear and from the oil of his skin.

The sticks of wood, when he could find them, were cut small
to fit the travois and then lashed down with rawhide. Each day
he searched the barren prairie. At times no more than sage or
skunk brush or the dried dung of buffalo could be found. And
each day he returned to camp where the women met him for
their share of fuel, chastising him if the load was sparse, spitting
on him and cursing him for his indolence. If the load was too
disappointing or late in coming, his share of food might be fed
to the camp dogs while he watched on, his stomach grinding
with hunger.

Often upon his return, he worked at the fetid buffalo hides,
the stink of tallow in his clothes and skin, his fingers splitting
from the blood and grease. At night he slept alone, curled onto
the hide tailings that he'd pilfered from the racks, and would
listen to the sounds of the camp, the bark of the dogs, the children playing, the warriors as they told their stories with unerring
monotony. Later, the laughter of the women stirred him as they
made their way to the teepees. When the smell of their fires died
away in the dampness of the night, he would sleep then, as alone
as the bear hibernating in his cave.

But as the days passed, he remembered his name, and Joan
Monnet's, and her smell of honeysuckle in the spring, and the
booming voice of his old friend Jim. He remembered Joshua with
his new stripe and pride, and Baud, with his smell of tobacco,
and he remembered, too, the trickling of dirt on his father's
casket. But even so, these things were distant and no longer of
him. He was still the wretched and stinking woodcutter.

As the weeks passed, the sun edged north, lingering hot and
profane in the cobalt sky. Caleb's arms bulged from the swing
of his axe, and his skin browned under the long summer days.
At times he would find quail, or dove, or even grouse. He would
cork their heads and roast their fat breasts on a stick. There were
berries and plums and wild onion to eat. Once, on a scorching
afternoon, he killed a rabbit with a rock as it panted unaware

in the shade of a log, and he ate it, roasted brown and delicious in his fire.

Fear and resignation gave way to the sweetness of the prairie and his developing strength. The thin soup of his captors lost its authority as his independence mounted with his newfound skills.

Watching his captors, he learned their secrets—how to forage like the coyote, to eat all that could be caught or killed, to use all that was accessible, and so from the birds' nests he pillaged eggs, or took molting chicks too young to fly, or roasted turtles in their shells. From wild mint he brewed tea, sweetening it with choke cherries, thickening it with scrapings from the buffalo hides.

He learned to crack the bones from old and abandoned buffalo carcasses, spooning out the life-giving marrow, or to strip away the lungs for roasting over his fire. Sometimes he covered the hides with earth, baking them in the embers, slipping off the fur as did the squaws, chewing the strips of hide until his jaws ached. Though tough, they gave him strength and, most of all, freedom from the whim of his enemies.

Once, in his enthusiasm for aged and tender meat, he ate the flesh of a deer that had sickened and died, its smell strong in the afternoon heat. Within hours his bowels roiled and by night's end bled in protest to his indiscretion. But without a rifle, or even a bow to kill fresh meat, it was the best he could do, and he determined to do it no matter the cost.

It was on a hot summer morning that Little River kicked the bottom of Caleb's foot, which stuck out of his lean-to.

"Woodcutter," he said, "catch up the horse. There's buffalo in the north. You are to come and bring your axe for cutting wood."

They rode out as the sun rose hot in the morning, and the women gathered, watching in silence from the doors of their teepees. Caleb rode behind the warriors, his hobble hoisted, his axe across his lap. Confident now with his riding, his body attuned to every turn and shift of his horse, he kept a close trail between. Once, Little River looked back, nodding his approval, and he did not look back again.

When the sun struck high overhead, they stopped for a drink, a buffalo wallow of tepid and doubtful water. Unlike before, when the others were finished, Caleb drank too and was given a piece of pemmican before they rode on.

Temperatures swelled in the afternoon, the sun a torrid and seething cauldron. The horses, lathered in sweat, gasped for air in the heat, their heads lowered as they drove ever northward. Caleb's ears seeped with sunburn, and his eyes crusted with dust from the trail.

At last they found water once more, and he drank with his horse from the creek, no more than a bog, alive with mosquito and larvae. He waited in the shade of a hackberry and rubbed at the weariness from the swing of the hobble. From all about him, locusts zinged in the heat, an invisible chorus, a crescendo and anthem from out of the sun. Caleb thought that in another time, peace would abound in this place, its quiet, its reach and exquisite solitude.

Dropping down from his horse, Little River too drank from the stream, pausing to check the horizon, always vigilant and cautious of his surroundings. He mounted and rode to the knoll to guard while the others rested. From under the shade of a tree, Caleb watched him, the red tails in his braid, his squared and powerful shoulders. There was about him the certainty of a man in his place, of freedom and pride in the lift of his chin.

When Little River signaled, the others mounted and drew their bows, their heads lowered as they rode up the knoll. Little River led the way into the cottonwood saplings that overlooked a ravine. Their horses danced with excitement, and Caleb knew that the hunt was on. Leading his horse, he drew up from behind, and below him was an ocean of buffalo. They filled the length of the canyon, and his heart raced at the sight.

Little River drew an arrow from his quiver and motioned for Caleb to move into the saplings. The others leaned forward into the necks of their horses and waited for the signal. Sweat ran into Caleb's eyes, and he rubbed away the sting with his sleeve. A breeze swept in from the south, rippling the saplings overhead. Below, the buffalo quieted, lifting their heads into the wind, and all knew that the time had come.

When Little River dropped his hand, the warriors bolted from out of the trees. Full out they raced down the hill, bows drawn, horses reined with knees and intent. Like wolves they circled the herd, fanning wide to bring them in, yelping and yipping and baying at their prey.

The buffalo churned, their great heads lowered, an eddy of strength and courage and unpredictable rage. Dust boiled from their hooves, and the sun was bloody in the blistering sky. With arrows shanked, mortal in their bellies, they ran on, slobbering and bucking as they fell away from the herd.

Caleb watched from atop the knoll, the smell of dust, blood, and carnage rising from below. Little River mounted an attack from out of the east, driving hard into the heart of the herd, his mark an immense bull with knotted neck and bloodied ruff. Tail straight with fury, the bull circled his cows. Little River came about to separate him from the herd, the bull's nose inches from the ground as he loped with immutable power, his nostrils flared, his head whipping from side to side.

Little River rode in full bore, speeding an arrow into the bull's flank. Spinning about, the bull shook his head, trembling from the assault. Little River circled and nocked an arrow for another shot. With braids flying he drove in once more, leveling his site at the bull, but it was not to be, his horse faltering, its leg dropping into a prairie dog hole and spilling him onto the ground.

The bull whirled about and pawed dirt high over his back. Blood dripped from his flank, and his bellow rumbled above the din of the herd. So involved were the others in the hunt that they did not see Little River's fall, nor could they hear his calls for help.

To ride into the fray had not been Caleb's intent, not for Little River, or for the goodness of man, or for God Himself, as far as that, but that's what he did, his hobble bouncing and clanking as his horse cut down the steep bank.

By the time he reached the bottom, the bull's back was covered with dirt, and his black eyes flamed with a shriveling fury. From the dust, Little River stood, shaken and confused from his spill. Caleb kicked his horse into a gallop and rode into the territory between the bull and Little River, sliding off in a running skid. With hobble dragging, he whirled about to face his foe. A final time the bull sprayed dirt into the air, then lowered his colossal head.

Caleb froze when he charged, his stomach buckling with the folly of his decision and the enormity of the creature now thundering toward him. But he waited, held his ground, his tongue clenched and bleeding between his teeth. When at last he swung his axe, he did so with all the accuracy and strength of practiced years, planting the blade between the bull's horns. The animal swayed like a grand tree, blood coursing from his nose, grunting in disbelief as he dropped in a plume of dust.

When Caleb looked up, the herd was gone, and Little River was at his side. The others, led by Red Nose, circled them on their horses, whooping and rejoicing at the success of their hunt, the enormity of the buffalo bull, and the bravery of the hunters.

"You saved my life," Little River said.

Caleb, dragging his hobble behind, retrieved his axe from the skull of the great bull before catching up his horse.

"It was this danged Cheyenne horse ran away," he said, pulling himself up on its back. "I'll fetch wood now for the night's fire."

As evening fell, the catch was butchered, choice cuts wrapped in hides and secured to travois made from the cottonwood saplings. A fire was built, and the warriors ate under the orange of sunset.

Caleb prepared his bed of cottonwood leaves and rubbed down his horse with a handful of bark. Lying down, he waited for Little River to come, as he always did, to check the hobble in silence.

Overhead, leaves rustled in the wind, and the stars broke into the infinite blackness of the prairie sky. Soon the chant of warriors rose from the camp, a litany familiar now to Caleb's ears. Next to his bed of leaves was his father's axe, the handle stained from the blood of the bull. Often he touched it, its warmth and memories, and thought of things past, of how far he'd come, of things yet to be. Today it had served him well once more.

When Little River came, the night was late, and moonlight danced in the oiled leaves of the cottonwoods. Smoke from the dying campfire drifted in on the scrubbed night air.

"Woodcutter?" he said, lowering onto his knees.

Caleb lifted himself onto an elbow and pulled up his pant leg so that the hobble could be inspected.

"Too tired to run," Caleb said.

"Take this," Little River said, "and eat of it."

"What is it?" Caleb asked, sitting up.

"The liver of the buffalo bull. You have earned the right."

"Oh, I didn't do nothing," Caleb said, "and I ain't much of a liver eater, what without onions to cover up the taste."

"Eat it," Little River said.

"Well," Caleb said, taking the liver, "couldn't be no worse than ripe deer meat, I reckon."

Taking a bite of the liver, he chewed with uncertainty. It tasted of the bull, of its sum and smell, and of the prairie soil from which it came.

"It is in respect for the life of the bull," Little River said.

"He was a piece of thundering lightning. I thought to choke before he was done."

"Why did you save the life of your enemy?" Little River asked, his arms encircling his knees.

"No disrespect, Little River, but I didn't set out to save no one's life. That blame horse just ran off down the hill, and next thing I know I'm face-to-face with that runaway bull. I didn't have no choice but to kill it before it killed me."

"Here is a slice of the hump," he said, "roasted to the white man's taste."

"Thanks," Caleb said.

Little River reached into his pocket and retrieved the hobble key, turning it under the light of the moon, and unlocked the chain before slipping away into the darkness.

For the longest time, Caleb lay awake on his bed of leaves, listening to the coyotes scrabble in the ravine below. Like them, he was free, he supposed, to go now, to roam, or to hunt, or to leave at will, but also like them, he was hostage to his heart, now chained and hobbled by the power of this land.

Chapter 14

No one mentioned the hobbles again, and even though Caleb still searched for wood, it was without restraint or rules. With complete freedom, he came and went as he pleased from the Cheyenne camp. No longer did the squaws switch his legs, or bring their buffalo hides for scraping. No longer did they serve him thin soup or taunt him at his work. No longer did the men turn their backs or fall silent as he passed. He was tolerated in their company, the woodcutter, the white captive who lived in the lean-to, the cripple who killed the bull buffalo with his axe. Even though Caleb knew less fear, he was still a stranger among them, their silence of tolerance but never of acceptance.

It was Little River who changed in those days, coming to his lean-to, squatting at his door to talk of hunting, or to show his new medicine bag, or to share a fresh cut of meat. Caleb looked forward to his visits, his own loneliness appeased if but for a few minutes each time. They never talked of Caleb's past, or of who he might have been, but instead of the day's events, or of summer drought, or of the needs of the band.

When the hunting forays were short, Caleb was left in camp. It was during those times that he most learned the customs, watching the women at work, listening to their talk, taking note of their ways, and soon he knew the words, at least a few, and then more as the days and weeks passed.

The summer heat flared, the sun rising in cloudless skies. Under its glare, the earth gave way, and the grass shriveled to yellow straw. Springs dried, first to wallows, stinking and foul, then to dust-blown holes of sand and bone. Caleb sweltered in his lean-to through the breathless nights, the baked earth still hot from the searing days, and each morning he rose to face yet again the scorching sun.

As the heat mounted, the need for wood dwindled, so while the men hunted for antelope, or scoured the country for horses to steal, Caleb spent his days watching the work of the camp. He made his first bow during this time, shaping it from seasoned bois d'arc, sizing it small, as he'd seen them do, smoothing its belly with the blade of his axe, stringing it with rawhide.

Afterward, he made arrows of cedar, measuring them with the length of his arm. From old buffalo hooves, he boiled up his glue, attaching turkey feathers for guided flight. But it was the points that proved most difficult. Try as he may, they were either too heavy, or too dull, or in the end shattered in his hand. In frustration, he sharpened the shafts into points as the children had to do.

As the days of summer passed, he practiced his aim, shooting at leaves, or at sparrows in trees, or at targets of hide or bone. At first he could hit nothing, chasing his arrows in the heat until his body dripped with sweat and his head whirled with exhaustion. But over time, he learned the bow's feel, its arch and flight, its strength and limited range. The day he killed his first rabbit, he danced in celebration with a hunter's pride and took of its liver so tiny and raw.

No one paid his bow any mind, and he carried it about the camp without fear. It was Little River himself who took him to the canyon of flint, who showed him the pieces free from flaw, who taught him to knap with antler and hide. Soon his quiver bristled with all manner of points, and his game grew larger in both size and number.

It was on such a summer morning that Little River came to his lean-to.

"Woodcutter, get your bow and horse. There's rumor of buffalo in the west. Their numbers and course must be scouted."

As they rode from camp, the sun lifted into the sky, searing its way into the clear morning. Unlike the times before, the pace was unhurried, and they rode side by side as equals do. At noon they ate pemmican under the shade of a sprawling elm, drinking water from a tepid and gypsum-laden stream.

Leaning back, Little River placed his hands behind his head, closing his eyes for a moment. "If there are enough buffalo for a hunting party, we will return and tell the others," he said. "The days are growing shorter. Soon, the people will move south where it is warmer, and the hunting is better during the winter."

Caleb took a drink of water, wiped his chin, and checked the position of the sun. "What will you do with me, Little River?"

"You will go south with the people," he said. "Black Kettle will join our band for the trip. There is plenty of wood on the Washita. It is a peaceful place and a quiet season. At night the moon fills the valley with silver. The horses grow weak without fodder in the winter, and the Cheyenne must wait for spring. It is enough to make it through the winter."

Taking another drink from the steam, Caleb walked to the edge of the shade and looked out onto the prairie. Heat quivered from the sand, and the zing of locusts rose and fell about them. "Why does Black Kettle come to us, I wonder?"

"He is a Cheyenne chief, but his warriors are few. Joining together makes us safer in the journey south. Many of his band were killed at Sandcreek by Chivington. They say the valley still stinks of death, and that Black Kettle's white flag still flies red with their blood."

"I wonder if it will ever end, all of this?"

Untying his reins, Little River mounted his horse. "What is your name again, Woodcutter?"

"Caleb."

"It will never end, Caleb," he said.

That evening they camped in the sands of a dry streambed, building a small fire of flood drift and roots, eating the last of the pemmican. The night was warm, and they slept stripped to catch the rare breeze. Stars burst into the heavens above them, touchable shimmers of light, and an enormous moon bobbed into the night. Neither spoke in its majesty—the sound of words would corrupt its splendor, take of its moment and diminish it with the irrelevance of man.

The next morning they rose before dawn, riding hard into the prairie. When sunrise came, it was a scorching inferno in the morning stillness. Little River spotted the tracks, a herd moving up the valley floor. Soon the ground was spotted with dung and craters of fresh-pawed earth. The smell of the herd was strong on the wind, even to Caleb's untrained nose.

At day's end they spotted them feeding in the valley below. Their numbers stretched into the distance as they grazed and drifted against the setting sun. Dropping from his horse, Caleb lay on his stomach, watching the sight below.

Little River moved to the ridge to estimate their numbers. "Hundreds, even more," he said.

"We should take them," Caleb said.

"A Cheyenne does not hunt alone, not for amusement or glory, but for food for the people. We will go back and tell the others and plan the hunt." Seeing the disappointment on Caleb's face, he added, "If one should fall behind, we'll have hump for our dinner. This is acceptable."

Evening fell, and as the herd moved up the valley to bed, an old bull, sore-footed and slow with years, dropped behind. Disgruntled, he stopped and pawed great clouds of dust into the air and bellowed his contempt for all to hear. But there is no waiting on the prairie, not for man or beast, and soon the others rounded the corner out of sight.

"Ride down slow to keep his attention," Little River said. "I'll circle about to cut him back. When I give the signal, you ride in hard and place the arrow, here," he said, pointing to a spot just behind the front leg.

"You want me to do this?"

"If it does not bring him down, circle about and come in again. As big as he is, it may take three arrows before he's finished."

As Caleb nocked his arrow, Little River hesitated. "Take care of the prairie dog holes," he said, kicking his horse into a trot.

Caleb worked his way down the hill, and the bull lifted his head. With eyesight fading, he sniffed the wind, snorting at the smell of his enemy, pawing at the dirt, covering his back in a shower of dust, and Caleb rode on, his heart pounding with excitement and fear.

Little River closed off the gap, reining up his horse to wait, and even as he did, the bull whirled in a fury, charging with undiminished courage into Caleb's uplifted bow. The first arrow hit its mark, its shaft buried and certain. Spinning about, the bull stopped, his black tongue lolling, his knees buckling, his eyes clouding in defeat. The second arrow struck but inches from the other, and the bull sagged onto the prairie floor, his battles over at last.

Little River rode up and dismounted, unsheathed his knife, and opened a jugular to bleed off the meat. Dropping down, Caleb steadied himself against his horse, his knees weak with spent excitement. "He's beautiful," he said.

"A warrior to the end," Little River said. "Tonight the herd will grieve his absence. Tomorrow, he will be forgotten forever."

In the waning light, Little River took the liver, the nose, and the tongue. He cut away the choice meat of the hump and detached the bull's enormous scrotum.

"Why must you do that?" Caleb asked.

"The sack is fitted as you can see and is the toughest hide of all. Our friend here gives it up without protest. It has served him well but is of no further use to him now."

That night, they camped on the open plain without so much as sagebrush for protection. Caleb scoured the countryside for chips, and they built a fire, its flame blue and pure and hot.

First they ate of the liver and then of the nose and tongue. A great slab of hump was roasted over the fire, and when they were done, their bellies swelled with meat.

Caleb said, "It was a shame in a way. He was such a beautiful and brave old man."

"There was no shame in his death," Little River said, "and today you hunted as a Cheyenne, with a bow and a courage of your own making."

"Well," Caleb said, dropping a chip onto the fire, "maybe so. Least I ain't just a woodcutter no more, or carrying slop in the Beer Bucket Inn."

Rising, Little River walked off into the darkness. Minutes passed before he returned, and Caleb wondered of his absence. It was his way, this sudden disappearance, the mystery and wonder of his manner.

By the time Little River returned, the moon had edged into the sky, and the land glowed like an ivory and boundless sea. Standing in the shadows of the fire, Little River was stripped of all but breechcloth and moccasins.

"I come to tell you of the great secret of the Cheyenne. I come to tell you of things that no other white man knows." Holding his arms into the moonlight, he said, "I come to tell you why, with all your bravery, you can never be as the Cheyenne warrior."

Caleb rubbed the smoke from his eyes, and his heart beat with disappointment. "What is it?" he asked.

Lifting his breechcloth, Little River grinned. "These," he said, pointing to the bull's sack, big as a church bell clapper, tied between his legs.

"Well, I'll be danged," Caleb said, laughing. "I reckon some things just ain't meant to be."

That night Caleb slept with a full stomach and a contentment that he had not known for many months. The saving of Little River's life had given him clemency, but today, Little River's joke had given him acceptance.

Chapter 15

The summer passed, days of heat and afternoon rest, of quiet and peaceful hours, days also of exhausting and rousing hunts. Caleb's skill with the bow improved under Little River's instruction, and soon he was as good as most of the other men. Though lacking in tracking ability, and the practiced stealth of the others, when it came to the strategy of the hunt, or to the hard drive-in, or even to the kill from the horse, he held his own.

Though accepted as a hunter of worth, Caleb was never a part of the clan, of this he was certain. Nights were the worst, alone in his lean-to with naught for company but memories and doubts. Although the squaws in camp deferred to his hunting ability, he was a captive as far as they were concerned, a stranger in their land, and they ignored him with the full conviction of that belief. The young girls just giggled when he passed, or lowered their heads, or watched him with rebuke in their eyes.

He stepped from his lean-to on a crisp morning and stretched the ache out of his muscles. His breath was a wisp in the cool morning air, and blue jays scolded him from the heights of the cottonwood. The grass shimmered in the sunrise, the morning dew laden with the smell of earth. Fall was in the air, the abdication of summer's grip, as liberating as the opened lock of his hobble, and Caleb breathed it in.

So accustomed was he to the routine of his day that at first he didn't see the package, the small stack of clothes there by his door. Unfolding them, he held them up in the morning sun, as fine a set of buckskins as he'd ever seen, and a pair of beaded deer hide moccasins.

He looked down at his pants, realizing his own condition, his clothes no more than rags, his shoes worn and frayed from months of wear. Taking off his old clothes, he shivered in the morning cool as he slipped on the buckskins, and the moccasins with their enduring softness. It was, he knew, Little River's doing, a thanks for saving his life. But Caleb was never to know for certain, not from Little River, nor from the others, not even from those who pointed, or smiled, or shook their heads in approval as he passed.

With the mornings cooling, the call for wood increased. Even with his new buckskins and hunting privileges, he was still the woodcutter, and it was his job to bring back the wood. So each day, he rode into the autumn morning with axe in hand and travois in tow, and each day, he returned with what the day had brought.

He returned from a trip on such an evening, the sun easing low. The camp dogs barked, and the children were astir with excitement. As he rode in, he saw them, warriors gathered at Red Nose's teepee, circled about his fire. Next to Red Nose a warrior sat with arms crossed, his face hardened from the years and hardships of the prairie. A pipe was passed among them, and they smoked with serious intent. Little River rose from behind, making his way to where Caleb stood.

"It is Black Kettle who has come," he said. "Leave your wood here and then go to your lean-to. Someone will bring you food tonight."

Caleb unloaded the wood and made his way to the lean-to.

It was not the time for questions. Soon a great fire was built, the smell of smoke filling the camp, and flames lifted into the blackness.

He pulled a blanket about his shoulders and drew into the darkness of his lean-to. As he awaited the night, his stomach tightened with uncertainty, and when the camp grew quiet, he could hear the warriors, Black Kettle speaking, his voice dark and deliberate.

"Our camp flew their flag," he said, "and a white flag at its side, but still they came. A hundred lodges were burned. Our women and children dug into the ground to hide from the bullets, but they killed them there, each in turn, like prairie dogs in their holes, until there was no sound or life left in all of the valley."

"They will know our wrath," Red Nose said.

"It is like fighting the wind," Black Kettle said, "invisible and boundless at every turn. It is time to go south to the Washita. Perhaps Black Kettle's band will not return in the spring. They say there is safety from the soldiers at Fort Cobb."

Even as the drums began, Caleb could hear the anger in Red Nose's voice. Throughout the night the drums beat as Caleb lay alone in his hut. Dread was in their cadence, an intercourse of fear and rage, a predilection and omen of things to come, of things too awful for the mere words of man, and in the late hours, a fog crept over the land, silencing all voices but the drum's, quenching all desire but the drum's, conquering all valor but the drum's, and when Caleb slept at last, it was but for a moment and void of both rest and solace.

Sunrise came as a bloody and furious eye. Caleb lifted himself on an elbow. The drums were silent at last, and his breath rose in the cold dawn. As Caleb was dressing, Little River stooped into the lean-to, his face drawn and weary from the night's ritual.

"We start our journey south to the Washita winter grounds today," he said. "Stay at the back and do not mix with the others. Do you understand?"

Slipping on his moccasins, Caleb stood. "I understand."

"Tonight when we camp, gather wood for the tribal fire. The women will take care of their own lodges on the journey south."

"All right," he said.

"And keep to yourself. Many of Black Kettle's band died at Sand Creek, murdered by Chivington. Be careful not to anger them more by your presence."

Putting on his buckskin coat, Caleb gathered up the few belongings he had accrued during his stay in the lean-to.

"You could let me go, Little River. I am but a simple woodcutter and have not done you or your people harm."

Little River studied the ground, his shoulders slumped. "Chivington's men cut off the people's fingers and ears for souvenirs, and took White Antelope's scrotum for a tobacco pouch. White Antelope was a great warrior and should not have borne such dishonor." As Little River rose to leave, he hesitated for a moment, bending with hands on his knees. "You saved my life from the buffalo bull, and no one can take away the honor of your bravery for that."

"Was just looking for a way to high-tail it out of there," Caleb said, "and got caught between you and that blamed bull."

"But you are the enemy of my people, Woodcutter."

"I've done them no harm."

"The harm you did was in the coming to our land. You killed us then, and you kill us now."

"All I wanted was to cut wood and to make my way," Caleb said.

"Last night I listened to the drums and to the prayers of the Cheyenne. There is courage in their hearts, but their hope is gone. You should have let me die with honor under the horns of the buffalo. Now I must die from the spit of a white man's rifle."

Before Caleb could protest, Little River was gone.

Without direction or orders, the camp was disassembled. Within the hour they were packed and on their way south out of the valley, a silent and efficient caravan.

Caleb took up the drag, distancing himself from the others, his axe secured by a rawhide strap, his bow and quiver slung over his shoulder. The women rode in front of him, their travois loaded with skins and lodge poles. Children walked at their mothers' sides, or led ponies or strings of bouncing dogs. Strapped to the backs of the colts were children too young to walk, tied there to fend against the dust, the weariness, and the ever-maddening gnats.

At the lead was Black Kettle, his hair braided, adorned with a single feather. His warriors rode behind, their paint horses dancing with energy and spirit, as high above, geese winged southward with honks small and distant in the infinite blue of the sky. The sun rose, burned keen, hot, and unchecked in the thin fall air.

Like flowing water the band wound through the ravines and the valleys, tracking ever southward in a slow but abiding gait. They were seldom visible on the open plain for more than a few hundred yards, moving with the swell and surge of the prairie, scouting ahead, checking ridges, outcrops, and tree stands, signaling assurances or cautions with silent gestures of the hands. Like the buffalo they hunted, they migrated across the land in a timeless course of custom and vigilance.

That night, they made camp in a rounded valley, a dry streambed running its length, but the wind was slight and the sands warm, a welcome relief from the rudeness of the day's walk. Caleb cut wood from a hackberry stand, arranging it in a circle for the common fire as Little River had ordered. Afterward, he moved into the shadows of the trees and waited for night to fall. At dusk, Little River brought him dried meat and a horn of water.

"We will move again at daybreak," he said.

Tearing off a piece of the meat with his teeth, Caleb chewed, leaning back against the gentle sweep of a hackberry tree. "How long is the journey?" he asked.

"Two weeks, maybe more, to the warm valleys of the Washita.

The buffalo are ahead of us by many days. They should be fat and waiting for our arrival. It is a sweet valley," he said, "soft and warm like the arms of a woman, and much wood grows on the banks of the Washita. To the north, the Antelope Hills sweep to the sky and bear against the coldest of winds. They are rich with winter grass and teem with antelope. Like giant jackrabbits they bound from the brush. It takes great skill to kill one with bow and arrow. As a child I hunted them through the snow until my toes were blue with cold, and my pony refused to climb another hill."

"It's a good valley, then?" Caleb said, taking a drink of the water.

"Yes," he said, "a good valley. It is the place that Cheyenne remember in their hearts, even as they grow old and faded with years." He looked out onto the camp and crossed his arms. "I am glad to be going now to the Washita."

"It's the feeling of home to you, I'm thinking," Caleb said.

"You sleep here in the trees tonight. I will come for you in the morning. It is best that you stay to yourself, Woodcutter."

That night, Caleb curled against the hackberry, the sand warm and soft beneath him. Unlike the night before, the drums did not beat, and the warriors did not dance. The fire died away, and the camp fell silent with weariness. Overhead, the stars sprayed into the blackness of the universe, and Caleb pulled his blanket over him against the cooling night air. Soon he gave way to his exhaustion, to the uncertainty and restlessness of the last few days, and he slept a deep and abiding sleep.

When he awoke, the moon hung in the sky, hallowed and unattainable with its light casting into the darkness of the tree stand. In the lateness of the hour was the smell of damp and decay and morning dew. Certain that something had awakened him, something deliberate and profane, he turned on his side to listen, the smell of mold and leaves and earth in his nostrils, and the voices rode down from the ridge, clear and certain English in the night.

"This is Lieutenant Gillian," a man said. "I've brought him as you asked, but he comes at great risk. The supply wagons will be leaving for Fort Larned in the morning, moving due south of Harker the first day out."

"What do they carry?"

Sitting up, Caleb leaned against the tree, his heart pounding. It was Sergeant Wins, of that he was certain.

"Ordnance," Wins said, "clothing, and three wagons of cornmeal."

And then the voices moved away, working down the ridge, growing smaller and smaller until there was but silence and darkness. Even now, Caleb wondered if he'd dreamed it, the result of fatigue and isolation and unending worry, but there was no denying the hatefulness and greed in the voice. It was Wins all right, out to get what he could, him and his Lieutenant Gillian, and at any cost to their fellow soldiers.

He thought of Joan Monnet, her green eyes, her smell of honeysuckle, her forthcoming nuptials to Lieutenant Gillian, and his stomach knotted with sickness. Turning back to his bed, he covered himself to await the arrival of dawn.

They left at sunrise, as Little River said they would, and moved south once more into the heart of the prairie. The day grew hot, and the breeze subsided as the band rode into dry land flats. Exposed now for miles in all directions, they were vulnerable to detection, so the scouts rode out until they were but specks, sweeping the countryside for tracks and signs of danger, staying far ahead to provide advanced warning if necessary. Caleb made his way from behind, weary and alone in the dust.

Camp was made in the lee of a rift that cut through the valley like a jagged scar. A search of the area turned up no wood for fuel. Gathering up what chips he could find, Caleb built a small fire near the rift wall and secured himself a place to sleep in the rocks. It was out of the wind and at the edge of camp, two requirements for a better night's sleep.

The choice had been a good one, because by the time the

sun edged down, a cold wind was blowing in from the north. Drawing into his shelter, Caleb pulled his blanket about him and trembled against the plummeting temperatures. The smell of winter and bitterness was in the air. How long ago, he wondered, how many months now since he had been plucked from his world and delivered into this place?

Caleb waited for Little River to bring his food, but he did not come. The wind, stinging and furious with sand, drove down the rift and into Caleb's shelter. When the drums started, Caleb buried his face in his hands and fought back the sorrow that lay black within him. There in his lair, he abandoned hope and surrendered to his despair.

"Woodcutter?" Little River said from above.

"What is it?" Caleb asked, peering from under his blanket.

"Come with me."

Climbing from his shelter, Caleb shivered against the wind. Little River's face was slashed with streaks of red grease, and his dark eyes snapped with resolve.

"Where are we going, Little River?"

"It is not for you to ask, Woodcutter, but to do what you are told. Get your horse and come to me."

In the darkness Caleb bridled his horse, leading him to Little River's place. Beyond, he could see the others, Black Kettle, Red Nose, the warriors from both bands. They were gathered about the fire, their faces painted with the colors of war, their horses bridled and dancing in anticipation.

Little River saw him and brought in tow a string of horses, each tied to the next with a rawhide rope. His bow was strung and slung over his shoulder, his quiver ripe with arrows, and there was a pistol stuck in his belt.

"You are to follow us with these horses," he said.

"I can't do this to my own people, Little River."

Little River retrieved the hobbles, locking them once more about Caleb's leg.

"Do not fall behind, Woodcutter," he said, mounting his horse.

They rode hard into the prairie, the beat of hooves, the blow and snort of horses in the icy wind. Caleb's arms ached from the drag of the lead, and his ankle throbbed from the onerous weight of the hobbles. But to fall behind could mean his life, of this he had little doubt. Little River was unpredictable at best, and when among the other warriors, he was perhaps dangerous. In any case, it was not Caleb's intent to test him now.

When at last they reined up, Caleb dropped his arms, his fingers long since dead from lack of blood, his backside afire with the scrub of his horse. Little River took up the reins, leading him and the string into a stand of elm high on a ridge. Sitting him on the ground, he snapped the hobble onto the leg of the first horse and handed Caleb the lead rope. After that, he removed the single action Colt from under his belt and dropped it in Caleb's lap.

"You are to guard the horses until we return," he said.

"You can't leave me hobbled to this string of broomtails, Little River?"

Even as he said it, the lead horse reared, scooting backward, stiff-legged and white-eyed into the horses behind, dragging Caleb into the thick of the trees.

"Whoa! Whoa!" he called out, pulling hard on the rope.

"We will be back by dawn, Woodcutter."

"By then I'll be dragged raw, or kilt," he said, anger in his voice.

"Then take good care of the horses," Little River said, mounting up.

With the lead rope in one hand and the Colt in the other, Caleb leveled the barrel at Little River.

"I could shoot you," he said.

"Yes," Little River said, "but Red Nose has the hobble key and a great desire for your scalp."

"It's a point," Caleb said, lowering the pistol. "Guess I'll just take care of these here horses until dawn, or until there ain't nothing left to drag around, either one."

And then there was only the wind and the ivory trek of the moon as it arched through the sky.

Caleb waited through the endless night, and with every stamp of a horse's hoof, or snort, or whinny, his heart leaped at the prospect of a frenzied ride through the night while hobbled to a herd of Cheyenne mustangs.

Morning came with frost shimmering in the grass and in the high branches of the trees. Hungry, the horses reached for dried leaves, or shook their heads, or nipped at each other's rumps in a perpetual round of tag. Time and again the hobble bit into Caleb's ankle until the wound was raw and his moccasin blood caked.

Little River rode up the ridge, and Caleb cried out, standing so that he might be seen. Dismounting, Little River took Caleb's revolver and unlocked his hobble. Little River's lip was swollen, and a tooth was broken, indelible evidence of the fierce battle he'd fought.

"We go now to the valley," he said.

As they rode from the ridge and into the hollow, Caleb's heart broke at what he saw—a half dozen freight wagons strewn about, wheels turning and ticking in the wind, broken barrels of cornmeal swirling in the icy wind, gathering against the soldiers' bodies. There was about the valley the smell of butchery and death.

"What has been done here?" Caleb said, his voice breaking.

"Tie the crates of rifles onto the horses," Little River said, "and the ammunition from that wagon there. When you have finished, wait by the horses until I am ready."

As Caleb carried the crates, a horse kicked out its life in the grass at the bottom of the hill, its leg broken, its cries rising into the valley. All around, the soldiers lay with fixed and dead eyes, frost gathering on the lapels of their coats and on their bloodied scalps. There they lay as if in jest, as if to jump out with a round of laughter at the fine joke they had played. But they did not jump out, or laugh, or move ever again from that final place. And so Caleb worked with eyes cast down, to look away from those quiet faces.

From across the way, Red Nose and the others broke up pieces of a wagon bed to build a hot fire. They gathered about and talked of their exploits, of the coup they had earned with their daring courage, and when all was finished, they ate pemmican and drank whiskey from a bottle found beneath a wagon seat.

When Caleb finished with the crates, Little River came from the fire to where the horses were tied. The wounds on his face had worsened with the hours, his mouth now swollen and inflamed.

"We go back to the camp," he said. "With these rifles the Cheyenne will have hope once more."

"There's a horse down there in the grass," Caleb said. "Its leg is broken, and it's suffering something terrible."

"It will die with the passing of the day," he said.

"Let me kill it, Little River. It's what ought to be done."

Reaching for his pistol, Little River took out all the bullets but one.

"Maybe you think to kill me now," he said, handing him the pistol.

"Yes," Caleb said, turning to what he must do. "It crosses my mind."

The horse lifted its head from the grass, its blazed face and eyes of glass. Caleb clicked up a round and cocked the hammer. Even as he fired, the horse relaxing in death, Caleb realized the terrible truth before him.

A few feet away, Jim Ferric lay dead, his red beard white with morning frost. An arrow grew from his throat, another from the calf of his leg, and his great chest lay opened and shamed under the prairie sun. Diligent black ants worked at his scalp wound, frenzied by their unaccountable luck. His powerful arms lay at his side, his hands opened and soiled from the black of his forge. When from up on the hill Little River called, Caleb touched his old friend's face.

He walked from that place with clenched fists and fought back his tears. This he swore to Jim and to all who had died that day: he would escape from this enemy and pay his dues. This he swore and damn the cost.

Chapter 16

For the next several days, the band drove south. Armed now with rifles, there was a renewed defiance and urgency among them. The drums raged at night, and the warriors danced, cast under their throb and spell. At the edges of the camp's light, the women moved to the beat, with arms linked, with eyes down, with bodies undulating to the pulse of the drum. But for Caleb, he was never more alone than in those moments, his own isolation heightened in the unity of their dance.

As the days passed, Little River grew more distant. The pressure for him to remove from Caleb increased with the anger and strength of the band. Even though Caleb pleaded with him to remove the hobbles, he refused, folding his arms, looking away as if not to hear. Soon he quit coming to Caleb altogether, leaving an old woman, who smelled of hides and rotting teeth, to deliver what food she may.

The band drove south as if obsessed, sometimes riding into the night under the full of the moon. Even so, there was little complaint from anyone, including the women who walked long hours alongside their travois, or the children who slept as they rode, tied to their ponies so as not to be lost in the darkness.

Without time to hunt, the food soon diminished, with little left to eat but cornmeal stolen from the supply train or an occasional rabbit or bird caught nesting in the brush. Caleb's meals were often no more than what pickings remained or were neglected altogether, and the arduousness of the trail soon took its toll. The new buckskins sagged on his thinning body, and his eyes sank dark and ponderous in their sockets.

On this evening, Caleb lay on the open prairie, his blanket about him against the chill. The old lady came and set down a bowl of cornmeal gruel, cold and tasteless and tainted with fly. Caleb ate it with his hand, sucking at his fingers for the last morsels of corn. The old lady watched on, the flare of sunset in the blackness of her eyes.

"I'm starving," he said in broken Cheyenne, pushing the empty bowl back to her with defiance. "I want more."

Grinning, she showed him the few remaining stumps in her mouth, worn low in her gums, sunken away in the absence of teeth.

"Here," she said, slipping a sagging breast from under her shawl, "it keeps our babies from crying in the night."

She laughed, scornful of his weakness, and turned back to the camp.

For the next several days the pace was relentless, as if now some purpose befell them or some deadline must be met. Camps were pitched late and without the comfort of fire in the cold fall. Too exhausted to search for protection from the winds, Caleb slept wherever they stopped, pulling his blanket about him to shiver through the night.

Sometimes he thought about what the old woman might bring. Sometimes he thought of Jim Ferric, butchered and dead, of his corpse so hopeless and still, of the swarming flies and open wounds. Sometimes he thought of the hobble cutting now to the white of his bone, but most times he thought of nothing at all, his mind numbed from the cold, the hunger, and the relentless trek south.

It was a windy and chill dawn that broke. Clouds, pink with sun, raced headlong across the sky. Standing over Caleb, Little River waited for him to stir.

"Woodcutter," he said, "gather fuel for a fire."

Climbing from under his blanket, Caleb shivered in the morning cold.

"We're going to have a fire?"

"There's a few buffalo stragglers spotted to the west," he said. "Red Nose will stay behind and is in charge of the camp. Gather enough wood to smoke the meat and for another night's stay."

"Reckon you couldn't take this hobble off?" he asked, showing his swollen ankle to Little River.

"We'll soon have meat," he said. "With these rifles the hunting will be easy."

"Could I ask what our hurry is, Little River? The Washita has been there a long time, ain't it?"

Little River mounted his horse and looked off to the south.

"The Cheyenne must know that they are still warriors. It is something you could not understand." Reining up his horse, he said, "When you have finished with the wood, make yourself small, Woodcutter. Red Nose's blood runs hot, as you know."

Caleb searched for wood throughout the morning. In a draw not far from camp, he found a dead elm, its wood light with decay, and down the hill, a hackberry of considerable size. The axe was heavy, his arms aching with weakness, but by noon he'd finished with the task.

Red Nose looked up at him with disdain and pointed to where the fire was to be built. And when the fire was roaring, the women gathered around, holding their hands to its warmth, and soon laughter filled the camp. Red Nose stood among them, folded his arms over his chest, a rooster among the hens.

Caleb kept to the edge of camp, as Little River said, and busied himself sharpening his axe on a chert fragment he'd found while gathering wood.

Walking about the fire, Red Nose watched him as he worked, turning to the women, who now sat about making repairs on their moccasins and clothing.

"We attacked them from above on the ridge," he said, "riding into their midst, and even then they did not know us." He looked over his shoulder and checked to see if Caleb listened. "The white soldier is like a jackrabbit who freezes in the face of his enemy." Squatting, he poked the fire with a stick and then blew the flame from its end. "He dies even before he fights."

One of the squaws stirred at a pot, the smoke from the fire finding her eyes. Rubbing them with the backs of her hands, she looked at the other women.

"Red Nose now has more coup than any warrior," she said. "He would make a brave leader."

"I killed three of the soldiers with my knife," he said, "one here in the heart, another here in the kidney, and the big one with the red beard here. Like a great stupid bear, he stood as I cut his throat."

Gathering up his hobble, Caleb turned his back against the words, his heart pounding at the lie.

"Red Nose is a fearless warrior," the squaw said, drawing her blanket about her. "Someday he will be chief, of that I have no doubt."

"He begged me to let him live," Red Nose said. "It's the white man's way to beg for his life in the face of his enemy."

"It's a lie," Caleb said, his own voice a stranger in his ears.

Red Nose stood, his rifle cradled across his arms. "Did you say something, Woodcutter?"

"I said it's a lie. The big one was killed with arrows, in his throat and another in his thigh. I saw it myself. I knew this soldier, and he would never beg for his life, and he would never lie about taking someone else's life."

Even as he said it, Caleb knew that he was dead, that his miserable life was at last at an end. There was relief in that knowledge, in the knowing of the moment of his own death.

Crossing the distance in an instant, Red Nose brought the butt of his rifle into Caleb's uplifted face, a stunning and pitiless blow. Caleb dropped like a felled tree, unhindered, onto the prairie floor.

The sky was the color of blood, red-clabbered clouds and flashes of light, and his stomach swelled with nausea. All he could see was the women's skirts as he hung upside down from Red Nose's lodge pole. Gasping for air, he tried to speak, but his lungs collapsed in panic, dry bags of fear, and his eyes bulged in their sockets. Blood oozed from his nose and dripped into the sand. Saliva drooled from his lips, gathering cool in the cups of his ears. Above him, smoke drifted and stirred in the sky, its succor lost in the knowledge of his demise.

"No man calls me a liar and lives," Red Nose said from somewhere above him.

Caleb coughed and spat blood from his throat, filling his ragged lungs with air. "Jim Ferric died a man to the end," he said.

At first he was not aware of the pain, so keen and exquisite was the blade that slid down his belly. But when it came, it was a fire, an unbearable inferno and anguish. Bile rushed his throat, and his bowels loosened under the collapse of his will. A scream of agony fell across the prairie, and all who heard could not but know the extent of its terror.

"Take him down," someone said.

Caleb searched for the voice, for the savior to release him from this torment, and he saw Little River's moccasins, the beading long since faded and worn from the trail.

"He's called me a liar and must die," Red Nose said.

"The woodcutter is my property."

"Then I shall trade for him."

"The woodcutter is not for trade. Take him down."

When the hobble was released, Caleb dropped in a heap, gathering himself up on shaking legs. Blood wept from the split in his stomach, and his eyes were blackened slits in his swollen face. Black Kettle watched on from across the way, his horse dancing with excitement.

"Did you call him a liar, Woodcutter?" Little River asked.

"He said that he killed the big soldier with his knife, that the big soldier begged for his life. He's a liar. The soldier was killed with arrows and was not Red Nose's coup. I saw them myself."

"The woodcutter has hunted with us," Little River said, tossing his knife at Caleb's feet, "has saved my life from the buffalo bull. I give him the right to defend his honor."

Even as Caleb bent for the knife, Red Nose whirled about, his own knife, still stained with Caleb's blood, held high at his side.

"It is good that I do not have to trade a Cheyenne horse for this worthless woodcutter," he said.

Caleb took his stance, mimicking his enemy, who now circled with knees bent and eyes fixed. Perhaps it was better to die fighting than to die hoisted on Red Nose's lodge pole, but at that moment, it seemed a meager choice. The fighting skills of Red Nose were renowned among the tribe, and Caleb knew that his chances were slim. It was in the power of his own arms, the swing of his axe, that Caleb was master, but he was weak from the lack of food and the burden of the trail.

The jump was swift and high, like a deer exploding from the bush, and Red Nose's knife slit Caleb's thigh, a gaping and white wound, but his rebound was off-center, leaving him vulnerable for that single moment. Caleb dropped his knife and pulled Red Nose in, his arm about his throat, his other hand warding off the thrust of Red Nose's blade. Entangled, they trembled in combat, one against the other, Red Nose pulling with all his power against Caleb's strangling hold. But even as Caleb's strength waned, and his mouth flushed hot with exhaustion, he did not let go or acknowledge defeat, because to do so was to die with certainty under Red Nose's knife.

How long they struggled Caleb did not know—hours and eons and mind-numbing eternities. But when in that moment his arms turned to stone, exhausted and bloodless stumps, when in that moment he no longer controlled their grasp, or knew them as his own, when in that moment the voices of his past whispered and wept in his ear, the first grunt of abdication issued from Red Nose's drooling lips, a gasp and resignation to his own impending demise. Caleb brought up the last of his will from deep within, and Red Nose's head fell forward, his muscles jerking in the final throes of death.

Afterward, Little River helped Caleb to the edge of camp and covered him with his blanket, and later, in the darkness, the old woman came, but this time with buffalo hump from the day's kill and a tender cut of the tongue.

"This is what we give warriors," she said, "who have proven their courage in the field of battle. This meat is for such a man."

From under his blanket, Caleb took the meat, chewing with swollen and fevered mouth. When he looked up to thank her for the meat, for the words, for the single act of kindness, she was gone.

That night as he struggled to sleep, his wounds throbbed, and the drums beat their farewell to the fallen Red Nose and to the courage that he had known.

When sunrise broke, the camp stirred with excitement. Caleb climbed from under his blanket and stood for the longest time, uncertain whether he dare try to move. The wound across his stomach was shallow but painful, and each movement of his body fired down its length like a streak of lightning. The cut on his thigh was deeper, having bled a large stain into his buckskins during the night, but at least the pain, too, was severed in the depth of the wound.

He paced back and forth to work the stiffness from his body and watched as the warriors strung their bows, or cleaned their rifles, or painted their horses with colors of war. The women, too, were busied in all manner of fussing, astir with the excitement of the day. Even the children, playful in the most difficult of situations, circled and jumped and shot blunt arrows at each other's feet.

When the old lady came, she brought a blood sausage cooked in the rennet of a buffalo calf and a bowl of boiled and salted cornmeal. The food was delicious, and life-giving, and Caleb ate with abandon.

"What are the men preparing for?" he asked, finishing the last of cornmeal.

At first the old lady said nothing, looking to the south, and then she bent low on her haunches, her breath smelling of sour, her hair falling dirty and heavy about her shriveled face.

"Soon the warriors will ride to the Santa Fe Trail," she said, pulling her skirt about her knees. "They will take a wagon train that has come from over there."

"How do you know this?"

She pushed the hair back from her face and looked up against the sun, squinting her eyes. "They've been blowing their bugle for days, Woodcutter, like a rutting bull bellowing for a cow. How could one not know of their presence?"

"I haven't heard anything."

Shrugging, she said, "A man must listen to hear."

By noon the warriors were readied, their horses with their streaks of color prancing in anticipation of things to come. Mounting up, Little River rode to where Caleb waited.

"I saw wood while hunting," he said, "a few miles west, enough for the night's fire. Make certain it is ready for our return."

"You go to make war on my people again, Little River."

"There is a horse tied at my lodge," he said. "He is old and toothless but will serve to gather the wood. Afterward, you can bask in the sun like the cat to heal your wounds." As he started to leave, he stopped, turning his horse about. "You have earned the respect of the other warriors with your fight against Red Nose," he said, "but do not mistake it, Woodcutter. In the end, you have killed a Cheyenne."

Little River joined the other warriors, circling the fire, their painted and fierce faces, yipping and howling and quirking their horses, weapons held high over their heads. Satisfied with their show, they circled one last time before riding off into the prairie.

The sun rose high overhead. Caleb waited, warming away the tension of the knife wound and the swelling in his face. When it was time to gather wood, he took up his axe and made his way to Little River's lodge. The horse was old, as Little River had said, with swayed back, protruding hip bones, and hooves split beyond repair. Its head hung inches from the ground, and as Caleb approached, it neither moved nor acknowledged his presence. A pitiful pair they made as Caleb led him across camp, both shuffling along in all their infirmity.

As they worked their way up the hill, the old woman sang out to Caleb, her hand shading out the sun from her eyes. "Woodcutter," she called, "bring plenty of wood because tonight the Cheyenne will celebrate their victory."

He acknowledged her with a wave and turned, looping the cold weight of the hobble over his shoulder. Using the axe as a walking stick, he gave the old horse a tug, and they moved up the hill, a tired and decrepit pair. Maybe the old woman was right. Maybe tonight they would celebrate their victory around the light of their fire, but this much he knew, this much he'd decided in the darkness of the night: they'd do it without him, because Caleb Justin was never coming back.

How long he walked he wasn't sure, nor did he know the direction he must take, whether it was south or west or straight ahead. If he were to intercept the wagon train before them, he would have to cut more north, at least that's what it seemed, and so that's what he did, keeping the sun over his right shoulder as he plodded along.

But in the end it was not to matter. As the sun dropped low in the western sky and the shadows stretched black and silent across the prairie, the old horse refused to go farther. Exhaling, it spiked both feet into the earth, lowered itself into the grass, and that was that. No amount of threatening could convince it to rise from that resting spot. Giving up at last, Caleb took off the old horse's bridle and tossed it into the grass.

"It's all right, ole friend," he said, rubbing it between the ears. "I've a good idea how you feel."

Caleb turned due south, determined to reach his destination. There was too little time for backtracking now. For hours he trekked across the plains, his wounds raw and agonizing under the relentless scour of buckskin and the weight of his hobbles. Evening descended upon him and, with it, all sense of direction. He wandered from hill to hill, lost and hopeless in the immensity of the plains. Falling to the ground, he buried his head into his arms. Like the old horse before him, his spirit was broken, and he could go no farther.

It was the smell of smoke, that unmistakable trace of peril, that brought him out of his stupor. There on the vista, flames flickered in the low-lying clouds, their bellies churning with the heat and devastation from below them. It was the wagon train, of that he was certain. With all his trying, he was too late, too late for himself, too late for the poor souls whose fate he could not imagine. So into the twilight he struggled, throwing caution aside as he navigated prairie dog holes, and ravines, and prickly pear cactus.

He stopped at the top of a hill and listened to the soldiers, their screams rising from the inferno, and the pitiful whicker of horses trapped in the carnage, innocent and helpless with cries like the screams of children. Gathering himself up, he ran on into the fray, because there was no turning back now. Whatever was to happen would happen down there with his own kind.

The heat from the fires burned his face and cast their hellish glow on the slaughter about him. There in a sage brush Sergeant Wins lay coiled in death, his jaw bulging with fresh tobacco twist, his denuded skull leaking into the prairie sand. Caleb dropped to his knees and brought about his carbine. Cheyenne circled all about, riding and whooping in a frenzy of death, firing again and again into the dying and convulsing bodies.

Death reeked in the clean dusk air as Caleb worked his way up the ridge, dragging his hobble behind, slipping and sliding in the viscera and gore of his comrades, searching in vain for ammunition among the bodies. The evening whined with bullets, and arrows, and cries for mercy, and there was a great sadness within him.

When once again his hobble caught up in the brush, he despaired, dropping to his knees to wait for the end. A moonless night descended in that moment over the battlefield, a dark and sallow shroud. From all directions the fires glowed as the Cheyenne burned the wagons and dragged the mutilated bodies into the flames for a final humiliation.

It was but a matter of time before they found him. His death would not be easy, this he knew with all the certainty of his experience, nor would it be fast. He heard the rustle of feathers above him and prayed for a bullet, for that sudden flash of light that would sweep him away. But it did not come, as he'd feared, and when he looked up into the yellow light of the flames, Little River stood over him.

"Woodcutter," he said.

Struggling to his feet, Caleb said, "I can't go on as it is, Little River. I'm dead sick of this hobble, and of standing by while my own are being kilt. Reckon you know how it is. I think you know better than anyone. I saved your life once, and I figure you owe me. That bow of yours can stall a two-ton buffalo at a hundred yards. I've seen you do it, so if you'd just kill me, swift and clean like that, we'll call it even for this world."

Little River nocked an arrow and brought about his bow, aiming it at Caleb's chest, his arm trembling with the power of his draw. Light from the fires flickered in his eyes, and in the red streak of grease across his face. Moments passed as Caleb waited for the flight of the arrow, swift and irrevocable, into his defenseless body, but it did not come.

Lowering his bow, Little River looked down on the slaughter and then back at the white man who stood waiting for death before him. He reached into his pocket and brought out the hobble key, tossing it at Caleb's feet, and then moved off into the smoke and misery of the battle.

When Caleb unlocked the hobble, it was as if the world fell away, and he ran into the darkness, for his life, for freedom regained at last, for that small flicker of hope so long extinguished in desperation. Neither the sting of thorns nor the uncertainty of his path nor the twist of his damaged foot could stop him from his flight. Not until the death fires faded behind him and the stink of smoke gave way to the clean night air did he rest, and then but for a moment, long enough to relieve the burn of his lungs before running on once more.

And when he could go no farther, he fell to the ground, the earth warm beneath him, its smell of decay and renewal in the night. The stars, still gallant and untouched by the evils of man, hung hopeful in the black expanse of the universe.

He slept then, even in his fear, and when he awakened, a full moon dangled overhead. The silvery orb lit the crevices and crannies of this alien land and cast shadowed specters in the night.

The cry was small in the vastness. Bolting upright, he listened, his ears ringing in the silence. It couldn't be Cheyenne. He'd come too far in the dark of night and in the heat of battle for them to have found him.

Rolling onto his hands and knees, he listened again, and it came as before.

"Who are you?" he called. And then he saw something, a bundle curled in the shadows. He moved forward with axe in hand. "I have a weapon," he said. Lifting the axe above his head, he waited to strike. "Ain't taking no more hobbles," he said, "not in this life."

But when she lifted her head, he could see the fleur-de-lis of rosewood and gold about her neck, the green of her tear-filled eyes, and the pale beauty of Joan Monnet's face in the moonlight.

Chapter 17

Scrambling into the darkness, she stared up at him. "Miss," he said, dropping onto his knees, "it's me, Caleb Justin." She drew her legs in and shook her head. "I've got a gun," she said.

"Miss," he said again, "don't you know who I am? It's me, the woodcutter. The feller what brought wood to your railroad car. Don't you remember?"

"Woodcutter?"

"Caleb Justin," he said again, realizing what he must look like in the darkness with his long hair, buckskins, and blackened eyes. "I cut wood for your pa and the track crew. Don't you remember?"

For the longest moment she looked at him, as if he were from some distant world.

"Did you bring my book back?" she asked.

"Book? Why, yes, Miss, I did."

"People never bring books back."

"I swear it," he said.

"You scared the life out of me," she said.

"I was took captive by the Cheyenne," he said, "and hobbled like a jack mule for the whole of the summer."

"You can trust a person who returns books."

"Yes, Miss."

She looked past him, searching the darkness. "It was horrible, you know."

"Yes, Miss, I know. There weren't nobody left alive, nobody at all, and now here you are, just like a miracle."

"Corporal Fitz saved my life," she said.

"Fitz from the railhead?"

"They killed him, but not without a fight. I loaded while he fired, and when there was no ammunition left, we threw rocks, and when there were no more rocks—" She looked up at Caleb. "But they just kept coming, over and over, and the dying was everywhere, and the cries, I'll never forget the cries."

"I'm sorry," Caleb said.

"We just stood there cursing, as if somehow we could stop them with the anger of our words, but we couldn't. Important things are never changed with words, Caleb, not things that matter. One minute Corporal Fitz was alive, and then he wasn't anymore." Folding her arms, she rubbed the backs of them as if a chill had swept through her. "You can't hear arrows when they come, and when they do come, things are never again the same."

He reached for her. She hesitated, then took his hand, her fingers still cold.

"What did you do then?" he asked.

"I fell to the ground, into a dry creek bed or buffalo wallow, I guess, and pulled Corporal Fitz's body over me. He was warm and heavy, I remember, and smelled of shaving soap. It was shameless of me, and there were the awful sounds of the arrows going into him as the Cheyenne circled and took their coup. I lay there waiting, but it never came. They never saw me."

"You did what you had to in order to stay alive. There's no shame in that. Now you and me better get out of here while we can. It's a rare opportunity we got. Take hold of my belt so we don't get separated in the dark."

"Are you taking me home?"

"I don't have a notion where we are," he said, "but I do know it's too close to where we've been. Now, come on."

Like hunted animals they moved into the night, the cool of her hand against his back. And when they could walk no more, they fell to the ground, where they slept, exhausted from their flight. In the early morning hours, the dew fell, and moisture gathered in their hair, and from the ridge a bitch coyote watched on with wheat-colored eyes. Squatting, she marked her territory before loping off into the sunrise.

A grasshopper, torpid with cold, clung to Caleb's brow and sat him upright in the morning sun. Flinging it away, he cursed its audacity and struggled to orient himself.

When he saw her curled in the grass, the night's events rushed back, and a great sickness welled up within him.

"Miss," he said, shaking her shoulder.

Covering her mouth with her hand, she gasped. "Who is it?"

"It's all right," he said. "We're safe, at least for the moment."

She wrapped her arms about herself, shivering. "Where are we?"

"As far away as we could go, Miss."

"I want to go home now, Caleb. I'm cold and hungry, and nobody knows where I am."

He turned about and studied the horizon, the blue haze of the plains. There was the smell of fall in the air and the coming of winter not far behind.

"I ain't all that certain where we are," he said, "and we ain't got that much to get by on. There's this here axe, but that's about all there is."

"We'll starve, or freeze, or—" she said, "or be taken by the Cheyenne. Now, maybe woodcutters don't mind that, but I find it a considerable inconvenience."

"We won't freeze, Miss, not so long as I can chop wood." Taking her hand, he helped her up. "We best figure us a place to hide until we can come up with a plan. Right now there ain't nothing between us and the Cheyenne but clear sky and flat land."

She spiked her hands on her waist, her eyes bearing down.

"I'm going to use that axe on you if you call me Miss one more time. I'm not some old lady, and I don't appreciate being talked to like I am. Now, call me Joan or just don't bother talking to me at all."

"All right, Joan," he said, testing out its sound.

So, ragged and lost, they struck out once more, the burden of the trail magnified with the uncertainty of what might await them. Even though Joan's endurance was weak with privileged living, her determination was strong as she followed behind.

Against his better judgment, Caleb would stop, "to check the sky," he said, or "to watch the horizon for movement," but he knew too well the Cheyenne's capacity for the hunt. They could rise like wolves from the prairie floor, leaving little but bloodstains in the grass to mark their passing, and so taking her hand, he would move out once more.

It was dusk when Caleb spotted the ravine. Carved from limestone, it cut into the belly of the prairie, a refuge and haven from the watchful eyes about them. If there was water, it would be there, and fuel for a fire.

"Come on," he said, "we can reach it before dark."

As they worked their way into the canyon, the winds fell away, and the shadows dropped about them like black curtains. Near the bottom of the ravine was a small alcove, sculpted by winds and floodwaters. It promised cover, and so they made their way down the tumble of rock and into its protection.

Trembling, Joan curled against the wall. "I'm so cold," she said.

"You wait here," he said. "I'll see if I can find something to start a fire."

She grabbed his hand to stop him. "You will be careful?"

"I'll be back before dark," he said.

And so he left her and searched the scattered trees for downed wood, finding an aged elm half-buried under a rockslide near the canyon entrance. He cut away the bark with his axe, stripping off the dry paper beneath it. After that, he cut a stick, fuzzing its end with the blade of his axe. Already the canyon darkened, and he worked as fast as he could to gather an armload of wood.

By the time he returned, the night had fallen black about him, and for one frantic moment he thought he was not going to find the shelter where he'd left Joan, but when he called out, she answered a few feet from where he stood.

He crumpled the paper in the darkness, spinning the fuzz stick against the bark with the palms of his hands. Again and again he worked at the stick, blowing into the bark paper as he'd seen the Cheyenne women do. When a curl of smoke rose, and the smallest red coal glowed, he yelped with gratitude and nursed the coal into a flame.

Never had fire been more welcome. Gathering about, they held their hands to its warmth and huddled against its flicker. The slightest hope returned in their hearts, the barest possibility that the world was not, at least for this moment, so desperate and dangerous.

The bed of coals glowed red and the chill was at last driven from his bones. Caleb pulled bunchgrass from the rock crevices and made them beds in the lee of the alcove.

Exhausted and weary, Joan fell on her bed, turning her back to the warmth of the fire. In the light he could see the blisters on her heels and the scratches on her legs. She was almighty tough for a little thing, and there was no complaining. Maybe he wished she wasn't so tough. Maybe he wished he could tell her that things would be all right, and that he, himself, was such a man to defend her from the cruelty and savagery of these plains. But even as he thought these things, her breathing slowed as she moved into sleep.

Dawn broke on a chill morning, its pink light skittering and dancing in the frost-covered grass. The fire had gone out during the night from want of fuel. Scraping away the layer of ash, a coal winked back, and Caleb's sprit rose. By the time Joan awakened, he'd gathered more wood, and a roaring fire warmed the tiny shelter.

"Good morning," she said, rising on an elbow.

"Good morning yourself. How are you doing?"

"I slept hard even in this cold," she said, running her fingers through a tangle in her hair.

"It was a fair long walk," he said.

"We were headed for Fort Dodge," she said. "How far do you think it is?"

Caleb scanned the sky. "That's east, sure," he said, "where the sun's coming up, and at night I can use the north star, but an hour after sunrise, all bets are off. These plains is like standing in the middle of the ocean."

Moving next to the fire, she warmed her toes. "It's no wonder you were captured by the Cheyenne, Caleb."

"Well, I've been thinking," he said. "We got fire, and that's a good thing, and we have shelter, too, in a fashion, but we need water for drinking, and food, because a person can weaken fast out here without food. Everything is such blamed hard work, see, and without food, things fall apart before you know it. Once the weakness sets in, then, well—it's the weak what gets eat or left behind."

The morning sun melted away the frost, and they worked their way into the canyon to see what they could find, discovering a clear stream trickling from under the rockslide. Having their fill, they explored the area for berries or nuts, but to no avail. In the ravine below the stream, they dug some roots. They tasted of bitter and dirt. In the marsh below the stream, cattails abounded, the dried stalks like skinny old men leaning and whispering in the wind.

"We'll cut them," Caleb said, "and haul them back to camp."

Joan pushed her hair back from her face and looked up at him.

Sunlight cut through the green of her eyes. "What for?" she asked.

He sliced off a half dozen of the reeds with his axe and handed them to her. "They make great bedding," he said. "We'll wrap them in bundles and lay them side by side. They're right comfortable and warm. Here, take one of those reeds and tie the others with it while I cut some more."

They'd gathered sufficient reeds for their beds by noon and hauled them back to camp. Lying down on her cattails, Joan covered her eyes against the sun with her forearm.

"They're wonderful," she said, "and they smell of clean air and sunshine."

Sitting down, Caleb hooked his chin over his knees and watched her.

"It's a powerful hunger I've got," he said. "We've got to figure something to eat, something quick."

"Couldn't you kill a buffalo?" she asked, her arm still covering her eyes.

"Sure I could," he said, "given one would come waltzing in here and let me whack him over the head with this axe. Course, it's hard to find such obliging buffaloes this late in the season, 'cause they already been eat up or took in as house pets."

Peeking from under her arm, she studied him. "So, do you have a better idea?"

"Well," he said, lying down on his bed, hooking his hands behind his head. "I been thinking on them grasshoppers."

She sat upright. "You've got to be kidding."

"One was perched on my brow this morning, shivering with the cold and slow as molasses, he was. I just plucked him right up like a nut off a tree."

"No, Caleb, I don't think so."

"Little River told me that the Shoshone eat them all the time, that a man can fatten his whole family in a good season, providing he don't have to chase them too far. Why, I'd rather run down a mule deer than a spry hopper."

"Caleb Justin, if you ate that grasshopper, I'll never speak to you again."

"Well, he had some growing to do, so I turned him loose."

Pulling her knees into her arms, she studied the fire smoldering under a growing layer of ash. "What, then, are we going to eat?"

"There's bullfrogs big as jackrabbits down at that stream. Frog legs ain't bad eating, and they're a sight easier to chase down than hoppers."

"Frog legs?"

"It's good clean meat and will keep us going until I get a bow made."

She looked at him, wondering if he was joking with her again. "You can't make a bow?"

"Course I can."

"Well, then, make one and kill us a buffalo."

"First we go frog hunting," he said. "Come on."

He cut a couple of sticks from a cedar tree on the way down the canyon and sharpened the ends with his axe. Once at the stream, they hid in the brush to wait. The sun lowered beyond the canyon wall, and a bullfrog croaked from somewhere in the reeds. Like enormous gray herons, Caleb and Joan edged forward, spears poised, but the frog fell silent.

Lowering themselves into the reeds, Caleb and Joan waited once more. Minutes passed as they squatted in the shallows, the smell of mud, the whine of insects swarming in their ears. The frog croaked again, and Caleb spotted him, big as a buffalo pie and sitting at the stream's edge. Taking aim, he chucked his spear, and the frog flew into the air, his great legs trailing behind like tails on a kite.

"Damn," he said.

"I see him," Joan said, whispering.

"Where?"

"There," she said. "Here, take my spear."

"I don't see him," he said.

"Just there, are you blind?"

"I can't see him."

"Oh, Lord, help me," she said.

Standing on her tiptoes, she threw her spear into the reeds.

"You got him," Caleb said, clapping his hands, holding the dancing frog up for her inspection.

"Ick," she said, "now I suppose we must eat him."

Caleb had a grand total of three frogs dangling from his belt by nightfall. In the waning light, he and Joan worked their way back to camp. Joan followed behind Caleb, her frog sticker slung over her shoulder like a hunter come home.

Caleb waited at the top of the slide as she picked her way through the rocks. Never could he have imagined her this way, in this place, her hair a tangle of dust and twigs. But here she was, and even more beautiful than he remembered, even with her muddied feet, her torn clothes, her arms welted from bites.

He took her by the hand and pulled her up the rest of the way, the surge of her breasts against her blouse, the fleur-de-lis of rosewood dangling from her neck.

"That was some shot," he said, letting her fingers fall cool and delicate from his own.

"Well, it was either that or grasshoppers."

"I missed on purpose," he said, "so you could work in a little practice."

"You did not," she said, giving him a push. "You were trying to find your way out of the reeds because you were lost again."

That night, Caleb built the fire high and extravagant. With his axe he cleaned the frog legs, spearing them on sticks for roasting. As they turned over the coals, the legs jumped with life, and Joan rolled her eyes.

After they were cooked, Caleb scraped charcoal on them from a burned stick. It wasn't salt, but it wasn't bad. He tasted his first, and then Joan tried a tentative nibble. They ate them then, with a hunger so fierce that they neither spoke nor looked up until there was nothing left but a small stack of polished bones.

Turning into the warmth of their cattail beds, they fell silent. Overhead, stars burst into the night, and the world rolled through the universe.

"Night, Joan," he said.

"Caleb, I've been wondering how you ended up out here on these plains?"

"I came to join Sheridan's outfit," he said. "That's the short of it."

Propping her chin in her hand, she looked at him. "Then why didn't you?"

"I'm a gimp, you see, and gimps can endanger the other soldiers."

Moments passed, the moon breaking in the distance, its ivory light spilling into the canyon about them.

"A person should know his own worth, Caleb," she said.

"It's a woodcutter, I am," he said. Reaching over, he tossed a couple of sticks onto the fire and watched the sparks quiver into the cold night air. "And why would you be in such a place, I wonder," he said, "a lady what with the world at her feet?"

There was a pause. "To get married," she said, pointing her chin, "as you know."

"Well, he's a lucky man."

"You think so?"

"Lucky indeed." Smoke stung Caleb's eyes, and he rubbed at them with the backs of his hands.

"Now they've sent him off again, to Fort Dodge this time, to prepare for the winter campaign."

"I reckon Sheridan's fighting mad over these raids and all?"

"He says that the Indians can't feed their horses in the winter, so that's the best time to teach them a lesson they won't forget. Now, he's called in General Custer to clean up the mess."

"It's their winter campgrounds they'll be going after," Caleb said.

"Lieutenant Gillian is stocking grain and fodder supplies at Fort Dodge for the drive south into the Territory. Cavalry horses have to eat, too, I suppose."

"Wasn't the lieutenant concerned about bringing you out on that wagon train, what with all the depredations about?"

Dropping her finger onto her lip, she let it rest there for a moment. "Well, he was very busy, wasn't he, and I'm sure he thought it safe enough."

"Yes," Caleb said, "he must have, because even Quartermaster Sergeant Wins was on that train. I seen him kilt myself."

"Lieutenant Gillian has lots of responsibilities, Caleb."

"We best get some rest," he said. "There's much to be done tomorrow."

She lay down and looked up into the stars. "You don't think he would have put me in harm's way?"

"How could he have known the Cheyenne were armed so well?" he said.

"Yes," she said, "how could he have known?"

Turning onto his side, Caleb closed his eyes. Even now he could hear the lieutenant's name as it was spoken in the darkness that night, the evil and telling whispers beyond the Cheyenne camp.

For the next few days, Caleb searched out every corner of the canyon, a vast ravine that stretched upstream for a couple of miles. Populated with heavy stands of hardwood trees, it provided an abundance of fuel, but food was another matter. Joan was mastering the skill of frog spearing, but the meat was spare and lean, and they both grew thin from want of fat.

To complicate matters, the days were growing shorter and colder, and the north wind blew with infuriating regularity. Sometimes at night he could hear Joan trembling against the chill. Neither spoke of it, but both knew that they must soon have larger game if they were to make it. Though he'd boasted of his bow making, what he hadn't said, hadn't admitted even to himself, was that he must first have rawhide to string the bow, but without a bow to kill the game, there could be no rawhide

for stringing. In the end, he'd still have to hunt without a horse,
something that even the Cheyenne were not wont to do.

Climbing onto the south side of a rockslide, he lay down to
rest, to warm in the sun and escape for a moment the eternal
wind. The blue of the heavens fell away like a vast and bottomless
sea. He shielded his eyes against the glare and gazed into their
expanse. Birds, no more than distant specks, spiraled through
the turquoise sky, soaring high with outspread wings, banking
and falling away like angels in the sun.

With each pass they drew closer to where he lay, but they were
not angels at all, now that he could see, but buzzards with craws
like red clots of blood, with beaded black eyes, and with nostrils
flared. He lay still and waited as they landed, gathering in the
rocks below him, their wings drooped like black-robed judges,
and when he stood, they lifted away with angry and scolding
calls. But in the end, it was their way to wait, and soon they
circled overhead once more to watch from privileged heights.

Caleb smelled it before he saw it, its sweetness and corruption
from out of the rocks, but he was unprepared for the sight of the
buffalo fallen from the cliff, its humiliation, its innards strewn
like wilted greens among the rocks. He examined it, and sweat
gathered cool and sick across his forehead. What they could
have done with this meat, how long they could have survived,
enough for weeks, if dried, but now it was no more than hide
and bone, no more than a fetid cauldron stewing in the sun. He
made his way down the hill, the stench trailing in his hair and
in his clothes. He'd not gone but a few yards when he stopped,
knowing all too well what he must do. Cursing, he threw his
axe into the rocks, and then had to retrieve it before making
his way back to the carcass.

The hide peeled away with disconcerting ease, like the skin of
a too-ripe peach, and blood clung like black mud to the bit of
his axe. Moisture dripped from Caleb's nose as if he had been
slugged, and his eyes watered with the insult of stench and

putrefaction. Twice he crawled to the edge of the embankment to purge the pathetic contents of his stomach so that he might continue with the grim task.

When at last the deed was done, he lay out the buffalo hide on the ground and in its center placed the horns and hooves of the unfortunate animal. Then he removed the stout hind leg bones, taking care to strip out the sinew to be used as backing for his bow.

He rolled up the hide, secured it with a piece of the sinew, and then hefted the whole business onto his shoulder. Its weight was imposing, and he weaved a little as he reached for his axe. Overhead, the buzzards descended, the waiting over yet again.

It had been a hard day, one Caleb hoped he would never have to relive, and there was still nothing to eat, this he knew with every squeak of his empty stomach, but now at least there was hide, and soon enough rawhide, and then a bow with which to hunt.

He approached Joan, who was standing at the fire with two frog legs dancing off the end of a stick.

"Oh my," she said, clamping her nose. "What have you done now?"

"It's a buffalo hide I've got," he said, setting it down, "and we can make rawhide for stringing a bow. I took it off a animal what's been lying in the sun awhile."

"Oh, " she said again.

"Well, I'm sorry, but there was no other way."

"It's just wretched, Caleb, really."

"I know," he said, rolling out the hide on the ground, "but it's the fat mostly. See, the hide's still strong and supple."

"Well," she said, "I suppose it has to be cleaned. I'll help since there's little point in just one of us stinking."

And so into the night they labored at the hide, scraping it over and over with the axe blade until all the fat was removed and the hide was shined and soft. Afterward, Caleb cut away a strip from the side for making up rawhide and placed it in cold ash from the fire.

"It will loosen the hair," he said, "and we'll save the fat, too."

"What for, Caleb?" she asked, holding her hands away from her as if they belonged to someone else. "It's too foul to cook with."

"Fire starting," he said, scraping it onto a flat rock, "if the buzzards don't take us first."

"Well," she said, sitting back on her pallet, "I suppose we could eat the frog legs now."

"I think my belly's been half-hitched with a hair rope," he said.

"Me, too," she said, lying down on her pallet.

Later, when the evening cooled, Caleb rose, laying the robe over her.

"I know it don't smell so good," he said, "but there's no one to know. My nose quit hours ago and ain't apt to ever work again. It will keep you warm, and that's the most important thing."

At first she started to protest, but decided against it, snuggling under, and was soon fast asleep.

Caleb lay awake for the longest time in his weariness, the temperature dropping in the cloudless night. Shivering and hungry, he pulled his legs into his arms to ward away the cold. There was a despair growing within him. They were lost, and in enemy territory, and not much closer to getting food than when they'd started. Turning over, he watched Joan. At least for this night she slept with a sweetness and warmth that she had not known for many days.

During the night, coons ate the buffalo fat, their tracks like babies' feet encircling the rock where he'd left it. It took an hour to bring up the fire, and even then, it smoldered like a wet blanket, giving out precious little heat for his trouble.

Joan awakened renewed, her night's rest evident in the brightness of her eyes and the bounce in her walk.

"I'll fix the frog legs for breakfast," she said, poking at the fire in the hope of bringing it to life.

"I'd as soon eat hoppers," he said. "Least they don't smell like fish bait, and they don't kick the roof of your mouth the whole blamed time you're trying to get one down."

"These legs have plenty of nourishment," she said, handing him one, "so just quit complaining."

"I'm going to make the bow today," he said, swallowing the meat as fast as he could. "Maybe you could soak that strip of hide in the creek. Tonight, I'll work off the hair."

"I'm hunting for frogs this morning," she said, "before the sun gets too high, and they head for the shade."

"You be careful," he said, "because where there's water, there're others who might be looking for a drink."

"I'll be careful," she said, picking up her frog sticker.

He watched as she walked down the hill, the bend of her back, the swing of her arms, the pride and toss of her head, and he remembered how she'd stood in the doorway of that railroad car, how she'd fixed him tea like he was a real person, and how she'd given him *Bleak House*, her very own book to read, as if it mattered in the whole wide world. Now, she was here.

He picked up his axe and held it before him, its heft and shape familiar to every muscle in his body, and he swore that no matter the cost, he would see her through and back to her people.

His search for wood brought him out of the canyon and into a hedge of bois d'arc that twisted from out of the cracks of a limestone table. Little River said that bow wood should be seasoned, but there was no time for such luxuries now. Picking out a healthy sapling, he chopped with wide swings of his axe, the bit ringing in the hardness of the wood. Afterward, he cut the bough to length and set the bit in its end. He struck the head of his axe with a rock and split the wood in equal halves. The grains were tight and dense and should make a fine bow. The bowstring would require constant tuning because of the wood's poor seasoning, its shape and tension changing as it dried.

By the time he'd reached camp, the clouds hung low in the sky, their bellies red and churning with sunset. A brisk north wind drove through the canyon, swirling eddies of leaves, their smell of earth and decay. Joan was stooped over the fire, fanning it back to life with a piece of bark.

"I'm back," he said, "and I've found bow wood."

She tossed the bark into the fire and dusted the ash from her hands. "Well, I'm glad," she said.

"What's the matter?"

"The frogs are gone."

"What do you mean?"

"Well, they called a meeting, packed up their bags, and left overnight. There's nothing to eat."

"It's all right," he said. "I've got the bow wood and rawhide, too. I will kill us a deer."

That night in the glow of the fire, he shaped the belly of the bow, taking care not to sever the grain, and when morning light came, they carried water from the stream in the buffalo horns, steaming the ends of the bow in the fire, bending them again and again until their shape was elegant and strong. After that, he boiled the hooves in a hollow stump, dropping in heated rocks until they melted into a stinking and vigorous paste. With the paste, he glued the sinew onto the back of the bow to increase its strength, placing it under heavy rocks to dry in the sun.

With his axe he crushed the leg bones of the buffalo, shaping the splintered pieces of bone into arrow heads with sandstone he'd taken from the slide. From cedar boughs, he fashioned arrow shafts, and a search of the cottonwood grove bore wild turkey feathers with which he fletched the arrows.

While the bow was drying, he showed Joan how to dehair the rawhide with a piece of chert and to weave the strips into a strong bowstring.

Two hard days and they were at last finished. Placing his foot on the belly of the bow, Caleb tested its draw, pulling the string to his stomach to check its balance, to make certain that both halves shared the tension. The bow fractured on the second pull.

"Goddang it!" he yelled, throwing it into the fire.

"It's all right," Joan said, "we'll do it again, won't we. That's why you brought two of them."

Hungry and despondent, they started over, and this time the bow tested the full reach of the string. Caleb's arms trembled under its tensile, and he knew the bow was good.

He rose at dawn and slipped the bundle of arrows over his shoulder. Stepping through the bow, he strung it over his leg, his fingers stiff with morning cold. If he was to kill a deer, it would have to be at dawn as they grazed in the tree line under the protection of early light. Joan's sleep was sound beneath the warmth of her buffalo robe, so he decided not to stoke the fire for fear of disturbing her.

The morning smelled of frost as he made his way through the canyon, and his stomach burned with an emptiness he'd never before known. There was a weakness within him, a frailty that shortened his stride and stole his breath. If he didn't get food soon, he'd be too weak to hunt, and their end would come with the bitterness of winter.

For an hour he worked his way out of the canyon to where the trees thinned into the prairie grass. When he was exhausted, he lowered himself into a plum thicket to scan the terrain. He laid his bow down and rubbed at the cold that pooled in his shoulders, his neck, and the small of his back. In that instant, a half dozen deer bounded from out of nowhere, knocking him backward into the tangle. By the time he'd unraveled himself, there was little left of the deer but their white tails flagging over the distant hill.

"Damn it," he said, kicking dirt onto his bow.

That's when he saw her, an old deer stalled in terror at the edge of the bramble, her raven eyes shimmering in the sunrise. He held his breath and reached for his bow, bringing it about and nocking his best arrow, his heart pounding with possibility.

Fearful of stampeding her, he leveled the bow from his waist, a shot fraught with inaccuracy.

The old deer did not move, her eyes rooted on his, and he loosed his arrow. There was a snort, and then another as she lowered her head. Caleb nocked another arrow with trembling fingers and stepped from out of the thicket, but there was no need for a second shot—his first arrow had shanked deeply into the white embroidery of her breast. She dropped to her knees and snorted once more before easing into the sand to die.

With his axe, he gutted her out, the gamy smell of butchery in the chill morning air. Afterward, he cut saplings for a travois, weaving them together with bark and grapevine taken from out of the draw, and then he loaded his deer, her head drooped and sweet over his shoulder, her tongue lolling from her mouth.

The travois was crude to be sure, but functional, and by the time the sun rose overhead, he was dragging home his catch. Even as he struggled with its weight, he was consumed with joy, because now there was meat, enough for weeks if they were careful, and there was deer skin for clothing, and horn for knapping, and bone for all manner of service. Tonight there would be roast for the spit, turned and blackened from the fire, and they would fill their bellies until they could eat no more.

Each time he rested, he rose again to his lading, overcome with the necessity to see the look on Joan's face when she saw the deer.

From the top of the canyon, he smelled the smoke from camp and knew she awaited his return. Getting down the rockslide was more difficult than he'd anticipated, the travois snagging again and again in the uprooted rocks. Each time he levered it out with the axe handle, only to repeat the procedure a few minutes later when it snagged once more. By the time he pulled out on level ground, his hands were raw and throbbing.

He could see the campfire from the trees at the edge of the stream, the blaze licking high in the dusky light. "Joan?" he called. When she did not answer, he lowered the travois. Moving into the camp, he stood next to the fire, its flames crackling and hot under a fresh stack of wood. Leaning against the embankment was Joan's frog sticker, and draped over the rock above the alcove was the buffalo robe. Each day she lay it there to dry in the warmth of the sun. "Joan," he called again, "I've killed a deer."

It was a feeling, no more, a sense of impending danger, or perhaps it was the silence, the kind that seeps from tombs, or pleads for mercy in moments of battle, or abandons old lives in the wee hours of dawn. Whatever the feeling was, he slipped his bow and strung an arrow and turned about. He searched the rocks, and there, looming in the shadows, a warrior stood, with his white-painted face, his shield of rawhide, and his knife at the ready. Caleb drew his bow and took aim, his mind centered on what must be done.

But there in the dimness of twilight, he saw Joan, with fear and resolve in her muddied face as she struggled against the warrior's hold.

Chapter 18

Joan said, "Caleb, watch out!"

The warrior looked up, and she shoved her elbow under his uplifted arm. Grunting from the blow, he slung her into the rocks and charged Caleb, his eyes fierce, his knife poised and readied at the hip.

It was the time Caleb needed, that single extra moment to judge the intent and danger of the situation. Pulling his bow to full measure, he loosed the arrow, the whine and certainty of its power, the pop and scald of the string as it burned away the skin of his forearm.

But the warrior's charge was unchecked, his momentum and resolve greater than the arrow that now grew from his belly. Like bears clutched in battle, they tumbled into the rocks. Caleb, stunned from the fall, struggled to unlock the warrior's hands from about his neck, but even as the warrior's blood dripped red and mortal from the arrow's shaft, his strength was steel, and death, and unrelenting determination.

The cry that rose from the warrior's throat was that of the wolf, the solitary howl from out of the wilderness, and his hands fell away, body slumping over Caleb, eyes clouding in his final moments.

The sweetness of breath came at last to Caleb, his mind cleared, and Joan stood above the warrior, her frog sticker rising from out of his back.

"I've killed him," she said, her eyes locked on the sway of her weapon from the final heaves and labors of the warrior's chest.

The warrior pulled himself up on all fours and crawled toward the rocks like an animal in search of a place to die. With head drooped between his arms, he struggled but fell backward, the frog sticker splintering away. He gathered himself up once more and struggled a few feet. But the wound was mortal, his life ebbing away, and he lowered himself on the ground to die.

With his eyes turned to the heavens, he howled, and Joan covered her ears, because in it was a warrior's cry of defeat, a cry of forfeiture and loss, a cry of a child lost in the darkness. None who heard could not but know the sorrow and shame that were in it. Collapsing onto the ground, his hands closed and then opened for a final time.

"He's dead," Caleb said.

"Oh my God, Caleb," Joan said, looking away from what lay before them.

"We had no choice, Joan. It was him or us. We both could be dead this very second."

Sitting down on a rock, she rubbed at her face and then looked over at the warrior once more. "The rest of my life I'll know that I've killed a man."

"No, no," he said, "it was my arrow, don't you see. He was a dead man, Joan, with a gut-shot arrow and a painful death ahead. There can be no doubting it. All you did was save my life by bringing his to a merciful end."

"It was hideous, Caleb. I would never have thought I could do such a thing."

"Well, I'm mighty glad you did. I was getting a little concerned about breathing again."

She wrapped her arms about herself. "He came out of the reeds and took me by the hair of my head. I didn't know whether to fight or go along. I went along."

"He would have killed you certain, Joan."

"I guess he smelled the smoke from the campfire, because he hauled me up the rockslide, and that's when I heard you call out. I thought we were both going to die."

Taking her into his arms, he held her for a moment. "It's over," he said. "Now, come help me go through his things."

They searched their victim in the fading light, taking his bow, splintered in the struggle, and a half dozen arrows from his quiver.

"He's made these points from an iron skillet," Caleb said, holding them up against the light. "They're a sight better than my bone points. And here's his knife. Boy," he said, shaking his head, "will this make life easier."

They turned him over and found a beaded medicine bag tied about his neck. In it was a river rock, rounded and polished, and a frayed turkey feather. Caleb put them back, tying the rawhide as he'd found it. Afterward, they stood over the body for the longest time, like pallbearers with folded hands.

"Can't you close his eyes, Caleb?" Joan asked.

Looking into the warrior's face, Caleb shook his head. "No," he said.

It was not until they were almost back at camp that Caleb took hold of Joan's arm.

"What's the matter?" she asked, looking into the darkness.

"I didn't even think," he said, "but he must have had a horse."

"But, Caleb—"

"We've got to go back. A horse could make the difference for us."

They climbed back up the rockslide as the stars eased into the sky, and the warrior watched them from his place in the rocks, his eyes shining in the rising moonlight.

At the reeds they stopped and listened. Caleb whistled, and they listened again. A horse whinnied beyond in the trees. "You were right," Joan said, taking his arm.

The horse was tied to a cottonwood sapling, a pinto with great brown and white splotches and eyes that shone wise and strong. When he saw Caleb and Joan, he pawed the ground and ducked his head in greeting.

"You're a beauty," Caleb said, rubbing his nose.

A canvas bag was tied through the empty shoulder sling of his black leather saddle, and a parfleche was strapped behind the cantle. In it was a horn spoon and a tin army mess pan. Caleb stuck his nose in the bag for a smell.

"What is it?" Joan asked.

"Cornmeal," he said. Lifting the stirrup, he examined the trademark in the moonlight. "And this is a McClellan saddle, cavalry, I'd say. Our warrior was pretty well equipped."

Taking the horse in tow, they made their way toward camp and came once again to where the warrior lay. Caleb handed Joan the reins.

"What are you going to do, Caleb?"

Kneeling, he placed his fingers on the warrior's eyes, cold now, like the rocks and earth about him, and he closed them. "Reckon his life might have saved ours. Come help me cover him with rocks, Joan, or there will be little enough left come morning."

By the time they got back to camp, the moon had faded behind drifting clouds, and a cold damp rode into the canyon. Caleb had forgotten altogether about the deer.

"Oh, Caleb," Joan said, clapping her hands together, "real food." Taking his face in her hands, she kissed him on the forehead. "You're a grand hunter," she said, and his forehead burned with the touch of her lips, and his spirit soared with pride.

He built the fire, and Joan helped clean the deer, cutting away a roast with the newly acquired knife.

"Be careful with the hide," he said. "It's your new coat, you know."

He propped the roast over the fire on a green spit, turning it now and again, and watched as Joan stroked the pinto's nose and held his big face to her own. When the roast bubbled into the fire and darkened in the red heat of the coals, the aroma filled their tiny camp. Both knew that this must be the most glorious meal man could ever know.

"I'll go for water," he said, handing the spit over to Joan. "We just as well have us a little cornbread, too."

He cut away what fat he could find from under the deer skin and rendered it in the mess tin. From the canvas sack, he added cornmeal, and then water from the horn, before slipping the tin into the bed of coals.

"Look it," he said, "he's cut the leg off of canvas army trousers and sewn 'em up with rawhide to make the bag."

"Oh, Caleb, when will it be ready? I don't think I can wait much longer."

"No eggs," he said, "no salt, no baking powder either, come to think on it."

"I don't care," she said, "as long as it isn't frog legs or hoppers."

And when it was finished, they took great slices of the blackened roast, still pink and delicious under the crust. Grease shone on their faces in the firelight as they ate like wolves, silent and insatiable at a fresh kill. Caleb tore off chunks of cornbread, stiff as hardtack, and gave one to Joan. She chewed with exaggerated motions, and he laughed, but both knew that it was real, that it was good, that it was substantial and life-saving fare.

Afterward, they lay on their reed mats, stuffed, and easy, and warmed against the damp. Somewhere upstream, a coyote yipped and then fell silent as the trail grew cold.

"How was the meal?" he asked, hooking his hands behind his head.

"The best I've ever had," she said, her eyes flashing, "and I've eaten in the finest restaurants in Kansas City. I better put this stuff up," she said, rising, "or the coons will have it before morning."

"I'll move the horse in closer to camp," Caleb said. "We don't want to lose him now."

He hitched the horse to a skunk brush within the camp's light while Joan cleaned the mess tin and put it back in the parfleche. She knelt and leaned into the light of the fire to tie the canvas bag. At some point her silence beckoned, and when Caleb looked over, Joan's hands were covering her mouth, and her face was pale.

"What's the matter, Joan?"

She turned the canvas bag into the light so that he could see. LIEUTENANT JOHN M. GILLIAN, QUARTERMASTER DIVISION, 7TH CAVALRY, U.S. ARMY was stenciled on the inside.

"What does it mean, Caleb?"

He told her then of what he knew, of Sergeant Wins, and of his suspicions about army supplies being sold out of Fort Harker. He told her of hearing Lieutenant Gillian's name in the darkness of the Cheyenne camp and how he was certain in his own mind of the lieutenant's involvement in the treacherous affair. He told her of the arms that Black Kettle soon after acquired and how it had cost the lives of so many soldiers, even the life of Sergeant Wins, and how it nearly cost her own life as well. He told her these things even though they struck deep and hurtful, even though she was shaken with disbelief, because he wanted her to hate Lieutenant Gillian as much as he did. He wanted her not to marry him and for her to feel the pain that his very name inflicted in his own wounded heart.

"He's playing a dangerous game, Joan. The only ones who could despise him more than his own would be the Cheyenne themselves."

"But we don't know if it's true," she said, looking up at him. "We don't know for certain."

He shut the canvas bag and tied it off, handing it back to her. "No, not for certain," he said.

That night they went to their beds full and satiated for the first time in many days, but their sleep was disturbed and uneasy, because beyond in the darkness, the warrior lay dead at their hands, and the question of Lieutenant Gillian's guilt was still alive and unresolved in their thoughts.

Chapter 19

The next morning, Caleb rose at dawn, his muscles aching from the battle with the warrior. By the time the fire was built, Joan was stirring under her robe.

"I'm taking the pinto down to the stream for a drink and to let him graze along the bank where the grass is still green," he said.

She pushed the hair back from her face and sat up. In the dim morning light he could see the shine in her eyes. The fresh deer meat had done its cure, and the warm rest had polished it to a glow. "I'll fix breakfast," she said, slipping on her shoes, looking up at him. "Be careful, Caleb."

A cool fog hung in the valley, silencing all but the familiar clop of hooves as he and the pinto picked their way through the rocks.

Caleb pulled up for a moment at the warrior's grave to wonder at the deed they'd done, at the life they'd taken, at the man who lay cold and still below. Morning dew glistened on the rocks, a grave now for all eternity, a timeless and immutable tomb. Pulling slack the reins, the pinto sniffed the mound and rattled his bit against his teeth.

"Sorry, ole boy," Caleb said, turning him about.

By midmorning the pinto had taken his fill of both water and grass, and they made their way back to camp. The smell of frying meat greeted them as they broke over the ridge.

Joan smiled up at him through the drift of smoke. "Morning," she said.

Tying the pinto to the skunk brush, Caleb squatted next to the fire. "You feel better today?"

"Better," she said, handing him the skewer.

"I've been thinking," he said, sliding off a piece of the hot meat, "now that we have food and a horse, that maybe we should be about moving on."

"Today?"

"Well, no, but after we get the meat jerked, you know, get things in order, then maybe we should head to Fort Dodge. The weather could turn bad on us at any time, and then, well, there's the Cheyenne. Every day is a risk, as we discovered yesterday."

Joan studied the fire and clenched her fingers around her knees. "Do you know the way to Fort Dodge, Caleb?"

"No, not exactly, but then it's got to be south, don't it?"

"Why couldn't it be north?"

Finishing off his meat, he stuck the skewer into the ground.

"Maybe it could be north, but we were north of Fort Dodge to start with, so I'd say it's got to be south. We ought to head south."

"Do you know which way is south, then?"

"Well, it's that way, at least at night."

"I think we don't know where Fort Dodge is, Caleb, or even north from south for that matter."

"Maybe we won't all the time, but at night we can set an arrow with the north star. It ought to keep us on the general track. One thing's certain, we can't stay out here forever. A man could be struck from the earth and never found again, just like that warrior out there."

"All right, Caleb. Then let's get things in order."

That afternoon they skinned the deer, cutting circles about its delicate ankles, working the hide back with strokes of the knife, peeling it away with exacting care.

"Oh, no," Joan said, holding the skin to the light, to show Caleb a hole the size of a man's fist in its center.

"How did that happen?" he said, shaking his head.

"That's where we took our roast last night," she said. "I guess we were intent on eating."

"Well, it will just have to do 'cause that's the only deer I kilt."

Afterward, they lay the skin over a round rock and fleshed it out, working it again and again with a sharp rock until it was supple and soft. Once they'd finished, they fashioned a drying frame from willow sticks, stretching the hide tight, tying it off with the buffalo rawhide. They set the hide in the sun to dry and turned to the meat, cutting away slices for curing, draping them about the camp. Cracking the bones open with a rock, Caleb scraped out the marrow into the army mess tin, and Joan wrinkled her nose.

"It's full of energy," he said, "and fat for keeping us warm. It tastes good, too."

"Oh, sure," she said, peering into the tin, "and this from a man who eats hoppers and heaven knows what else."

They walked down to the stream to wash their hands as the evening set and to water the pinto once again. With sand from the streambed they scrubbed the blood and grease from their fingers, splashing the icy water onto their faces. Joan wiped her face dry with the tail of her shirt and shivered against the evening chill. The red sunset cast in her hair and turned the white of her skin to pink. There was a stateliness about her, in the way she held her head, an untapped strength beneath the delicacy of her manner.

On the way back, they stood for a moment to watch the sun as it fumed on the horizon. He reached to help her up the rockslide, and she dropped her hand, cool and extraordinary, into his own. No matter the distance between them, or the impossibility of their circumstance, his heart gave way. In that moment he knew with the clarity of a man who'd faced his own death that he was in love with Joan Monnet, and wherever it took him, he must follow.

That night they sat about the fire and talked. The prairie night darkened and closed over them, their fire but a point of light in a sea of blackness. With legs crossed, Joan combed at her hair and listened to the wood snapping in the heat.

"I've been wondering, Caleb," she said, "about those scars on your ankles."

Pulling on the cuffs of his pants to cover the marks, he shrugged. "Oh, that. It's from the hobbles, you know."

"Hobbles?"

"The side hobbles taken off my mules by the Cheyenne when I was captured. It's how they kept me to home. A man can't run far with them side hobbles on."

"They must have been painful. Look what they've done to your legs."

"The Cheyenne could turn me out to cut wood and know I wasn't going to go far. It was a inconvenience all right, but then they'd have kilt me right off without them, I figure. Anyway, I won't never hobble a mule again, that's certain."

"How was it you were taken?" she asked, pulling her feet to the side and away from the heat of the fire.

"I was living in a root cellar, cutting wood for Fort Harker, and for the railhead camp, on occasion, as you know. The signs were everywhere, and Jim told me, too, told me that living out there alone was going to get me kilt. But there's no accounting for ignorance, you see, and I just kept on cutting wood until it was too late."

"Jim?"

"Jim Ferric, the blacksmith at Fort Harker and a good friend of mine." He fell silent and looked out into the blackness. "Course, it was Jim what got kilt in the end and Red Nose hisself what did it."

"I'm sorry, Caleb."

"It's been atoned, but it weren't an easy death, and it's there in my head forever, I suppose."

Walking to where the firelight lapped the darkness beyond their camp, Caleb turned his back to the warmth of the fire.

"There's something I been needing to say, Joan. I wouldn't say it at all, 'cept the way things are out here. What doesn't get said now might never get said at all."

"Caleb, maybe you shouldn't."

"I'm in love with you, and there ain't nothing either one of us can do about that, because that's just the way it is. That's the way it's always going to be."

"Caleb, no. Let's talk about this some other time."

"All along I've loved you, since the first time I saw you, but it was like a dream then, you see, like waking up with your heart aflutter from the sweetness of a dream. But now, out here, it's different. It ain't a dream no more but a world with just you and me, and it's got to be said."

"You know that I'm engaged, Caleb. If I were untrue, I would not be the same person you care about. You must understand that?"

Picking up a couple of sticks, he added them to the fire before speaking.

"I stood at that warrior's grave out there, and I wondered if there was something he'd like to have said before he died, if there was just one last word to make things right with someone, or to tell someone he was sorry, or that he would love them for all of the eternity that he was about to enter." He dusted his hands and turned. "Anyway, I've said my words, and I'm glad I did. I think I'll go to bed now."

The next few days they worked at the deer hide, scraping and softening it yet more as it dried in the sun. Each day, Caleb rode out on the pinto, cutting a wide circle about the canyon in search of tracks. Even though the likelihood of spotting anything was slim, the effort was comforting.

Joan discovered a pecan tree upstream and gathered a shirttail full of nuts for their journey. The meats were shriveled and tasted of bitter, but they were a welcome addition to their supplies. They pounded them into powder with rocks, added bone marrow, then toasted the concoction over the fire in the mess tin.

"Tastes a little like hoppers," Joan said as she took a sample from the end of her finger, "but with a woman's touch."

Satisfied that the hide was soft enough to sew, they set about making Joan a coat. Cutting a hole in the center, Caleb placed it over her head.

"It smells of death," she said, holding her nose.

"It smells of spring and warmth," he said, "and I got this here knife to fight off the coyotes if it comes to it."

"Oh, thanks," she said.

Using a sharpened stick and rawhide, he laced it down the sides. Turning her about, he whistled. "Why that's a fine coat. None better in all of Kansas City, I'd say."

"If the wind catches me, I'll sail to Dodge City like a great deer kite," she said. "And what about this?"

"What?"

"This hole dead center of my front where we cut away that roast?"

"Oh, that. Why, that's the latest fashion in buckskin wear," he said, "and right proper ventilation against the heat of the day."

"Right proper way to freeze," she said.

It was two weeks past when Caleb rode out at dawn on his circuit about the canyon. At the plum thicket where he'd killed the deer, he slid off the pinto's back and examined the area for tracks. A cold wind whipped up his shirt, sending goosebumps racing up his back. Winter was waiting just beyond the day, its sting and smell in the air.

He swung a leg over the saddle horn and pulled himself up. Dipping his head, the pinto pranced in a circle.

"Whoa, boy," Caleb said, patting him on the neck.

Laughter, sudden and alien, rose from out of the rocks where the trail descended into the canyon. Caleb's heart froze at the sound, and he slid off the pinto, ducking into the center of the plum thicket. Tying off the horse, he drew down and listened. Again voices rose from out of the draw and then faded into the distance. He didn't move for the longest time, his ears trained against the silence, but the voices never came again.

The sun rose warm in the thicket as he mounted the pinto and rode toward camp. Not far from the slide, he spotted the tracks of unshod horses, three, he guessed, maybe four, perhaps a hunting party searching the stream for deer out to water. Whether they were Cheyenne or someone else he didn't know. At this point, he didn't care. The stay in the canyon had come to an end.

That night they left in the darkness, their belongings lashed in bundles on the pinto's back. Carrying the quiver of steel-tipped arrows and his bow, Caleb took the lead, keeping the north star to his back, while Joan followed, the knife tethered with rawhide about her waist. The night was black and the going slow as they worked their way out of the canyon. Caleb stopped to listen from time to time, or to sniff the air for camp smoke, or to scan the darkness for firelight.

When at last they broke out on the plains, they stopped to rest and to eat a piece of dried meat from their stash. It tasted of blood and horse sweat, but they ate it anyway, washing it down with tepid water. Their hunger satisfied, they pushed on into the night.

When they found themselves in sand hills shot with badger holes, the going was slowed for fear of the pinto breaking a bone. But for Caleb there was relief in the open expanse and in the darkness of the night. Here at least they were less vulnerable to surprise attack. He was happy to be rid of the canyon and the fear that lurked in every shadow.

They found a break at dawn along a dried streambed where

the sand was soft and the cover was good. Tying the pinto to a mesquite sapling, they crawled onto their buffalo robe. Exhausted from the journey and the uncertainty of their course, they were soon hard asleep.

The sun rose through the leaves of the mesquite and into Caleb's face. He squinted and pulled himself onto an elbow, rubbing at his eyes. Like a fawn hidden in the grass, Joan lay curled on the robe next to him, her head nestled in the bend of her arm. He watched her sleep for some time, the rise and fall of her chest, the sweep of hair across her ear, the turn and pout of her mouth.

"Joan," he said, taking hold of her shoulder. She turned over and dropped her arm across his knee, and her breath fell hot and unnerving on his leg. "Joan," he said again.

Opening her eyes, she looked about. "Oh, sorry."

"The sun's overhead. We better be moving on. The farther away from that canyon, the better off we are, as I see it. Sooner or later someone's going to figure out that Cheyenne warrior's missing, and they just might come looking."

"All right," she said.

"I'm going to see if I can find some water for the pinto. Maybe you could fix us a little to eat and pack up the robe."

"You won't go far?"

"No," he said, hooking the bow over his shoulder, "not far."

After saddling the pinto, he mounted up and rode down the dry streambed. Soon it twisted into a small ravine where a rank stand of cottonwood grew. The streambed disappeared from there under a weathered limestone outcrop. Caleb peered into the blackness of the cranny, but he was unable to see. Reaching his arm under the bank, he explored the darkness with his fingers. It was cool and had in it the promise of moisture.

"Well, ole boy," he said to the pinto, "let's give it a go." He searched out a stick and dug a trench as far back into the bank as he could reach, forming a reservoir from the sand at its end.

"Nothing to do but wait now," he said, taking up a place against the bank.

The day was soft about him, gentle with noon sun, and he dozed for a moment in its warmth. When he awoke, a cottontail, with eyes as black as ink, watched him from under a pile of driftwood. Confident in its seclusion, it hopped into the open and then disappeared under the rock ledge. Caleb took his bow, nocked an arrow, and waited. The wait was short, and within moments the cottontail reappeared, rose onto its hind legs, and commenced cleaning the mud from its front paws. With deliberate slowness, Caleb drew his bow and sent the arrow dead center into his prey.

"All right!" he said in a yelp.

He left the rabbit to kick out on the end of the arrow and checked his reservoir, finding it swirling with murky water. After taking his drink and filling the horn flask, he led the pinto over to drink. The contents were soon drained with the slurps and gulps of a mighty thirsty horse.

He knew that Joan was hungrier than she would admit and so rushed back to camp with his catch. "Dinner," he said, holding out the rabbit for her to see.

"Oh, Caleb," she said, taking her face between her hands, "you're wonderful."

"There was little else to do since he jumped in my lap. Didn't want to be tromped to death by no demented rabbit."

"Well, I was not prepared for bone marrow and bitter pecans, I must admit."

After building a small fire, Caleb skinned out the cottontail and set aside the hide. When the coals were hot, he roasted the rabbit off the end of a cottonwood spit, the aroma sending Joan circling the fire in anticipation.

"All right, all right," he said, breaking the rabbit in half and handing it to her. "Sorry about the fingers."

"Manners never counted for so little," she said, tearing away chunks of meat with her teeth. Watching her eat filled Caleb with a contentment, and he smiled. "Would you like some of mine?" he asked, holding out the last of his rabbit.

She sat back on her heels and looked up at him through the hair that had fallen across her face. "I've made a pig of myself, haven't I?"

"You're just woodcutter hungry, that's all."

"I wouldn't dream of eating your share," she said. "Now, you finish while I pack up."

They secured their supplies and climbed from the break. As far as they could see, grassy hills swelled and surged in the wind. There were no landmarks, no horizons, no directions to mark their way. Inside, Caleb withered at the hopeless distances.

"It looks to be a fair walk," he said.

Shading her eyes, Joan stared into the haze. "It's a walk we can make, Caleb."

They tramped for hours through the hills, Caleb leading the pinto, Joan trailing behind. One hill was as another, to swell and to dip and to swell again, and the mind-numbing monotony of dried grass, yellowed with fall, and the lizards with their arrogant stares, and the hoppers, stupefied with cold and impending death. When they were too tired to go on, Caleb would dig a rock from the ground and set it on the pinto's reins while they rested. But soon the silence, and the discouraging lack of progress, would drive them once more on their journey.

As evening fell, the sky flared with the orange of sunset, and the winds retreated for dawn. Caleb waited as Joan worked her way down the hill.

"Let's camp here," he said.

"It's so in the open, Caleb."

"Over this hill, there's another one just like this," he said, "and another and another right into eternity; besides, the grass is good here for the pinto, and I've seen a few buffalo chips about for making a fire."

"All right, Caleb, I'll get out our things."

"Maybe you could graze the horse while I gather up some chips? He'll weaken on us without proper time to graze."

"Caleb," she said, wrapping her arms about herself, "do you think we're lost?"

Caleb looked into the sky. "We're headed south," he said, "certain as certain. Anyway, we can check the stars again tonight. Now, I'll tie this rabbit pelt onto a arrow and stick it on top of that hill. Won't be any missing you then, will there?"

"No," she said, smiling.

Caleb set the arrow at the top of the hill and waved to Joan, who was leading the pinto into the draw. For an hour he walked, keeping the arrow in view to his right. The chips were few and light as paper, but there would be enough for heating water and cooking up a little meat.

It was in the first shadows of nightfall, as he was approaching camp with his arms stacked with chips, that he spotted something at the base of a hill, a deer carcass, or a buffalo perhaps, or a Cheyenne pony run to death in some brutal chase. But as he came closer, he could see the burned-out army wagon and a human body crumpled into the grass. Setting the chips down, he took a deep breath and clenched his jaw against the dread within him.

He parted the grass, and black flies swarmed in a disgruntled hum. Caleb's stomach lurched with the stench of carnage and spoil. A naked body lay contorted in death, his head back, his mouth agape in a final and agonizing scream. Eyes stared from the dusk, the fear still in them, burned there forever in those final and terrifying moments. A scalp lock had been hacked away, a vengeful wound running from the bridge of the nose to the nape of the neck, and the blackened stumps that were once his legs, the disquieting smell of burned meat, and the shin bones like ivory canes in the ash.

U.S. 7TH CAVALRY, FORT HARKER QUARTERMASTER DIVISION was

still decipherable on the half-burned side boards of the freight wagon. Nearby, a forage cap hung over a dried sunflower stalk, the crossed swords of the cavalry insignia untouched on its crown. A single steel-tipped arrow lay next to the body, dropped away with evisceration.

With one of the side boards, Caleb pushed the pitiful carcass from the ash, a chill racing through him at the sight of the army carbine shoved to the trigger guard between the buttocks of the hapless soldier, its stalk splintered away in that violent and final humiliation.

"Caleb, what is it?" Joan asked from behind him.

"Joan, don't come over here."

"Oh, my God," she said, covering her face with her hands.

"Joan, please, go back to the camp."

She leaned into him, taking hold of his arm, her face stricken at the tangled and mutilated corpse. "It's John, Caleb."

"Who?"

"Lieutenant Gillian," she said, her voice singular and trembling, like a bell in the prairie night.

Chapter 20

Silent in her grief, Joan turned her back and looked into the darkness. Once, Caleb thought to tell her how sorry he was, how dreadful for her to see the dead and mutilated body of her fiancé. He thought to take her in his arms, to console her, to hold her against the shock and horror of the moment. He thought all these things, but in the end, he stood mute and powerless, with his hands shoved into the depths of his pockets.

"What you said about him was true, then?" she asked.

"I'm sorry, Joan."

"I guess I don't understand why."

"No," he said.

"I couldn't see beyond the idea of marriage. I never saw what he was."

"Greed is a powerful and ugly call," he said. "Once it takes hold of a man, he loses all that matters in the end."

"What do we do now?"

"There's no shovel for digging, so a cross will have to do, I suppose."

"Yes," she said, "a cross then."

As a cold moon eased into the blackness, they built Lieutenant Gillian a cross from the side boards, tying them together with the last of the buffalo rawhide. Caleb drove it into the ground with his axe. He took Joan's hand, and for a moment they stood in silence. When the pearl moonlight washed overhead, Joan gripped his fingers until they ached, and her green eyes were wet and shimmering.

"It's a lonesome death, Caleb," she said.

"Anybody finds him, ought see the markings on these side boards," he said. "We best be on to camp. There's a hard journey ahead and no more we can do here."

"Well, then," she said, straightening her shoulders, "I'll help with the carrying."

There were just enough chips for hot water and for toasting out the raw smell of their pemmican. Joan nibbled at her food without enthusiasm, offering Caleb the last of it.

"I've had a harvest share already," he said, tucking her piece back into the parfleche.

"It's all so strange," she said, holding her hands in front of her. "I've lived a hundred years in this land, a hundred years. It's like I've never lived anywhere else."

Rolling out the robe, Caleb lay down, pulling in close to the blue flame of the chip fire.

"Couldn't have been no more than fifty years to my count," he said. "Course, I been busy what with mule hobbling and fighting Cheyenne every which way, so guess time might have slipped by."

"I'm sorry," she said, pushing the tangle of hair back from her face. "I didn't mean to complain."

"Takes more than a few days on the trail to change the likes of a lady, Joan, a real lady like yourself, and it don't matter a whit whether she's living in a fine railcar and smelling of honeysuckle, or sitting around a chip fire eating half-raw pemmican with a woodcutter. Don't make no difference in the breeding, I'd say."

"I thought I had everything figured out, Caleb, knew where I was headed, had picked the right man, had my future packaged, wrapped, and tied up in a bow." Pulling her knees into her arms, she looked at him through the smoke. "Everything I planned is changed. Now, I don't even know if I'll eat tomorrow, or if I'll be alive, or dead, or–" she paused, "wish that I was dead. It's like the world I knew has just vanished forever."

"It was a right proper life, too," he said, "and coming off green grass is the hardest of all, and then losing someone you loved. I'm right sorry." He hooked his chin in his hand and said, "It don't take much for an ole woodcutter like me, long as I got wood to cut and a dry place for laying down my head. Course, I admit to a dislike for mule hobbles, and Cheyenne revenge parties, and the Beer Bucket Inn. Aside from that, where I am ain't that much different from where I been. But for you, a lady like you, sleeping in a fine bed, and drinking tea, and reading books morning to night, well that's different, ain't it. That makes you special, you see, the way you stand up to this land, taking on what gets in your way, giving back what's dealt and the matter be damned. That makes you strong and fine in a place you never intended to be. That makes me right proud to be in your company."

Joan adjusted the pins in her hair and looked away. Even in the waning firelight, he could see the red scrapes under her arms, scoured there from the stiffness and ill fit of her buckskin coat, and her ankles were cut and swollen from the infuriating drag of dried weeds and grass. A streak raced across her neck where the pinto had swatted her with his tail full of cockleburs. To top it off, not a hundred yards from where they sit lay the body of the man she'd intended to marry.

When she looked at him again, her eyes shone with tears. "Just shut up, Caleb," she said.

"I was just trying to–"

"I know what you were trying to do, and you can stop now. Things are no harder for me than they are for you, so you can just stop with all that."

He rolled onto his back and looked for the north star. Figuring out women was proving to be more difficult than he'd thought.

He guessed a man could live too long in the woods with nothing but mules for conversation.

"I didn't mean no harm, Joan."

"I'm sorry to have yelled at you, Caleb, but I'm not some fragile lady whom you have to pamper. Fact is, I lost my mother when I was young, and I've learned to take care of myself quite well, thank you."

"What happened?" he asked, sitting up.

"She died during childbirth, my birth, if you must know."

"My ma's died, too," he said. "Seems an empty spot right there in the pit of my stomach ever since."

"My papa met her in Paris. He claimed that she was the most beautiful girl in all of France. This was her necklace, her fleur-de-lis," she said, holding it to the firelight for Caleb to see. "This was hers, and I've worn it all my life. I think it's beautiful, don't you?"

"I've admired it from the beginning. Makes me think of faraway places," he said.

"My papa never got over her death, not to this day, and he did what most men do when they can't face the realities and emptiness of their lives. He turned to his work, leaving all else behind, including me. I went off to boarding school, and he went off to build railroads somewhere."

"Seems a sad thing for a child," he said.

"Yes," she said, "at first, but even children can learn to cope with life. I was a good student, you see, and I found my way in books. It can be a seductive world. In any case, it sustained me through a rather forgettable childhood."

"I worked with my pa every day of my life," Caleb said, "and it's a thing I hold on to, like you hold on to that necklace of yours."

"When I graduated, I went to Fort Leavenworth to stake claim on him," she said. "He was there to build the railroad west. As it turned out, he got his railroad, and I got Lieutenant Gillian."

Somewhere from down the draw, a coyote yipped as it slid through the night.

"I best bring the pinto in close tonight," he said.

"Oh, damn this hair," she said, pulling the pins, first from one side and then the other, shaking her head, letting it spill black and beautiful down her back. "It needs braiding or cut."

Caleb worked at the fire with a stick, orange sparks racing up the column of heat. "Don't cut it, Joan. I can braid a horse hair halter. My pa taught me how."

"You want to braid my hair into a halter?"

"No, no," he said, "but I can braid a tail, the same as them Cheyenne squaws wear, 'cause I seen them do it plenty of times."

"Well, then, do mine."

"You mean now?"

She loosened her hair with her fingers and swept it to the side.

"I'm worn out trying to keep it stacked on top of my head in this endless wind."

"But my hands," he said, holding them up for her to see the dirt and grime.

Turning around, she leaned forward, her hair a cascade down her back. "Braid it," she said.

Caleb sat down and crossed his legs, gathering up the strands, winding them into a braid, taking care to shape and round each of the loops as he brought it about. In the firelight, the sassy curls lay like sleeping kittens against the white of her neck. Her breathing steadied under his touch, and she fell silent.

"I'm sorry about the lieutenant," he said. "I can't figure a man to give up so much for so little."

"I could never forgive him for what he did to those men, or what he did to us," she said, "but I could never wish him to die. I could never wish anyone to die like that."

He brought the braid down and drew the strands snug with his fingers. "It's a cruel thing, I know, but for the Cheyenne it's different. Most of that's done after the enemy is dead, you see, a way for a warrior to mark up his bravery for the others. They don't think about it the same way as you and me."

"Well, it's horrid, nonetheless."

"There," he said. "Now, give me the knife, I'll cut off a piece from your coat to tie it off."

"Here," she said, "take all you want. Take this from under my arms, or you could enlarge this hole across my stomach."

He tied off the braid and sat back on his heels. "I believe that's the finest halter I ever braided."

She turned to face him, her eyes lit in the dying flames, a girl again with her braid down her back. "It feels wonderful."

"Looks that way, too," he said, standing.

"Caleb, I want you to know something."

"Know what, Joan?"

"I want you to know that, if I had to be stranded out here with anyone, in these circumstances I mean—well, what I'm trying to say is that I'm glad it's with you."

Heat rose into Caleb's face. "We're going to get through this, you and me. We're going to make it," he said.

"You better bring in the pinto, Caleb," she said. "I'm going to rest now."

By the time he got back, the fire had died away. Joan lay with her arm outstretched, her breathing even and certain in sleep. He eased the pinto into camp and tied him off to a sagebrush that grew out from under a rock. Pulling an arrow from the quiver, he studied the sky, arranging the point to the north star. It was a foolish hope, he knew, the direction accurate but for a short time at best, but it gave him hope, and there was little enough of that to spare.

He took his place on the robe and curled against the evening chill. The smell of damp and fog drifted over the hills and settled about them. Somewhere a coyote bayed its lonely vigil. What Joan said tonight had filled him with joy. With the tips of his fingers, he touched her braid, ivory moonlight casting in the white of her skin. Back there in that other world, they were separated by money, power, the advantage of education and breeding. Out here they were but two souls on the prairie, each reliant on the other in a cruel and unforgiving place. There, he was a woodcutter, ignorant and small. Here, he was full measure and worthy in her eyes.

Once, he thought he heard something in the grass below, perchance the legless corpse, scorched and sanctified under its makeshift cross, or a Cheyenne warrior with black eyes shining in the moonlight. He turned his ear into the night and listened again, and nothing came.

Perhaps it was his conscience, his heart of blackness, his lie of regret upon the early death of Lieutenant Gillian, that disturbed him the most.

Chapter 21

With no fuel for the fire, Caleb's teeth chattered as he packed their belongings onto the pinto. Joan rolled up the buffalo robe and secured it with rawhide and handed it to him.

"Each day is colder," she said.

He brought the pinto around and checked the direction of the arrow he'd placed the night before. "But each day we're closer to Fort Dodge," he said, "and all we have to do is keep one step ahead of old man winter, I'm thinking."

"I hope we come into trees by night, Caleb. I want a hot fire and hot food."

"If we can make it to a creek somewhere, there will be trees enough all right."

"A roaring fire, that's what I want."

"Surely would be nice," he said, "and that's a fine braid you're sporting, if I do say so."

"Thanks," she said, lifting it from her shoulder. "I rather like it myself."

As they climbed out of the draw, neither spoke of what lay in the grass beyond, the still and frost-covered body of Lieutenant Gillian, but as the miles widened behind them, their spirits rose.

Back there was an end to treachery and lies. Ahead was hope and beginnings, and they both sensed the possibilities.

Even in their short time together, a routine had been established, him taking the lead, Joan following behind, her head down against his steady and unbroken pace. They spoke little in these moments, intent on the trail, on the hope of civilization somewhere on the horizon. Ever mindful of her plight, Caleb adjusted his pace, or stopped to secure their supplies, or to gauge their direction anew, whenever she fell behind.

They rose onto a plateau, and he pulled up to wait as she climbed the last few feet.

"Oh," she said, taking his hand, "that was a hard one."

"Better let the pinto take a breather," he said. "He's hard-pressed for a feed of grain, and his disposition is going sour."

Turning about, Joan took in the distances, her breathing labored yet from the climb. There was the smell of fall in the air, of decay and ebbing life.

"There's no end to it," she said, "and there's not a tree for a thousand miles."

"I ain't up to a thousand miles just now," he said, "so we got to find another way. You see the swell to these hills?"

"I feel their tug," she said, "like an ocean tide."

"When a man looks across that span, he doesn't see what's under his nose. Canyons and ravines and streams abound, and there's trees, too, plenty of them, wherever there's water. You have to look, that's all."

"Oh, really," she said, holding her hand over her eyes, "then why can't I see them?"

"'Cause it takes practice and a good eye. I've seen Cheyenne travel fifty mile in one of those ravines and never pop up a single time. Once I watched a hunting party sneak within a hundred yards of a cavalry detachment. Why, they thumbed their noses and danced around with their bums out like they didn't have a worry in the world. All the while those soldiers didn't even know anyone was about."

"Oh, Caleb, I never know when you're telling the truth."

"It's a true fact," he said, "and common knowledge amongst those of us with such experiences."

She wrapped her arms about herself and looked into the thin, blue distance. "This time I hope you're telling the truth and not just showing off, Caleb Justin."

"Course I'm telling the truth. There's water and wood out there just waiting." He picked up the pinto's reins and winked at her. "You ready now?"

By noon they'd made good headway, and Caleb found a clearing under a run of skunk brush. Even with the noon sun, the wind was sharp, and they huddled with their backs against its cut like buffalo in a blizzard. They ate from their store and lay back for a rest. Dried grass clung to Joan's braid, and he picked it away.

"Caleb," she said, looking up at him, "did you mean what you said?"

"About them Indians' bums? Course I did."

"No, silly, about the other, about how you feel? You know, how you feel about me?"

"I never spoke truer words in my life."

"I'm so mixed up," she said, dropping her chin onto her knees. "It's like I no longer know who I am."

Taking her hand, he held it in his own. "You take your time about how you feel, because a lot has happened since you and me been tramping across these plains, a lot of hard things."

"Thanks, Caleb," she said. "I do wish my papa knew I was all right. He'll be so worried."

"I wish that for you, too," he said, "and for your pa most especially. It's an aching heart he must have."

She brushed away the sand from her hands. "Come on, Caleb. Let's see if we can find one of those Edens before I freeze to death."

For the next few hours they walked in silence, and when the

sun drooped and wobbled in the distance, its light cold and remote like the distant flicker of a lantern, a bitter gale swept in at their backs. There was despair lying in wait, in the gray and monotonous miles. Each time a hill was topped, yet another presented itself with a predictable and exhausting summons. Even the pinto lagged, pulling the reins taut again and again to nibble at some morsel or sniff some foreign scent.

The sunlight waned to twilight, and clouds raced in on the winds, their bellies laden and full as they sped through the sky. Ahead, the sand hills gave way, and mesas rose like pyramids against the setting sun. He handed the reins to Joan and studied the changing terrain.

"What is it?" she asked.

"Looks like we're out of these hills at last."

"Oh, thank God," she said. "I thought they were to go on forever."

"It looks like rough country ahead," he said, "but it's open, and the walking should be easier. Look over there. See where the brush darkens and grows thick?"

"Yes, I see."

"Well, that's our Eden," he said. "Come on."

As they entered the brush, the prairie dropped away into a great chasm, a rift twisting into the soft belly of the land. A buffalo trail wound its way into the weathered rock below, and cedar trees sprouted from the cliffs, daubs of green in the white, weathered rocks.

"Trees," Joan said, patting him on the back, "just as you said. We'll have a warm camp tonight."

"I'm mighty glad to see it," Caleb said. "I'd about decided I was a no-good liar."

They made their way down the trail as the winds diminished, and the evening grew still and peaceful. The going was slow, at times so steep that the pinto balked, his eyes white with fear at the descent. Ledges of gypsum protruded from the canyon walls, eroded into odd and unpredictable shapes, some with dark and ominous openings that led away into the heart of the earth.

"Listen," Caleb said, drawing up. "Do you hear it?"

"Hear what?"

"Water."

She hooked her arm through his and turned her head to listen. "I hear something, I think."

Parting the brush that grew rank under the ledge, he knelt down. "Over here."

A stream of water the size of a man's arm surged from the canyon wall and into a pool that gathered and swirled in a worn rock basin.

"Spring water," Joan said, tightening her grip on Caleb's arm, "and watercress. Look, Caleb, it's everywhere."

They dropped down on all fours and cupped their hands into the pool, drinking until their faces ached from the icy water. Even the pinto joined them with ill-mannered slurps at the pool's edge.

"Look," Caleb said, wiping his mouth with his sleeve, "there's turkey tracks and coon, too. I reckon they've been coming in for water. We best camp down the canyon a ways."

After a last drink, they found a clearing on the south slope where the morning sun would warm their camp. Caleb gathered wood while Joan went back to the spring for watercress. Wood was plentiful, and he built a roaring fire, spreading out the cedar boughs to soften their bed. He cut green cottonwood saplings down-canyon, spared from the frost by the sun-warmed walls, and delivered them to the pinto, who munched at them with contentment.

When Joan returned, Caleb roasted the meat, nestling it in the peppery watercress when it was finished. The night darkened about them as they ate their fare and washed it down with quantities of spring water.

Caleb stacked on more wood and stirred the fire, the fragrant cedar filling the camp. As the sky darkened, stars exploded overhead, dazzling and unfathomable in the pristine night. From somewhere up-canyon, an owl hooted, its voice singular and irrevocable in the silence.

Joan lay back on the boughs and watched the flames sputter and flare in the darkness.

"It's a wondrous place," she said, "this Eden of yours, and I'm warm for the first time in days."

Caleb took the arrows from his quiver and checked their points before aligning one to the north star. In the morning, he would try for a turkey when they came in to the spring for water.

"I figure a day or two stay," he said, "before we move on."

"Couldn't we make it a little longer? There's game and fresh water." Pausing, she looked up into the yawning branches of the trees, "And no wind."

"Wouldn't do to get caught by winter."

She drew her knees into her arms and watched him. The first light of the moon shimmered in the treetops, and shadows bolted across the jagged rocks of the canyon. "Come sit by me," she said, "to talk while the fire burns down."

His heart lurched. "All right," he said, taking a place next to her. The heat from her body slid keen and delicious into his own.

"I've been thinking," she said.

"Me, too, and I'm sorry," he said. "I shouldn't have said those things. Just mean and selfish and ought be forgiven."

"Now you're the one who started this, Caleb Justin, so just keep quiet and listen."

"But I'm just a ignorant woodcutter what don't know when to keep his mouth shut, and then all what's happened, I mean with the lieutenant and all. Well, I just had no right saying those things."

She spiked her hands on her waist and said, "You don't want to hear what I have to say?"

"I'm afraid to hear, because I know what I'd say if I was stuck with some ignorant woodcutter what didn't own anything in the world but his pa's bit axe and a stole Indian pony."

Taking his face between her hands, she turned his head toward her, her eyes like liquid jade in the moonlight. "I've thought about this all day, Caleb, and it needs to be said. I'm in love with you, too. I think I've been in love with you since that day you brought wood to the railcar. Maybe it was because I was engaged, or I just didn't want to admit it, or maybe I thought I was too good. Whatever it was, I can't deny how I feel any longer."

A lump formed in his throat at her words. "Maybe it's 'cause you're lonely and scared and heartsick," he said. "Maybe it's 'cause the lieutenant is dead, your very own fiancé, and there's no one to fill the emptiness inside you. Maybe it's 'cause there's no one left standing in your life but a gimp woodcutter, that your world has just shriveled up to that. Maybe the day we walk into Fort Dodge, you'll see what a terrible mistake you made."

"You think me frivolous, or confused, I suppose, but I know my own heart. Once considered, I follow it to the end. Do you understand?"

"Yes," he said.

"You and I might not make it back, Caleb. It's a dangerous land, and we're lost. I've known that all along. Maybe we won't make it back."

"I was hoping you hadn't thought on it," he said, "but I guess neither one of us would be telling the truth to say otherwise."

She took the fleur-de-lis from about her neck and held it in her hand. "Do you love me like you said, Caleb?"

"Yes."

"Then put your hand on this."

"What?"

"Just do it."

"All right," he said, laying his hand on the fleur-de-lis, still warm from the hollow of her neck.

"Do you love me?"

"Yes."

"And would you marry me if you could?"

"Yes."

"Then swear it on my mother's necklace."

"I swear it."

"And I swear it, too," she said, laying her hand on top of his, "and now we are married."

"Married?"

"Yes, and you can kiss me."

"I never kissed a girl before, Joan," he said.

Slipping the fleur-de-lis back on, she put her arms about his neck and brushed her lips against his. "It isn't all that difficult," she said.

Lightning struck, molten and unsettling, and pooled in the depths of Caleb's soul. Mystified, he traced the arch and fulsomeness of her mouth, the cedar fire snapping in the night, embers quivering into the blackness.

"It's a fearsome thing," he said.

"Take down my braid, Caleb," she said, her voice full and certain.

And so he did, untying the strip of hide, separating the strands with trembling fingers. Rising, she turned away, slipping off her buckskin coat, and then her blouse, letting it fall away unheeded at her feet. Caleb swallowed and stared into the fire. But as she unlaced her skirt, he was taken to look, as one looks at a glorious sunset, or at a beautiful and quivering horse, with mesmerizing and unwitting fascination. Shadows danced across her marbled shoulders, the exquisite curve of her hips, the breathtaking arch and grace of her back.

She turned to him, and Caleb's heart stalled, her hair fallen and dark about her shoulders, her lush breasts, her fleur-de-lis with its immutable promise.

"You're beautiful," he said, his voice strange and hollow in his ears.

"And now you," she said.

"But I'm not beautiful," he said, turning his hands in the firelight.

"This is our place and our time, Caleb," she said.

And so he did, and they lay on the buffalo robe, unclad in the way and order of Edens. About them the night smelled of cedar boughs, and the fleece embraced them with its warmth, and against their trembling and innocent nakedness.

With her promise, Joan came to him then, this woodcutter, and with her fervor took him into her, and the night fell away about them as their bodies joined and their voices rose against the loneliness and extent of the prairie.

Chapter 22

T he sun fell warm against the canyon wall, stirring Caleb from his sleep. Rolling over, he pulled Joan against him, snuggling his face into the warmth of her throat. She smelled of cedar and of earth, and her breasts were abundant against his arm.

"I'm going to see if I can bag us a turkey," he said, his groin stirring against his will.

"Be careful, Caleb," she said, turning back into the glow of her sleep.

Dancing against the morning chill, Caleb slipped on his clothes, hooking the bow and quiver over his shoulder. From the high branches of an elm, a mockingbird sang out its repertoire, random and stolen choruses long since claimed as its own.

The morning was still, and bits of fog clung in the crevices and crannies of the canyon. As he neared the spring, he cut high up the cliff wall and onto a ledge that gave him full view of the approach. Steam rose from the spring as it gurgled into the morning cold.

He squatted behind a fallen walnut and nocked an arrow. Patience was the soul of the hunter. This he'd learned from Little River. With patience, the world will come to your door. As he waited, he thought of Joan, the pleasure of her, the smell and taste of her, and of the oath they'd sworn, of love and marriage, and how in his heart it was a true and right thing and would be so forever. It was their time, as she'd said, and no man or god could ever take that from them now.

A line of turkeys pranced from out of the bramble as he thought these things, led by a splendid tom, his tail flared, his step high and proud, his great wattle red as blood in the morning sunlight. Bringing about his bow, Caleb waited as they drank from the spring, dipping and preening and stretching their necks.

He took a deep breath and drew his bow, melding hand and eye and target. In that silence between heartbeats, he loosed his arrow, and the tom dropped, his feet kicking out the remaining seconds of his life. In a great flutter of feathers and squawks, the flock disappeared into the bramble once more.

The tom was heavy and warm against Caleb's back as he walked to camp, and he was happy, not so much for the kill, or for the food that would sustain them for a few more days, but for the look on Joan's face when he presented her with the tom. It was the hunter's pride, that pride he'd seen on the warriors' faces when they rode in laden with bounty.

Holding the tom at the end of his arm, Caleb grinned as Joan clapped her hands with glee.

"You're wonderful," she said, beaming.

He plucked the tom and cleaned him, setting aside the entrails for bait at the spring. Afterward, he searched out a downed pecan tree that had been uprooted by floodwaters, dried and perfect for smoking the meat. By midmorning, the aroma of roasting turkey filled the canyon.

"Here," Caleb said, handing a tail feather from the tom to Joan, "a gift. I wish it was gold instead of an ole turkey feather."

She kissed him and tied it into her braid. "It's a grand gift, and I'll keep it always," she said.

That day they explored the canyon, wandering hand in hand through the labyrinth of rock, laughing as they leaped like children from stone to stone. Near the end of the canyon, Joan discovered an apple tree, its fruit darkened with cold and bruised with bird pecks. But they tasted of glory and sweet as they munched them with their backs against the tree trunk. With pockets full, they strolled campward, and when the noon sun flooded the canyon, they made love in the warmth of the rocks. Afterward, they lay in each other's arms and dozed.

That night they ate smoked turkey and watercress, and apples roasted over the coals. Joan fed the cores to the pinto, laughing as his great tongue slithered into the palm of her hand for the last of the delicacies. The evening fell still and glorious, and they made love once more on the buffalo robe, the future's uncertainty far from their minds.

For three days they lived such, exploring, laughing, making love in the freedom of the moment, and each day Caleb took something at the spring, a coon, a jack, a squirrel from the high reaches of a tree. But with each day, the weather grew colder and the inevitability of their leaving more certain.

One morning they awoke to find their robe dusted with snow, no more than a powdering that skittered and faded before the wind. Caleb walked the perimeter of the camp while Joan fixed their breakfast. Afterward, he led the pinto out to where the canyon broke onto the mesas.

"I'm going to see if I can find a little grazing for the pinto," he said, but when he returned, Joan had packed their things. "It's time to go, isn't it?" she said, rolling up the buffalo hide.

"Yes."

"I hate leaving," she said.

"I know."

"Things will change."

"But these days we've had won't change," he said, taking up the pinto's reins.

At the mouth of the canyon they both looked back, but neither spoke as they moved on to the trail ahead.

Soon the soil turned the color of blood, a lifeless clay, blistered and ruined from summer heat. An occasional boulder shot from its depths, shoved from the earth's bowels by evils below, a bleak and unforgiving land. But the walking was unhampered, and the miles passed with uncommon speed.

By day's end, they had yet to reach the mesas, their distance and size far greater than either realized. The sun slid below the hills, and they camped in the open, without comfort of fire or protection from the wind. When the blackness dropped over them, a wet gale swept in and set them to shivering.

They huddled under their buffalo robe and ate the last of the smoked turkey, drawing into each other's arms against the chilling night. Caleb rubbed at the soreness in his ankle, the old wound having worsened with the dropping temperatures. Outside, the pinto stamped his hooves against the cold and the ever-present howl of coyotes.

For two days they trudged across the flats, their water low, their food dwindling, their spirits numbed with the tedium and the maddening winds. Pickings for the pinto were slim, an occasional yucca or thorned mesquite, and his sides grew gaunt from lack of water.

On the second day, as the sun hung low in the sky, they climbed at last onto the mesas. Buttes stretched across the land, sheared away by some colossal scythe, rocks the size of houses tumbled and strewn into the valleys below. Mesquite twisted from out of the gypsum, tortured with lack of water, and paddle cactus sprouted about like shriveled and deformed hands.

They stood at the precipice and looked out into the expanse, their faces burning from the cold, their eyes watering with its sting.

"Well," Caleb said, "at least we'll be out of the wind tonight."

"Out of everything," Joan said.

"I've seen a few mesquite. Maybe I can round up enough for a fire."

And so they made camp on the lee side of a gypsum boulder. While Joan unpacked, Caleb scoured the area for mesquite, an armful of limbs no larger than a man's finger, but they were hard and would make a steady fire. He cut paddle cactus with his axe, carrying them in by the thorns and stacking them next to the fire.

"I never eat cactus without a good wine," Joan said.

"These are for the pinto, just the same," he said.

Starting the fire was difficult without proper tinder. Exasperated, Caleb cut dry sage, and within moments, a spark glinted and sputtered to life.

"It's just a matter of time before you want my braid for tinder, I suppose," Joan said, holding her nose against the pungent smell of the weed.

Blowing on the ember, still tenuous and shimmering in the sage, Caleb smiled. "Sacrifice is expected from the least of us."

"I'm all paid up on sacrifice, thank you," Joan said.

When the fire at last blazed into life, they took refuge in its light and warmth.

"Anything you want cooked, you best get on it," he said, holding one of the paddles in the fire. "It's a short heat at best."

He dug through the parfleche for the squirrel, and she looked over at him. "What are you doing?" she asked.

"Searing off the pricklies. The pinto wants cactus pie, wine or no wine."

Joan heated the meat on a spit, while Caleb finished burning away the cactus thorns. Without complaint, the pinto wallowed the paddles into his mouth, happy enough for the green that drooled from his lips as he chewed.

Caleb warmed his back at the fire and said, "There's coyote droppings about and cougar tracks leading up that draw. Maybe that ole cat could lead us to water."

Taking a piece of meat from the stick, Joan leaned back against a rock. "I hope he's on his way to Fort Dodge for a drink at the sutler," she said.

That night, Caleb dreamed that Red Nose rose up from the grave and forced him to eat quantities of paddle cactus. Much to his distress, great thorns erupted from his intestines and stomach, painful and bloody pustules that sent Red Nose into peals of laughter.

Morning came, and they ate the last of the apples Joan had brought. Shivering in the cold, they tied their belongings on the pinto and picked up the cat tracks at the base of the mesa. Joan checked the faded tracks and shook her head. "They look like they've been there a while to me, Caleb, like a hundred years or so. If we find anything, it will be its carcass where it died of thirst."

"It's either trailing this thirsty old cat or a blind walk out there," he said, pointing into the mesas. She hooked her arm through his and said, "I'm with you, Woodcutter. Let's go." For several hours they followed the tracks, a winding and unpredictable trail through the jumble of rocks. Once, the tracks faded away altogether, and it was sheer luck and providence that they stumbled across them.

"We've lost them again," Caleb said, searching the ground, his hands on his knees.

"No, there," Joan said. "See, it looks as if he's climbed up in those rocks."

They followed the tracks as Caleb worked his way into the rocks that had eroded and slid from the heights of the mesa. "Will you look there," he called out. "This ole feller knew his way around after all."

Water shimmered wet on the face of the rock and gathered in a shallow pool at its base. From there it disappeared once more on its subterranean journey. All about were cat droppings filled with rodent bones and indiscernible seeds.

"It smells of dung," she said.

Cupping his hand, Caleb sampled the water.

"She tastes of gypsum, but she's wet, and she'll get us down the road, won't she. We'll make camp up there in those rocks tonight. It's out of the cold, and the smell, too, if the wind don't shift. There's a good bit of mesquite about in these rocks, and a hot fire is in the making, I'd say."

"And tomorrow?"

"With a little luck the sky will clear enough so's we can locate the north star. It ain't much of a compass, I admit, but it's all we got."

"What about the pinto?" she asked, looking down the embankment where the horse waited.

"He ain't got a compass either," he said.

Picking up a rock, she threatened to throw it at him. "Caleb, you know what I mean."

"I can lead him up here for a drink, but he'll have to be tied below. It's a rare horse can sleep standing on his hind legs."

After the pinto drank, Caleb led it back to level ground and by nightfall had built a roaring fire. They boiled water to warm their stomachs and ate squirrel while huddled about the fire. The flames settled away and a wind set up, howling down the draw, a dirge from out of the mesas.

"It's a lonesome call tonight," Joan said.

Drawing her under his arm, Caleb kissed her cheek. "It's no more than the wind," he said.

Moments passed, neither speaking as they stared into the fire, but there was sadness in the wind that neither could shake, a foreboding and hopelessness that had crept into their camp.

"Caleb," she said, "I didn't want to have to say this, but I guess I must. We are out of food, you know. There's nothing left."

"I was wondering about that," he said, "but we have water. We can get by for a few days without food if we have to."

"What are we going to do, Caleb, if we are going the wrong way? We don't know where we are for sure, and winter's coming on."

"We'll find food," he said, pulling her in close. "We got the bow and the knife, and this here axe, too. Soon enough there will be a jack or maybe even a deer, something to get us by."

"There's no deer out here, Caleb. There's nothing but cold and wind and loneliness. It couldn't be any worse, could it?"

When she looked up, Caleb's face was blanched, his jaw set, his fists doubled at the two men standing silent and wary in the shadows of their fire.

Chapter 23

Caleb reached for his bow, his eyes trained on the strangers.

"I got armed men posted," he said, "so step into the light and make yourself known."

Coming forward, the men held their hands in the air. One of them was tall with high cheekbones and haunting dark eyes. The other was short and stood a pace behind, as a servant might stand, his cuffs frayed, his beard clotted with dust from the trail. There was little in his eyes, shallow and absent of character. Every now and again he would scratch under an arm or in the thick of his beard. Both wore overcoats and field caps, the cavalry's crossed sword insignia pinned on the front. Even in the dim light, their poor condition was apparent.

"We ain't armed," the tall one said, "just hungry and in need of fire."

"We ain't got food," Caleb said, "but there's a spring just down there if you're in want of water before you move on."

"Maybe we could warm a little at your fire?" the tall one said.

"How is it I know you boys are alone?" Caleb asked, standing up. "For all I know there's a pack waiting over the hill."

The tall one held his foot up to the fire and showed Caleb

the hole worn through the sole of his boot. "Mister, we been walking in these hills near on a lifetime. There ain't nothing left of my feet, as you can see. If I had a pack of men over that hill, I reckon I wouldn't be standing here asking to warm at your fire. Besides, you got us covered with them boys of yours, ain't you?"

Glancing over at Joan, Caleb shrugged. "I reckon it's a point, but fact is, there ain't but me and this here bow, although it's a mighty good one. We'll heat a little water for warming your innards. That's the best we can do. It ain't coffee, and it ain't food, but it's better than the north wind blowing up your skirt."

"We near thought you was Indians at first," the tall one said, "what with those buckskin clothes and that gal with a turkey feather in her braid."

"We ain't Indians," Caleb said.

"Mighty proud you ain't," the tall one said, "given their particular dislike for soldiers."

Caleb moved to the other side of the fire and kept his bow at the ready as he sat back down. If worse came to worse, he might get a shot off. Taking one out would at least keep the odds right.

"I'm Caleb Justin," he said. "This here's Joan Monnet."

"Well I'll be dogged," the tall one said. "You're that railroad man's daughter, ain't you?"

Joan put the water onto the coals. "Yes, I suppose that would be me," she said.

"Why, I seen your picture tacked up over half the country. They say your daddy's threatened to shut down the whole of the railroad if you ain't found soon. Course, most figured you been kilt by now or ruined by the Cheyenne."

"You ain't introduced yourselves," Caleb said.

"Well, sir, I'm Roscoe Blue, and this here's Scratch Howson. He ain't too clever, and he eats more than a short man ought. Don't say much either, which you'll find as a blessing soon enough."

"That's a funny name, ain't it?" Caleb asked.

Scratch grinned a toothless grin and stuck his hands in his pockets. Joan poured the hot water and handed it to Roscoe.

Roscoe nodded his head as he took a slurp. "It's a tad thin for a shriveled stomach such as mine, but it's good and hot, and I thank you the same, Miss."

"That your real name?" Caleb asked Scratch.

"No, it ain't," he said, digging for something elusive in his beard.

"Well, what's your real name then?"

Looking over at Roscoe, Scratch shrugged. "I forget."

Roscoe took another drink of the water and turned the palms of his hands up. "You see what I mean? Say, you folks wouldn't have a little flour and lard, would you, enough for a biscuit or two?"

"We ate the last of our squirrel," Caleb said, "and there ain't a crumb of nothing left to be had. I'm hoping to shoot a jack or deer come tomorrow."

"My name's just 'Scratch' and nothing more," Scratch said.

Caleb lifted his brows and glanced over at Joan, who was busy adding wood to the fire.

"Scratch is a little dim," Roscoe said, "as you can see. They've called him Scratch ever since I've known, 'cause he's had the itch near all his life, I guess. Digs at his parts like an ole hound dog, don't he. Gets downright unsettling after a time."

"Right practical name," Caleb said.

When the hot water was nearly gone, Roscoe handed it to Scratch, who drank it without comment.

"I wouldn't be figuring on no deer, or jacks neither, for that matter," Roscoe said. "We ain't seen a living critter for three days, 'cept a skinny ole kangaroo rat, and he was too fast on his feet for me or Scratch either one."

"You boys with the cavalry, I figure?" Caleb said.

"The Seventh," Roscoe said, "under ole Autie Custer, 'til the no-good son of a bitch left us behind to starve, begging your pardon, Miss."

"Why would a man be left behind?" Caleb asked, adjusting his bow across his lap.

"We ain't deserters, if that's what you're figuring," Roscoe said. "Are we, Scratch? Hell, a man what deserts Custer can reckon with a bullet for his trouble. Course, enlisted's all right for marching the rogue's hump, or for being left behind for the Cheyenne to scalp, ain't they?" Easing down in front of the fire, Roscoe crossed his legs and studied the flames. "That fire sure feels good," he said. "Hell, I thought me and Scratch was going to freeze stiff as carps last night. Ole Scratch couldn't even get on with his itching, could you, Scratch?"

"It's a odd commander what leaves his men behind to be kilt, ain't it?" Caleb said.

Roscoe pulled a pipe from his coat and sucked on the empty bowl before putting it back in his pocket. "Sure miss my tobaccy,'" he said.

"Maybe you got that big 'D' branded on your hip, what keeps you from enlisting somewheres else?" Caleb asked, glancing over at Joan.

"I can see where you might think that," Roscoe said, "but you'd be mighty mistaken. Show him your cheeks, Scratch, but keep it decent 'cause there's a lady present."

Scratch eased his trousers down on the sides and turned into the firelight for Caleb to see. Joan rose to busy herself with packing the parfleche.

"How is it you got left behind?" Caleb asked.

"Me and Scratch happened on a little liquor what came in on a grain wagon. Missed inspection, didn't we, Scratch, and stable call on top it. Well, ole Autie was some mad about the whole mistaken business. He said that by goddamn if all a man can do is drink and scratch he ought live with his own kind so he put us in charge of his wolf hounds."

"Wolf hounds?"

"Big as horses, weren't they. Ole Autie run them bastards day and night. It's a wonder there's a antelope left what ain't had his flanks tore out by them mean sons of bitches. The general was mighty particular about them hounds, wasn't he, Scratch?"

"Mighty so," Scratch. said.

"Hand fed 'em like babies, didn't we, and picked their ticks, and wrapped their feet at night so's they'd be ready for running the next day. Hell, we ate with them, slept with them, and combed out their tails like they was goddamn royalty, didn't we, Scratch?"

"Goddamn royalty," Scratch said.

"So what happened?" Caleb asked.

Roscoe took out his pipe again and knocked it against his foot, looking into the empty bowl. "We had ole Roman Nose cornered just out of Harker, or so we thought, and ole Autie got afeared them dogs would give away our position. 'Stay behind and strangle them dogs,' he said. Didn't he, Scratch? Said he couldn't take no chance of them dogs making a racket and him losing out on ole Roman Nose. 'Couldn't we shoot them, sir,' I asked. 'Do what you're told, Blue,' he said, 'or I'll hang you and that ignorant partner of yours off a cottonwood.'"

"We strangled them," Scratch said, "just like he said."

"It was a murdering we did," Roscoe said, "and one I ain't likely to forget. Then the son of a bitch left us behind to make our way back without no horses, no carbines, and no goddamn rations. We been lost ever since, I reckon, ain't we, Scratch?"

"Ever' day," Scratch said.

Coyotes struck up a chorus somewhere in the mesas, and the pinto whinnied below the spring. "Guess that was that pinto tied up down there in the draw," Roscoe said, "or a spirited coyote?"

"How did you know we had a pinto?" Joan asked.

"Saw him coming in, didn't we, Scratch. No offense, Miss, but I ain't never seen a horse with a scrawnier tail."

"Well, he's an Indian pony, earned the hard way," she said. "Now, we'd like to help you soldiers out, but as you can see, we have no food and precious little else to share."

"Must be a comfort having a horse, even if he is a broom tail. Me and Scratch walked the danged prairie out on foot, didn't we, Scratch?"

"Ever' day," Scratch said.

Roscoe put his pipe away and said, "I wonder why folks like yourselves is wandering around out here in the prairie with nothing but a Indian pony, if you don't mind me asking?"

"I was woodcutter for Harker," Caleb said, "before the Cheyenne took me to home and hobbled me up like a jack mule. Figured each day was my last, 'til I broke loose. That's when I happened on Miss Monnet in the night, still alive she was, in a sea of dead soldiers. We've been walking to Fort Dodge ever since with winter nipping at our heels."

"I ain't never heard of a man be mule hobbled before," Roscoe said, shaking his head. "Sure glad ole Autie hadn't thought on it, or Scratch and me would have been living with the mules instead of them wolf hounds, I'm thinking." Standing, Roscoe dusted his pants. "The hot water and the fire was mighty nice, folks. We wouldn't want to put you out none, so we'll be on our way. Maybe we could borry' a few lucifers so we can start up a fire?"

"We don't have any matches," Caleb said.

Pushing back his hat, Roscoe looked at him. "I reckon lightning striked your wood pile and set her afire then? That's mighty good luck, I'd say."

"Learned how to use a fuzz stick from the Cheyenne," Caleb said. "Be glad to wrap up some coals for you boys, though."

"Yes, sir," Roscoe said, "coals would be mighty nice. I'd rather sleep at a hound's back than with ole Scratch here."

Caleb pulled out some of the coals while Joan packed them in ash, wrapping them in a piece of hide.

"Here," she said, handing Roscoe the bundle. "Maybe you could help us in return?"

"Why, I'd be proud too, Miss. What did you have in mind?"

"Maybe you would give us a map, or some landmarks, something to help us in finding our way to Fort Dodge?"

"I sure would like that, Miss, but me and Scratch ain't figured our way back to Larned yet, much less Dodge. You still lost, ain't you, Scratch?"

"Ever' day," Scratch said, digging under his arm.

"Best I can say, Miss, is that the Cimarron cuts south between Fort Dodge and Indian Territory. That much I know. You come to the Cimarron, you come too far."

"The Cimarron?"

"A river, Miss, with a foot of water and a mile of quicksand, they say. There ain't nothing but rattlesnakes and Indians in the Territory, not until you get down to Fort Cobb. It ain't no place to be, Miss, not with Cheyenne on the run and ole Autie in charge of the winter campaign. It's a son of a bitch what strangles his own dogs, a man likely to stop at nothing, ain't he. Then there's ole Black Kettle with his back to the wall and nowheres to go and with winter setting in. Hell, Miss, the whole caboodle could blow like a wagonload of black powder, as I see it. Why, I'd as soon be chasing kangaroo rats and having dinner conversation with ole Scratch here."

"Well, thanks anyway," she said.

As they made their way into the darkness, Joan hooked her arm through Caleb's. "I don't trust them," she said.

"I'd bet my pa's axe that them boys are deserters," Caleb said. "Can't say I blame them much for wanting out of Custer's outfit, though."

"It was strange talking to people again, Caleb. I'd grown accustomed to just the two of us, I guess."

"I'm going down to check on the pinto," he said. "Better stoke the fire high, Joan. I got a feeling it's going to get cold tonight."

As a precaution, Caleb moved the pinto higher up the embankment, tying him out of the wind as best he could. Deep in the canyon, coyotes picked up a trail, their voices pitched and frenzied in chase. The pinto danced with anxiety.

"It's okay, boy," Caleb said, rubbing his nose.

Even from afar, Joan's fire licked into the blackness. She was waiting for him under the robe when he got back. Shivering against the cold, he joined her there, their lovemaking desperate and fierce with the uncertainty of their future. Afterward, they held each other, naked and warm under the robe, their breaths rising into the cold, black night.

Morning arrived with an icy gale that drove ash and sand into their eyes as they struggled to dress in the cold dawn.

"Couldn't we have a fire?" Joan asked, slipping on her shoes. "I'm freezing."

"It's gone out," Caleb said, digging into the ash with a stick, "and there's nothing to cook in any case. We best just move on out, Joan."

By the time they'd packed, the sun had edged over the canyon wall, but its warmth was distant and meager against the frigid wind. With arms loaded, they worked their way down the trail, the watering hole now shimmering with a thin layer of ice. They made their way to the bend where the pinto was tied; Caleb's heart sank, and he threw his axe onto the ground.

"What's the matter?" Joan asked, alarm in her voice.

"The pinto's gone," he said.

"The coyotes must have spooked him," she said. "He can't be far. We'll find him, that's all."

He pointed to the boot tracks that led away into the mesas and shook his head. "Them deserters must have been watching when I moved him last night. They've stolen him, Joan, and killed us in the doing."

Chapter 24

Without the pinto to carry their supplies, they culled them to the minimum, fashioning packs, loading what they could on their backs, but from here on they'd have to take food as they found it and pray for a quick delivery to the gates of Fort Dodge.

They followed the tracks into the mesas with spirits broken. The gale blew from the north, a bitter wind, a wind that wormed into the marrow of their bones and eroded their strength and their will. The boot tracks of the deserters soon enough faded and with them the last of their hope of finding the pinto.

Mesas rose about them and into the sky, the impenetrable red clay beneath their feet, the stunted and knurled mesquite, starved and desperate with lack of rain. An occasional yucca struggled from the rocks, or a shriveled cactus purple with cold, or a sage, battered and ragged from the ceaseless winds. What animals might have lived there were long since gone, driven to warmer fields, or burrowed under the rocks, or curled in caves to await the spring.

At midday, Caleb pulled up, sliding his pack from his shoulder.

"What is it?" Joan asked. "Why are we stopping?"

He rubbed at his ankle and looked upward, as if the answer

lay in the blue of the sky. "I'm thinking the army was right about taking on gimps," he said.

"It's your foot, isn't it? Let me see, Caleb."

"It's nothing what a little rest won't cure."

"Let me see, please."

He rolled up his cuff, hiked his trouser leg up to his knee, and pulled down his sock. Under the strain of the walk, the old wound had given way, blood gathering under the skin, dark and ominous, the ankle swollen and pathetic.

"Oh, Caleb," she said, "it looks awful."

"Looks worse than it is, I figure," he said.

"I've been thinking that you packed my load a little on the light side, Caleb."

"Packed 'em even up, didn't I. Not much walking time left today at best. There's mesquite to be rounded up before dark, or it will be a cold night for certain."

She opened his pack and transferred some of the heavier items into her own. "There, now," she said, "that will do, and like you said, there's not much walking left today in any case."

Taking her by the hand, he lifted her up and rolled her into his arms.

"You're my heart's dream," he said, "and the bravest person I know."

"I'm not brave at all," she said, dropping her head against his shoulder. "Each day I think I will crumble with fear from what might lie ahead. I would perish before sundown without you."

"Let's go," he said. "We can make a few miles yet."

That night they camped in the rocks once again. Joan prepared their bed, while Caleb gathered wood. As the sun settled in the west, the day's meager warmth faded, and a bitter cold descended over them. The pain in Caleb's ankle crawled up his leg and settled in the emptiness of his stomach. Unlike most nights, the wind did not abate, or relent, or lament the misery it cast upon the prairie. Instead, it rode in hard, cresting with dust, turning the sunset to blood and ice.

Each time Caleb worked an ember to life with the fuzz stick, the wind snuffed it away. He placed Joan on the upside with the buffalo robe outstretched to ward off the wind. When at last the tinder burst into flames, they both sighed with relief. They huddled before the fire and pulled the buffalo robe about them, their stomachs knotted with hunger and despair.

"Aren't you going to set the arrow?" she asked, curling against him.

"There ain't a man alive don't know north from south tonight," he said.

"But we've got each other," she said, snuggling into him, "cold or no cold."

"I can't think of anyone I'd rather freeze to," he said.

"I'm exhausted, Caleb. Maybe I'll try to sleep."

Laying the robe over her, he brushed his lips against her ear. "You sleep. I'll stoke the fire and stand watch a while."

Joan slept before the wood had burned high, her breathing steady beneath the robe. Drawing in close to the fire, Caleb listened to the wind as it swept through the mesas, and he thought of home, of the trees that grew green and lush along the banks of the Ohio, and of his pa, the way he'd died in the backwash that day, and he thought of Joshua Hart, and of their journey to Leavenworth, and of how they'd been separated in the end. He thought of Jim Ferric, and of Baud, and of ole Sophie and Ben lost now forever.

The wind moaned through the valley once more with its dirge, its tale of misfortune and ruin, and he despaired in his heart at what might happen to them, at what might happen to her.

The next morning, the cold light of a new day drove them from their bed. Grateful that the wind had subsided, they struck out once more across the mesas, their breaths rising into the icy dawn. Caleb struggled to keep pace, his foot swollen and painful, his toes strutted and blue. Joan insisted on carrying the heavy share of the load once again, but without food, without shelter from the plummeting temperatures, they would both weaken soon enough—of this Caleb had little doubt.

The noon sun brought relief, and as they climbed onto a plateau, Caleb spotted a rattler basking in the warmth of the rocks. Too cold to move or to strike, he was an easy target for Caleb's axe. "Lunch," he said, holding the snake high for Joan to see.

"Oh, Caleb," she said, "I can't."

"Think of it as legless chicken," he said, "one what's been plucked and ready to cook."

They stopped in a wash and built a small fire. Caleb skinned the snake, threading it onto a stick to roast over the coals. When it was finished, he handed her a piece. Wrinkling her nose, she closed her eyes and sampled it.

"Well?" he asked.

"It's not so bad, actually," she said.

Caleb, too, found it not so bad, but neither spoke of its oily smell or of the way it writhed on the roasting stick long after it was blackened from the coals.

With renewed energy they bore on, Caleb searching the crevices and crannies for snakes as he walked, but with waning light and falling temperatures, there were none to be found.

That night, they slept under a clear and star-filled sky, and when they awoke, their buffalo robe shimmered under a layer of frost, their ears stinging with the burning cold. By noon the next day, water blisters had formed on the tops of Caleb's ears where they had frozen in the night.

"I told you to keep them covered," Joan said. "Now they're frostbitten. If they fall off, you will look like that snake we had for lunch."

Two more days they walked the mesas, sleeping in the open with naught but the robe for protection. Without food, or hope of food, their spirits and their strength waned. Again and again they pulled up to rest, their bodies aching with weakness and hunger.

They found water on the third day, a puddle gathered in a wallow with its smell of dung and slime and creatures unknown.

"No," Caleb said, pulling Joan back.

"But, Caleb, we have to have water."

"It's too tainted," he said, "even for the likes of starved-out pilgrims. There will be water ahead."

"It's called the ocean, I think," she said, "and I hear that it's salty."

"Wait," Caleb said, pointing. "Will you look at that?"

"What?"

"If I ain't mistaken, those are boot tracks, deserters' tracks, I'd say. Looks like ole Roscoe and Scratch ain't particular about their watering hole."

"And there're horse tracks," Joan said, "leading off that way."

"The pinto," Caleb said.

"What are we going to do?"

He strung his bow, took an arrow from the quiver, and nocked it. "Going to get our pinto back, ain't we."

Within a hundred yards, the tracks took a sudden turn to the right and disappeared into a gulch. The sandstone was smooth, scoured and worn by turbulent floods, the horse tracks fading and then reappearing in the sandy bottom of the gulch. Caleb crouched down and scanned the rocks overhead.

"They might be waiting for us," he said, whispering.

"Caleb," Joan said, taking hold of his arm, "over there."

Near the bend of the gulch, the pinto lay on its side, its legs strutted, its belly bloated, its head pitched and tortured in death.

Caleb said, "The sons of bitches have kilt the pinto, kilt our way home for a bellyful of meat."

They approached with wariness, drawing into the mesquite that grew from the bank of the gulch. Next to the pinto's crushed skull was a rock, its jagged point bloodied and telling of violence. The pinto's end had been a slow one, the sand swept and churned beneath its thrashing legs. A slab of meat was hacked from its rump, and its tongue was cut away. Nearby were the remains of a campfire, as cold and dead as the pinto itself.

"Reckon they're still making use of our coals," Caleb said, holding his hand over the ashes. "Probably this morning's fire. We just as well camp here for the night."

"But Caleb—"

"The pinto's dead, ain't he, and no reason for us not to have a cut of the meat. It will spoil soon enough anyway. Them deserters' tracks lead out just there, so guess we'll be safe enough."

"All right," she said, "but let's camp somewhere else if you don't mind. I'd rather not have to sit by my old friend while I'm having him for dinner."

They took what meat they could use, and Caleb wrapped it in a hide, tucking it away in the parfleche. Searching out a campsite near the mouth of the gulch, they built a hot fire and roasted the meat, the aroma spurring their hunger until they could no longer resist. They tore away chunks of half-cooked roast and ate with abandon, blood dripping from their chins. They ate past their uncertainty, and their reluctance, and their shame. They ate until their stomachs ached and they could eat no more. Like lions at a kill they preened, sucking grease from their fingers, wiping their mouths on the sleeves of their shirts.

Afterward, they lay in the soft sands of the gulch, their stomachs full for the first time in days, their bodies curled under the warmth of the robe. Sleep came soon, an abiding and healing sleep that sustained them through the deepening cold of the night.

The next morning, they left at dawn, as had become their way, but with renewed energy, their pace steady and unbroken. Caleb's foot, while yet tender, was less swollen, his gait stronger and more certain.

"Why are we following these tracks?" Joan asked. "What's the point now, Caleb? We can't retrieve our horse, you know. We ate him last night."

He adjusted his bow on his shoulder and shrugged. "It's as good a direction as any, I guess. Maybe they'll take us to Dodge, or Larned, maybe."

"Maybe they'll take us into an ambush," she said. "Strikes me that Roscoe and Scratch make for unlikely pathfinders."

"Who's to know?" he said.

"Maybe you're wanting revenge, Caleb Justin, like those Cheyenne you've been living with. Maybe that's what you're after."

He turned, looking into the green of her eyes. "Maybe," he said. "I don't know anymore. It's them Cheyenne's world we live in, you and me. It's their world we might die in, and I'm beginning to see that the things they do are for a reason."

They hadn't gone a mile when Caleb drew up. Taking an arrow from the quiver, he scanned the horizon. Ahead, rocks heaved from the earth, their edges worn and rounded from the enduring winds. Crows lifted into the sky, their frantic jeers breaking the silence.

"What is it, Caleb?" Joan asked.

"I'm not sure," he said. "Stay here while I have a look around."

"Caleb, be careful."

Slipping from rock to rock, he listened for the prairie sounds, listened from within for the subtle and telling changes, the unexpected call of distress, the shifting rhythms of the order. But there was no sound, no breathless sigh or call, no sinister telling. There was but the stillness of death, and in that what Caleb most knew.

"Joan," he said, "I think I've found them."

Joan gasped and covered her mouth at what she saw, the hapless deserters lying dead in the rocks, their bodies distended and smelling of decay. "Oh, Caleb," she said, "what's happened to them?"

Caleb took the hat from Scratch's face, and Scratch stared back, his eyes sunken and blank and swarming with ants. In death, as in life, Scratch had little to say. He rolled Roscoe onto his back and kneeled at his side, studying him for the longest time.

"There's mud collected in his teeth," he said, "and in the corners of his mouth. I'm thinking they had a fill from that buffalo wallow after they finished up with our pinto."

"Shouldn't we bury them or something?" she asked.

His jaw rippling, Caleb stood, drawing his bow and aiming it at Roscoe's distorted corpse. "No," he said.

"Caleb," Joan said, laying her hand on his shoulder. "Don't."

Several moments passed, his eyes locked, his face fierce, his arm trembling from the bow's draw. Lowering it at last, he walked away. "There's a few hours' daylight left," he said over his shoulder. "We best be on our way."

They walked in silence for the next several hours as the sun rode down in the western sky. Already the temperature fell, and another bitter night was in the making. But there was meat in their parfleche and mesquite for fuel, and for these things they were grateful.

They climbed onto high ground, and a valley opened before them. A small stream meandered down its length, the sunset casting orange in its shallow waters. Sand skirted the stream as far as the eye could see. Like a desert it stretched into the distance, void of life and of hope.

Caleb scanned the valley, hand over his eyes against the final light of day. Joan slipped off her pack. "Wonder how far to Fort Dodge now?" she asked.

Taking her hand, he looked away. "It's a far piece," he said, "back there somewhere."

Her hand tightened on his as she looked up at him. "What do you mean?"

"'Cause down there's the Cimarron," he said, his voice falling, "and out there, the Territory, and the end of the line."

Chapter 25

The next morning, Caleb and Joan stood at the banks of the river and looked across the expanse of sand. Ahead was likely Indian Territory, unknown, untamed, and fearful. Behind them, back there somewhere on the frozen Kansas plains, was Fort Dodge.

Caleb picked up a stick and drew in the sand where he figured they might be. The blisters on his ears had burst, the skin peeling away like a boy too long at his swimming hole. She knelt beside him, leaning into him, her body warm and reassuring as she studied his drawing.

"What are we going to do?" she asked.

"If them deserters were telling the truth, then Fort Cobb is out there somewhere ahead, but it's smack in Indian Territory. It's like stepping barefoot into a rattlesnake den and hoping you don't stir none awake in the doing. Behind us is Fort Dodge," he said, scratching out his map with his stick, "but we missed it once, and there ain't no guarantee we wouldn't miss it again. The weather ain't getting no better either. Heading back strikes me as mighty hard business."

"Which way do you think, Caleb?" she asked.

Throwing his stick into the shallow water, he watched it turn and drift downstream. "Fact is, I don't know which way to jump no more."

Joan dabbed at her cracked lips and looked back at the mesas, silent and shrouded in the morning cold. "I don't think I can go back there," she said.

Caleb pulled off his moccasins and stuck them in his pocket. "Come on, Missy," he said, "we got a river to wade."

That day, they followed the meander of the river as it wound and twisted into the forbidden land. From somewhere above them, geese honked out warnings as they winged away to safer homes. Soon the land gave way to sand and sage and bullhead sandburs with spiny thorns that penetrated their shoes and set their feet to throbbing. Devil claws clung to their legs like blind and soulless fiends, and the wind, laden with river sand, eroded the skin from their ankles and from the bridges of their noses.

They camped in a salt sage stand that evening and ate the horse meat from the parfleche for supper. Already it tasted of spoil, its smell cankerous and unholy, but they ate it anyway, rubbing their hands into the sand to scour away the odor from their fingers.

During the night, water seeped up from the depths of the sand and into their bed, soaking their clothes and the buffalo robe. They rebuilt the fire in the wee hours of the morning, their teeth chattering as it smoldered back to life.

The next day, they abandoned the river, heading straight into the sand hills. Caleb had long since given up navigating by the north star, relying instead on dead reckoning and prayer. But the weather held, and so for two days they drove on, collapsing at night with little energy left for anything but rest. By the third day, the last of the horse meat was gone, and their water was low. The coyotes gathered each night, frenzied packs of them beyond the horizon, their demonic yelps filling the couple with dread and fear.

On the fourth day into the Territory, the weather worsened, a stinging wind that churned and cut its way across the sand hills. Clinging to each other, Joan and Caleb pressed on, their heads down, their strength and resolve dissolving under the wintry blast. As they topped a hill, Caleb scanned the horizon, the distances as cruel and hateful as the wind that bore through their clothes.

Hanging on to his coattail, Joan stood silent. He was strengthened in her need and determined to see her through. Without her, he would have long ago lay down in the sand and joined the legions who had done so before him.

"Caleb," she said, pointing into the valley below, "look down there."

Blinking the water from his eyes, he stared into the wind. "Heaven save us," he said, "if it ain't wagon tracks."

"Oh, Caleb, are you certain?"

"Come on," he said, "let's go take a look."

Just as he thought, the wagon ruts cut deep through the valley and out into the plains. "Who could it be, Caleb?"

"They got to be cavalry," he said, laying his hand into the ruts, "with right many freighters, I'd guess. See those mule tracks there, all shod and dainty, ain't they?"

"What does it mean, Caleb?"

"They must be headed for Fort Cobb with supplies, and they can't be that far ahead. I can still smell the sage where it was crushed by the wheels."

"Do you think we can catch up?"

"Catching up to a mule is a might harder than it sounds, but there ain't nothing keeping us from following them home, is there."

"It's like a miracle," she said.

"We still could have a hard walk ahead, Joan, and without food. But at least we ain't lost no more, not with these tracks to follow."

The wind whipped at their backs as they stared off down the trail. Pulling a strand of hair from the corner of her mouth, Joan looked up at Caleb. "What happens when we get there?"

Caleb fell silent as he studied the situation. "Between us, you mean?"

"Yes," she said, "between us."

"Maybe we won't be married no more, not in that way, I mean, and there will be your father, too. Having a woodcutter in the family ain't all that inviting."

Taking the fleur-de-lis into her hand, she held it for a moment. "Come on, Caleb," she said, "no one's ever going to separate us. It's written in the stars."

All day they followed the tracks, their energy renewed with hope, and when the sand turned to clay, they rested. Red hills rolled into the distance ahead of them, the earth swollen and distended, void of form, except for the roundness of the hills, or the sporadic outcropping of rock, or the occasional ravine that descended into its heart like a red and vital artery.

At dusk they camped in a dry wallow, too tired to look for better. There was no fuel to be found, no mesquite, no chips even to drive out the day's chill. They crawled under the robe and clung to each other for warmth as the wind howled through the hills.

Sleep came hard without food, and Caleb rubbed the tension from Joan's shoulders, pulling her into him against the icy wind that seeped into their bones. And when at last sleep came, it was fitful and worried and absent of rest. Above them, clouds rode in with the night, their bellies laden and ominous, and a blackness descended over the Territory. All life fell silent to await the dawn.

Caleb pulled back the robe, and snow sifted into his face and down the collar of his shirt. He sat up and brushed it from his hair. As far as he could see in every direction, snow glimmered under the morning sun.

"Joan," he said, shaking her shoulder. "It snowed last night."

Sitting up, Joan looked about, rubbing the sleep from her eyes. "It must be a foot deep," she said.

He shook the snow from the robe and rolled it up before

speaking. "It's the wagon tracks," he said. "They're covered with snow. We won't be able to follow them for long."

"Oh, no, Caleb," she said, "I hadn't thought about that. What will we do? Maybe we ought to wait for it to melt."

Fixing the robe across his pack, he hefted it onto his shoulder.

"There's no way of knowing how long it will stay, Joan, and there could be more on the way. Without food, well, a feller could get in trouble pretty fast. We know we've been headed in the right direction, so let's just keep moving."

Slipping on her pack, Joan looked out into the frozen morning. "Well," she said, "we've got plenty of water for drinking."

The going was slow as they made their way through the snow. Even on high ground, it was deep, the crust giving way with each step, and in the draws it was even worse, four and five feet of impassable drifts.

Caleb soon spotted rabbit tracks in the snow, skidding holes where they'd leaped in futile attempts to stay topside of the unstable crust. And then rabbits were everywhere, bobbing from out of the snow, disappearing again, resurfacing a few feet away like seals in the ocean. Within moments, Caleb's arrows were spent, the snow pocked with the blood of his kills. Afterward, they gathered them up, their bodies warm against their arms as they searched for wood.

With luck they found a fallen elm, its limbs poking from the snow near the crest of a hill. They cleared a place for their fire in the draw. As they waited for the coals to redden, they peeled their rabbits like ripe bananas, tossing entrails to the crows who gathered beyond in the snow.

Caleb cooked all of the bounty, five in total, and after having their fill, packed the remainder in the parfleche for the trail. Sunset fell across the plain, its dazzling colors rupturing from the snow-covered hills.

"Let's camp here," Caleb said. "We have our fire, and it's out of the wind."

"Let's do," Joan said, smiling for the first time in days.

So in the majesty of sunset, they melted snow for water and sipped its heat and watched the sun as it faded away.

That night they made love, their bodies alive with verve and hope, and in the immense quiet of the Territory, they moved into each other, as if for the first time, as if for the last, their love as singular and resplendent as the ivory moon above them. Afterward, they lay in each other's arms, both knowing the rarity of such love and such moments.

A bitter cold descended during the night, and when Caleb awoke in the early hours of morning, his ears stung from the chill. Rising, he worked at the ashes, but the fire had waned, and there was nothing to do but gather more wood.

"Joan," he said, "the fire's gone out."

"Wait," she said, "I'll go with you."

Their breaths fogging, they climbed the hill where the elm lay buried beneath the snow. Caleb listened for morning, for the caw of crows, or the chatter of sparrows, or the fume and rant of blackbirds banking against the dawn, but it was silence that replied, a mounting and unerring silence that sent Caleb's blood racing. "Something isn't right," he said, taking hold of Joan's arm.

"What?' she said, looking about.

"I'm going to the top of that hill for a see."

"I'm going with you," she said.

"You stay," he said, crouching to string his bow.

"I'm going with you, Caleb."

"All right, but keep it quiet."

As they reached the crest of the hill, Caleb lay down in the snow, pulling Joan beside him. He eased up for a look, and his heart sank at what lay below. A valley twisted through the hills with a small tree-lined river skirting its length, its waters frozen in the winter morning. Cheyenne lodges cropped like mushrooms from the snow, fifty, maybe more, smoke twisting from dying fires. A pole with a white cloth tied to its end leaned against the center lodge, and a warhorse stood hip shod at its entrance.

"It's the Washita," he said.

At the far end of the encampment, a makeshift corral encircled horses and mules, hundreds of them, with their breaths steaming as they milled about. A single warrior sat on a stump, his robe gathered about him, his rifle crouched in his arm. Even from Caleb's vantage, there was no doubting the red cloth tied in Little River's braid.

It was then that Caleb saw the soldiers, flanked on his left and on his right below the crest of the hill, their carbines at the ready, their horses prancing in anticipation. As far as he could see, there were but the dark uniforms of cavalrymen against the breaking dawn.

Amassed in the night, they now stood poised for attack on Black Kettle's winter camp. There was no mistaking General Custer as he rode among them, his saber drawn, his blond hair flowing from beneath his cap. At the summit, a signalman crouched to await the dawn, his Spencer trained on Little River below.

"Joshua Hart," Caleb said, his heart breaking at the unfolding scene.

The sun came up, and light spilled into the valley. A dog darted from the Cheyenne camp, its bark certain and sharp with alarm. When Private Hart fired, Little River stood, his arms outstretched with surprise, and then he dropped, dark and bloodied and silent, like a rabbit in the snow.

Chapter 26

T he cavalry band struck up "Garryowen" from out of the hills, its drums thundering through the valley, its trumpets raw and horrifying, its song profane with Irish merriment.

Like wolves at the chase the soldiers rode from on high, and from all directions, snow spewing from beneath their horses' hooves. The caustic drift of powder and smoke steeped the valley as they fired with abandon into the sleeping lodges.

"Oh, my God!" Joan said, crying and struggling to stand.

"No!" Caleb said, yelling, pulling her back down.

A warrior, naked to the waist, ran from the center lodge. Caleb recognized him at once as Black Kettle. Following behind was his wife, her hands covering her breasts, her hair black against the blinding snow. Black Kettle dropped to his knees and fired into the onslaught of soldiers, but the odds were too great, the charge too fierce. He abandoned his position and leaped onto his warhorse, pulling his wife up behind. Digging his heels into its flanks, he reined it about. He drove toward the river with head down and reins full slack.

A dozen soldiers bore in from the east, their carbines ablaze as they closed the gap. Cutting down the riverbank, Black Kettle pulled up, scanning the hills as if looking for help. A bullet tore through the jaw of his horse, dropping it to its knees, its head plowing into the snow. Black Kettle and his wife spilled across the thin ice of the river.

They scrambled to stand, but the ice gave way, plunging them into the frigid waters of the Washita. Against the volley of rifle fire, their bodies leaped and jerked, and as they slipped under the frigid waters, their hands lifted for a moment, eddies of blood moving away in the unhurried current beneath the ice.

Women and children ran unclothed and terrified through the crusted snow, their telling and bloody footprints behind. From all sides the soldiers rode, firing into the innocence, their shining and lopping sabers, their yells of victory and bravado.

From the hillside, "Garryowen" played on, but from the valley, there were but cries of terror, and of disbelief, and of prayers falling unheard into the blackness of eternity.

The warriors were few, the old and the bent, or the young with children's bows, but they died as they stood, their scalps taken, or their heads, or their scrotums for favored trade. Within a few short minutes, there was none left to stand, all dead and dying in the bloodied snow.

A woman, great with child, fled toward the river, and a soldier mounted his horse, hat cocked, saber drawn, gait slow and deliberate behind. With a backward swipe of his sword, he felled her into the grass. Dismounting, he held high the fetus, his trophy, for all to see, the precision and sorrow of his blade. He mounted and pranced his horse in a turn, hat held high in triumph, spinning back in a dead run.

Caleb rolled over and stared into the blue of the sky, his stomach frozen and knotted. Next to him Joan trembled with cold and with horror at the carnage below.

"They're butchering them," she said, her voice shaking with disbelief.

"We can't go in," Caleb said. "There're warriors gathering up there on the ridge. They ain't Cheyenne, and they ain't Custer's scouts. Looks like they're drifting in from up the valley, maybe another winter camp. Little River said that the Kiowa and Arapaho sometimes wintered in the Washita. Maybe they are a hunting party, I don't know, but if we move, they will see us, sure. We got to hold on here."

"We will," she said, "like we have from the start."

Below, Custer's Osage scouts rounded up the scattered and frightened women. With willow switches they drove them back from the grassy knolls, their cries of anguish like coyotes on a moon-filled night. Soldiers gathered up hides, hundreds of them, jerked meats, winter blankets and bows, stacking them about the camp. They piled drums, buckskins beaded for dance, headdresses, and toys on top of these. Anything that could be moved or lifted was placed on the growing piles. The pole with the white cloth was lit and the pyres struck.

Then there was smoke from the lodges, dark clouds bellowing from their tops, and flames, flickering and playful from out the doors, and then raging infernos as they sighed and groaned into the snow. From the corrals, the horses churned, their eyes wide with fear at the inferno about them, and from behind the Osage guards, the women wailed and pulled their hair as the last of the teepees withered under the roaring fires.

"They're destroying everything," Joan said, her hand over her mouth.

"To the last," he said, "until there ain't nothing left."

The sun rode high in the sky as Caleb pulled himself behind a sage to scan the valley. On the distant ridge, warriors still gathered, more now than before. He watched as two of them mounted their ponies and rode off in a gallop through the snow.

"They're going for reinforcements from upriver," he said. "Things could turn sour mighty fast."

"I can't feel my feet anymore, Caleb," she said.

He crawled back down and pulled her against him, warming

her face with his hands, kissing the blue of her mouth. "We got to wait," he said. "We wouldn't make it a hundred yards without being spotted. If we can hold out 'til dusk, maybe then."

"What if they come back with more warriors?"

"Custer ain't even seen them yet," Caleb said. "He ain't even got lookouts posted. It's a fine trap he's in if they show up."

"It's a fine trap *we're* in," she said.

Huddled there in the snow, they listened to the sounds from the valley, the whoop and holler of soldiers as they gathered their souvenirs.

"Joan," he said.

"Yes, Caleb."

"A woodcutter don't get to talk much, being alone all the time, I mean, and, well, he don't learn how to say what's on his mind. He don't know how, you see, and everything he says comes out ignorant, even when he don't mean it to. But there comes a time it's got to be said."

"It's the trying that matters, Caleb," she said.

"I just wanted to tell you that I love you and that life was mighty thin before you came along."

She brushed the snow from his collar and turned into him, holding his hand against the warmth of her throat.

The sudden whinny and clamor of horses came from the valley, and Caleb lifted up to see over the crest. "The women are leading the horses out," he said.

"Maybe they're getting ready to leave," Joan said.

As she spoke, a soldier took the rope of the lead horse from the woman. It was a bay with white blazed face and trembling flanks. Pulling his saber, he slit its throat with a quick downward draw. In disbelief, the bay bolted, its eyes white, its front feet pawing the air as blood pumped from its neck with each throb of its great heart. The horse's scream was that of a child, a piteous and desolate cry, and chills raced down Caleb's back.

The other soldiers joined in then as the horses were taken

from the corrals, an extermination of hours and of hundreds as they were led to the slaughter. The cries of the horses, and of the women, and even of the soldiers, rose in sorrow and shame. The valley churned with the dying, and the snow was crimson with their blood.

Caleb and Joan covered their ears and wept in their hearts for humanity, and for themselves, and for the evil that befell the valley of the Washita on that godless day.

As dusk fell, a cavalry scout spotted the warriors on the ridge. The order came with a bugle call. Custer was at the lead, his saber drawn, and when the charge sounded, the Seventh rode in pursuit. Certain now that help was too late, the warriors turned, riding hard in retreat up the Washita.

The Seventh topped the hill, and as the warriors disappeared over the ridge, Custer pulled up, his hand held high to halt the charge. Turning, the column rode back against the fading light.

"They've called it off," Caleb said. "They're coming back. We've made it through, you and me."

He hooked the bow over his shoulder and lifted Joan from the snow. Waving his axe over his head, he called out to them.

The column halted at the top of the ridge, their voices clear and certain against the snow-covered hills.

"What is it?" Custer asked.

"Goddamn stragglers," someone said.

Rising in his stirrups, Joshua Hart held his hand over his eyes against the setting sun. "Wait," he said, as shots rang out, first one, and then another. Crumpling into the snow, the figures lay still.

Joshua dismounted, his heart pounding. "God help us, they were waving for help, sir. I'm sure of it. They aren't Cheyenne at all."

Custer turned in his saddle. "You don't know Cheyenne when you see them, soldier?"

"Permission to go back and check, sir."

"I'm not holding up this regiment for you to go wandering off.

You're on your own if those others return with reinforcements."

"I'll catch up soon enough, sir."

Custer held up his hand, the bugle sounded, and the Seventh moved off. And when they'd gone, Joshua made his way to where the bodies lay. Caleb's axe was at his side, and the girl had a fleur-de-lis necklace about her throat. Their hands were clasped in death.

Joshua dug a stone into the newly covered grave to mark their place and, with the tip of his knife, scratched in a fleur-de-lis. It was not his way to mourn or rail against wrong, not anymore. He'd have to go soon if he were to catch the others.

As the moon rose over the bloodied valley of the Washita, he stood for a moment, his breath rising in the bitter night.

Acknowledgments

Thanks to my publisher, Holly Monteith, and the staff at Cennan Books for their enthusiasm, insight, and patience as this work passed through the editorial process. It's gratifying to have such support and expertise on my side. And, as always, thanks to my wife, Nancy, who has listened patiently to my ideas and stories all these many years.